Young Jack Duluoz seems all set for a fairly ordinary future. But he is catapulted into another world when he wins an athletic scholarship to New York University. His adventurous education is launched, and it takes him far and wide, from the football fields to the high seas in World War II ('what I have to tell you about the US Navy will knock your head clean off') back to a wild time in New York City, where the underground scene is just beginning to simmer. Duluoz throws himself into a frenzy of nonstop experience, an explosion of drugs, writing, love – and eventually murder.

Jack Kerouac is the late lamented Daddy of the Beat Generation, the 'strange solitary crazy Catholic mystic' whose writing has influenced the lives of thousands and will go on doing so for many years yet.

'Mr Kerouac has talent of an enviable sort. He writes with clarity, compassion, and force. What is even more important, he has something to say' – *Chicago Tribune*

OTHER BOOKS BY JACK KEROUAC
AVAILABLE IN QUARTET EDITIONS

Satori in Paris
Maggie Cassidy
The Town and the City

VANITY OF DULUOZ

An adventurous education, 1935–46

JACK KEROUAC

QUARTET BOOKS LONDON

Published by Quartet Books Limited 1973
27 Goodge Street, London W.1

First published in Great Britain by
André Deutsch Limited 1969

ISBN 0 704 31003 1

Printed in Great Britain by
Hunt Barnard Printing Ltd., Aylesbury, Bucks

DEDICATED TO

Σταυροῦλα

Means 'From the Cross' in Greek, and is also my wife's first name – STAVROULA.

Extra, special thanks to Ellis Amburn for his empathetic brilliance and expertise.

BOOK ONE

I

All right, wifey, maybe I'm a big pain in the you-know-what but after I've given you a recitation of the troubles I had to go through to make good in America between 1935 and more or less now, 1967, and although I also know everybody in the world's had his own troubles, you'll understand that my particular form of anguish came from being too sensitive to all the lunkheads I had to deal with just so I could get to be a high school football star, a college student pouring coffee and washing dishes and scrimmaging till dark and reading Homer's *Iliad* in three days all at the same time, and God help me, a WRITER whose very 'success,' far from being a happy triumph as of old, was the sign of doom Himself. (Insofar as nobody loves my dashes anyway, I'll use regular punctuation for the new illiterate generation.)

Look, furthermore, my anguish as I call it arises from the fact that people have changed so much, not only in the past five years, for God's sake, or past ten years as McLuhan says, but in the past thirty years to such an extent that I dont recognise myself as a real member of something called the human race. I can remember in 1935 when fullgrown men, hands deep in jacket pockets, used to go whistling down the street unnoticed by anybody and noticing no one themselves. And walking *fast*, too, to work or store or girlfriend. Nowadays, tell me, what is this slouching stroll people have? Is it because they're used to walking across parking-lots only? Has the automobile filled them with such vanity that they walk like a bunch of lounging hoodlums to no destination in particular?

Autumn nights in Massachusetts before the war you'd always see a guy going home for supper with his fists buried deep in the sidepockets of his jacket, whistling and striding along in his own thoughts, not even looking at anybody else on the sidewalk, and after supper you'd always see the same guy rushing out the same way, headed for the corner candy store, or to see Joe, or to a movie or to the poolroom or the deadman's shift in the mills or to see his girl. You no longer see this in America, not only because everybody drives a car and goes with a stupid erect head guiding the idiot machine through the pitfalls and penalties of traffic, but because nowadays no one walks with unconcern, head down, whistling; everybody looks at everybody else on the sidewalk with guilt and worse than that, curiosity and faked concern, in some cases 'hip' regard based on 'Dont miss a thing,' while in those days there even used to be movies of Wallace Beery turning over in bed on a rainy morning and saying: 'Aw gee, I'm goin back to sleep, I aint gonna miss anything anyway.' And he never missed a thing. Today we hear of 'creative contributions to society' and nobody dares sleep out a whole rainy day or dares think they'll really miss anything.

That whistling walk I tell you about, that was the way grownup men used to walk out to Dracut Tigers field in Lowell Mass. on Saturdays and Sundays just to go see a kids' sandlot football game. In the cold winds of November, there they are, men and boys, sidelines; some nut's even made a homemade sideline chain with two pegs to measure the downs – that is to say, the gains. In football when your team gains over 10 yards they get another four chances to gain 10 more. Somebody has to keep tabs by rushing out on the field when it's close and measuring accurately how much ground is left. For that you have to have two guys holding each end of the chain by the two pegs, and they have to know how to run out according to parallel instinct. Today I doubt if anybody in the Mandala Mosaic Meshed-Up world knows what parallel means, except brilliant nuts in college mathematics, surveyors, carpenters, etc.

So here comes this mob of carefree men and boys too, even girls and quite a few mothers, hiking a mile across the meadow of Dracut Tigers field just to see their boys of thirteen and seventeen play football in an up-and-down uneven field with no goalposts, measured off for 100 yards more or less by a pine tree on one end and a peg on the other.

But in my first sandlot game in 1935, about October, no such crowd: it was early Saturday morning, my gang had challenged the so-and-so team from Rosemont, yes, in fact it was the Dracut Tigers (us) versus the Rosemont Tigers, Tigers everywhere, we'd challenged them in the Lowell *Sun* newspaper in a little article written by our team captain Scotcho Boldieu and edited by myself: '*The Dracut Tigers, age 13 to 15, challenge any football team age 13 to 15, to a game in Dracut Tigers field or any field Saturday Morning.*' It was no official league or anything, just kids, and yet the bigger fellows showed up to keep official measurement of the yardage with their chain and pegs.

In this game, although I was probably the youngest player on the field, I was also the only big one, in the football sense of bigness, *i.e.*, thick legs and heavy body. I scored nine touchdowns and we won 60-0 after missing 3 points after. I thought from that morning on, I would be scoring touchdowns like that all my life and never be touched or tackled, but the serious football was coming up that following week when the bigger fellows who hung around my father's poolhall and bowling alley at the Pawtucketville Social Club decided to show us something about bashing heads. Their reason, some of them, to show was that my father kept throwing them out of the club because they never had a nickel for a Coke or a game of pool or a dime for a string of bowling, and just hung around smoking with their legs stuck out, blocking the passage of the real habitués who came there to play. Little I knew of what was coming up, that morning after the nine touchdowns, as I rushed up to my bedroom and wrote down by hand, in neat print, a big newspaper headline and story announcing DULUOZ SCORES 9 TOUCHDOWNS AS DRACUT CLOBBERS ROSEMONT 60-0! This newspaper, the only copy, I sold for three cents to Nick Rigolopoulos, my only customer. Nick was a sick man of about thirty-five who liked to read my newspaper since he had nothing else to do and was soon to be in a wheelchair.

Comes the big game, when, as I say, men with hands-a-pockets came a-whistling and laughing across the field, with wives, daughters, gangs of other men, boys, all to line up along the sidelines, to watch the sensational Dracut Tigers try on a tougher team.

Fact is, the 'poolhall' team averaged the ages of sixteen to eighteen. But I had some tough boys in my line. I had Iddyboy Bissonnette as my center, who was bigger and older than I was but preferred not to run in the backfield, liked, instead, the bing-bang inside the line, to pen holes for the runners. He was hard as a rock and would have been one of the greatest linemen in the history of Lowell High football later on if his marks had not averaged E or D-minus. My quarterback was the clever strong little Scotcho Boldieu who could pass beautifully (and was a wonderful pitcher in baseball later). I had another wiry strong kid called Billy Artaud who could really hit a runner and when he did so, bragged about it for a week. I had others less effectual, like Dicky Hampshire who one morning actually played in his best suit (at right end) because he was on his way to a wedding, and was afraid to get his suit dirty, so let nobody touch him and touched no one. I had G. J. Rigolopoulos who was pretty good when he got sore. For the big game I managed to recruit Bong Baudoin from the now-defunct Rosemont Tigers, and he was strong. But we were all thirteen and fourteen.

On the kickoff I caught the ball and ran in and got swarmed under by the big boys. In the pileup, with me underneath clutching the ball, suddenly seventeen-year-old Halmalo, the poolhall kickout, was punching me in the face under cover of the bodies and saying to his pals 'Get the little Christ of a Duluoz.'

My father was on the sidelines and saw it. He strode up and down puffing on his cigar, face red with rage. (I'm going to write like this to simplify matters.) After three unsuccessful downs we have to punt, do so, the safety man of the older boys runs back a few yards and it's their first down. I tell Iddyboy Bissonnette about the punch in the pileup. They make their first play and somebody in the older boys' line gets up with a bloody nose. Everybody's mad.

On the next play Halmalo receives the ball from center and starts waltzing around his left end, longlegged and thin, with good interference, thinking he's going to go all the way against these punk kids. Running low, I come up, so low his interference thinks in their exertion that I'm fallen on my knees, and when they split a bit to go hit others to open the way for Halmalo, I dive through that hole and come up on him head on, right at the knees, and drive him some 10 yards back sliding on his arse with the ball scattered into the sidelines and himself out like a light.

He's carried off the field unconscious.

My father yells 'Ha ha ha, that'll teach you to punch a thirteen-year-old boy *mon maudit crève faim!*' (Last part in Canadian French, and means, more or less, 'you damned starveling of the spirit.')

II

I really forget the score in that game, I think we won; if I went down to the Pawtucketville Social Club to find out I dont think anybody'd remember and certainly do know everybody'd lie. The reason I'm so bitter and, as I said, 'in anguish,' nowadays, or one of the reasons, is that everybody's begun to lie and because they lie they assume that I lie too: they overlook the fact that I remember very well many things (of course I've forgotten some, like that score), but I do believe that lying is a sin, unless it's an innocent lie based on lack of memory, certainly the giving of false evidence and being a false witness is a mortal sin, but what I mean is, insofar as lying has become so prevalent in the world today (thanks to Marxian Dialectical propaganda and Comintern techniques among other causes) that, when a man tells the truth, everybody, looking in the mirror and seeing a liar, assumes that the truth-teller is lying too. (Dialectical Materialism and the Comintern techniques were the original tricks of Bolshevist Communism, that is, you have the right to lie if you're on the Bullshivitsky side.) Thus that awful new saying: '*You're putting me on.*' My name is Jack '(Duluoz') Kerouac and I was born in Lowell Mass. on 9 Lupine Road on March 12, 1922. 'Oh you're putting me on.' I wrote this book *Vanity of Duluoz.* 'Oh you're putting me on.' It's like that woman, wifey, who wrote me a letter awhile ago saying, of all things, and listen to this:

'You are not Jack Kerouac. There is no Jack Kerouac. His books were not even written.'

They just suddenly appeared on a computer, she probably thinks, they were programmed, they were fed informative confused data by mad bespectacled egghead sociologists and out of the computer came the full manuscript, all neatly typed double-space, for the publisher's printer to simply copy and the publisher's binder to bind and the publishers to distribute, with cover and blurb jacket, so this inexistent 'Jack Kerouac' could not only receive two-dollar royalty check from Japan but also this woman's letter.

Now David Hume was a great pilosopher, and Buddha was right in the eternal sense, but this is going a little bit too far. Of course it's true that my body is nothing but an electromagnetic gravitational field, like that yonder table, and of course it's true that the mind is really nonexistent in the sense of the old Dharma

Masters like Hui-Neng; but on the other hand, who is he that is not 'he' because of an idiot's ignorance?

III

This recitation of my complaints aint even begun yet; no fear, I wont be longwinded. This beef I'm putting in here is about the fact that Halmalo, or whatever his name really was, called me that 'little Christ of a Duluoz,' which was a blasphemy that went with his secret punch in the mouth. And that today nobody believes this story. And that today nobody walks hands-in-pockets whistling across fields or even down sidewalks. That long before I'll lose track of my beefs I'll go cracked and even get to believe, like those LSD heads in newspaper photographs who sit in parks gazing rapturously at the sky to show how high they are when they're only victims momentarily of a contraction of the blood vessels and nerves in the brain that causes the illusion of a closure (a closing-up) of outside necessities, get to thinking I'm not Jack Duluoz at all and that my birth records, my family's birth records and recorded origins, my athletic records in the newspaper clippings I have, my own notebooks and published books, are not real at all, but all lies, nay, that my own dreams dreamed at night in sleep are not dreams at all but inventions of my waking imagination, that I am not 'I am' but just a spy in somebody's body pretending I'm an elephant going through Istanbul with natives caught in its toes.

IV

All footballers know that the best football players started on sandlots. Take Johnny Unitas for instance, who never even went to high school, and take Babe Ruth too in baseball. From those early sandlot games we went on to some awful blood-flying games in North Common against the Greeks: the North Common Panthers. Naturally when a Canuck like Leo Boisleau (now on my team) and a Greek like Socrates Tsoulias come head on, blood will fly. The blood my dear flew like in a Homeric battle those Saturday mornings. Imagine Putsy Keriakalopoulos trying to dance his way on that dusty crazy field around Iddyboy or a crazy charging bull like Al Didier. It was the Canucks against the Greeks. The beauty of it all, these two teams later formed the nucleus of the Lowell High School football team. Imagine me trying to dive off tackle through Orestes Gringas or his brother Telemachus Gringas. Imagine Christy Kelakis trying to lay a pass over the fingers of tall Al Roberts. These later sandlot games were so awful I was afraid to get up on Saturday mornings and show up. Other such games were played in Bartlett Junior High field, where we'd all gone as kids, some in Dracut Tigers field, some in the cowfield near St Rita's Church. There were other, wilder Canuck teams from around Salem Street who never contacted us because they didnt know how to ask for a game via the sports page of the newspaper; otherwise I think the combination of their team with ours, and the combination of other Greek or even Polish or Irish teams around town . . . O me, in other words, Homeric wouldnt have been the word for it.

But as an example of where I learned football. Because I wanted to go to college and somehow I knew my father would never be able to afford the tuition, as it turned out to be true. I, of all things, wanted to end up on a campus somewhere smoking a pipe, with a buttondown sweater, like Bing Crosby serenading a coed in the moonlight down the old Ox Road as the strains of alma mater song come from the frat house. This was our dream, gleaned from going to the Rialto Theater and seeing movies. The further dream was to graduate from college and become a big insurance salesman wearing a gray felt hat getting off the train in Chicago with a briefcase and being embraced by a blond wife on the platform, in the smoke and soot of the bigcity hum and excitement. Can you picture what this would be like today? What with air pollution and all, and the ulcers of the executive, and the ads in *Time* Magazine, and our nowadays highways with cars zipping along by the millions in all directions in and around rotaries from one ulceration of the joy of the spirit to the other? And then I pictured myself, college grad, insurance success, growing old with my wife in a paneled house where hang my moose heads from successful Labradorian hunting expeditions and as I'm sipping bourbon from my liquor cabinet with white hair I bless my son to the next mess of sheer heart attack (as I see it now).

As we binged and banged in dusty bloody fields, we didnt even dream we'd all end up in World War II, some of us killed, some of us wounded, the rest of us eviscerated of 1930's innocent ambition.

I wont go into my junior year in Lowell High School, it was the usual thing about the boy too young, or with not enough seniority, to get to play regularly, though because coach Tam Keating thought I was a sophomore because I was fifteen he didnt let me play but was 'saving me up' for junior and senior years. Also there was something fishy in the state of Merrimack because in practice scrimmage he ran me pretty hard and I made perfectly good hard gains and could have done the same in any official games, or there are politics involved, none of which my father countenanced as he was so honest that when a committee of men of Lowell came to him in about 1930 to ask him if he'd run for mayor he answered 'Sure, I'll run for mayor, but if I win I'll have to throw every crook out of Lowell and there'll be nobody left in town.'

V

All I know is how my senior year season went and judge for yourself, or if you dont understand, let a coach judge: I started the first game of the year only because Pie Menelakos had an injured ankle. Granted he was a nice tricky runner but he was so small that when somebody hit him he flew 10 feet. Granted again, he was slippery. But because, somehow, the coach figured he needed a blocker, a 'fullback' like Rick Pietryka, and that neat little passer Christy Kelakis, there was no room for me the runner, in the starting backfield. Yet as for being fullback I, in scrimmage, could put my head down and ball right through for 10 yards without even looking. As for being halfback, I could catch a badly thrown pass that was zipping behind me by simply pivoting, gathering it in, and whirling back to my run and go all the way. I admit I couldnt block like Bill Demmons the quarterback or pass like Kelakis. Somehow they had to have Pietryka and Menelakos in there and my father claimed somebody was being paid. 'Typical of stinktown on the Merrimack,' he said. Besides he wasnt very popular in Lowell because whenever somebody gave him some guff he let em have it. He punched a wrestler in the mouth in the showers at Laurier Park after a wrestling match had been thrown, or fixed. He took a Greek patriarch by the black robes at the bottom and shoved him out of his printing shop for arguing about the price of circulars. He did the same thing to the owner of the Rialto Theater, Buck-a-Thousand Grossman he called him. He had been cheated out of his business by a group of Canuck 'friends' and he said the Merrimack River wouldnt be cleaned up before 1984. He'd already told the mayoral committee what the hell he thought about honesty. He ran a little weekly newspaper called the Lowell *Spotlight* that exposed graft in City Hall. We know all cities are the same but he was an exceptionally honest and frank man. He was only Mister Five-by-Five, 5 foot 7 tall and 235 pounds, yet he wasnt afraid of anybody. He admitted I was a lousy hitter in baseball but when it came to football he said they hardly came better as runner. This opinion of his was later corroborated by Francis Fahey, then coach of Boston College and later of Notre Dame, who actually came to the house and talked with my father in the parlor.

But he had good reason to be sore as the record will show. As I say, I started the first game. Let me say, though, first, we had a magnificent line: Big Al Swoboda was right end, a 6 foot 4 Lithuanian or Pole strong as an ox and as mild. Telemachus Gringas (aforementioned) at right tackle, nicknamed Duke and brother to great Orestes Gringas, both of them the toughest, boniest and most honest Greeks to meet. Duke himself actually a boyhood buddy of mine in the short month's duration at age twelve or so we'd decided to be friends, Saturday nights walking a mile and a half leaning on each other's arm over shoulders from the glittering lights of Kearney Square, Duke now grown into a quiet fellow but a 210-pound blockbuster with merry black eyes. Hughie Wain right guard, a big 225-pound quiet fellow from Andover Street where the rich folks lived, with the power and demeanor of a bull. Joe Melis center, a Pole of dynamic booming dramatic crewcutted tackles, later elected captain to next year's team and destined to play fullback and a good 300-yard runner in track. Chet Rave left guard, a strange talkative rock of a man of seventeen destined to be the only other member of this Lowell team besides myself to be seriously sought after by bigtime college teams (in his case, Georgia University). Jim Downing left tackle, a 6 foot 4 lackadaisical Irishman and beware of them. And Harry Kiner left end, speedy and good on defense and made of rocky bones.

So I started the first game of the year against Greenfield Hi (and here's the record I spoke of, the whole year) (game by game) and made two touchdowns that were called back, actually made five of the seven first downs in the whole game, averaged about 10 yards a try, and made a 20-yard run to within inches of a touchdown and Kelakis assigned himself the honor of carrying it over (he was the signal caller).

In the second game of the season, despite this performance of mine, Menelakos' ankle (Menny's) had healed and he started in my place. I was allowed to play only the last two minutes, at Gardner High in western Massachusetts, carried the ball but twice, hit for first down both tries, for 12 and 13 yards respectively, got a bloody nose and ate some Chair City ice cream after the game (it's made in Gardner).

(Both those first two games won easily by Lowell.)

In the third game I wasnt even assigned to start but was sent in for the last half only, against Worcester Classical, and ran back a punt 64 yards through the whole team for a touchdown, then knocked off two more touchdowns of about 25 yards apiece, carrying the ball only seven times for 20.6 yards per crack. This is in the newspaper records. (Lowell won that, too.)

Nevertheless, when the 'big test' came for Lowell against Manchester even then I was not a big heroic 'starter' but sat on the bench as now the kids of school in the stands took up a chant 'We want Duluoz, we want Duluoz.' Can you beat or figure that? I had to sit there and watch some of those bums prance and dance, one little leg sprain and there's heroic Pietryka making sure to remove his helmet when he was helped limping off the field so everybody could see his tragic hair waving in the autumn breeze. Supposed to be a piledriving fullback he really plowed and plumped like an old cow, and without the grim silent blocking of Bill Demmons in front of him he wouldnt have reached the line of scrimmage in time for an opening. Vaunted Manchester was overrated however, Lowell High won 20-0 and I was allowed to carry the ball just once in the last moment, the quarterback's call being for a line dive when what I wanted to do was sweep the end, so I got buried in tackle and the cry 'We want Duluoz' died and the game ended a minute or less than a minute later.

I admit they didnt need me anyway in that game (20-0), but when the fifth game came, I didnt start that either, but was allowed to play one quarter of it during which I scored 3 touchdowns, one called back, against Keith Academy, which we won 43-0. But quite understandably, if you understand football, either by now or before, quietly in the background I was now being scouted by Francis Fahey's men at Boston College who were already preparing to move to Notre Dame, in other words, I was getting interested attention from the highest echelons of American football, and on top of that the Boston *Herald* ran a headline on the sports pages that week, right across the top, saying DULUOZ IS THE 12TH MAN ON THE LOWELL HIGH SCHOOL ELEVEN, which was strange no matter how you slice it. Even in my own sixteen-year-old dewy brain there lurked the suspicion that something was wrong though I couldnt altogether (or wouldnt) believe my father's claim of favoritism. The coach, Tam Keating, seemed to glance at me sometimes with a kind of distant rugged regret, I thought, as though this misattention to my palpable straight powers was out of his hands. My father by now was enraged. A sportswriter, Joe Callahan, who was later to become publicity director at Notre Dame in the Francis Fahey regime and then president of the Boston Patriots in the American Football League, began to hint in his sports column about me that 'figures dont lie.' An enemy sportswriter who hated my Pa wrote of me as 'looking' like a football player. Wasnt that sweet?

VI

The next game against Malden was a meeting of the titans of Massachusetts high school football that year, tho I'd say Lynn Classical was tougher than both of us. Malden's huge beefy guards and tackles with grease under their eyes like war-painted Iroquois held us to a 0-0 tie over the whole afternoon (I still say Iddyboy Bissonnette should have been there but the coach told me his marks were not good enough, they'd sent Iddyboy home after a few practice sessions where he clobbered everyboy and coulda clobbered Everyman too). Nobody was hardly in possession of the ball all that Malden afternoon. But our magnificent line of Swoboda, Wain, Rave, Downing, Melis, Gringas, etc. brooked no boloney from them either. This afternoon made no difference whether I carried the ball, or started, or played just a quarter or not; it was a defensive pingpong BLONG of a game: dull enough but watched by interested observers.

My only real goof of the season was in the Lynn Classical game: they beat us 6-0 in Lynn, but had I not dropped that damned pass with my slippery idiot fingers at the goal line, a pass from Kelakis straight and true into my hands, we might have won, or tied, one. I've never gotten over the guilt of dropping that pass. If there had been no pigskin in football but just a good old floppy sock like you play with at ten. In fact I used to carry the pigskin with one hand while running and fumbled often. This was one thing the coach may not have liked. But it was the only way for me to run hard and dodge hard with full trackman's range and I didn't fumble any more than anybody else, anyhow.

Malden game was followed by a ridiculous game to be played

at New Britain Connecticut, big team, with all our whole squad screaming in hotel suites the night before the game, not drinking beer or anything like the kids must do nowadays but just no chance to sleep like at home on Friday nights, and so we lost that one cold. (Some had sneaked out to a dance.)

So now, being all discouraged, the great starters of the team, the heroes, had to rest after that fiasco in Connecticut, so I was left with a bunch of second-string kids to face Nashua (hometown of both my parents) in the raining mud, and as I say, it was an example of how they were treating me. After the game, mind you . . . well wait a minute. It was the toughest best game of football I ever played and it was the game that decided Fahey and also caught the attention of Lu Libble of Columbia and other sources like Duke University. Naturally, the heroes resting in Turkish baths at the Rex, I started this one, in mud that smells so sickly sweet, facing a lot of big tough Greeks, Polocks, Canucks and Yankee boys and collided with them till we were all caked beyond recognition of face or numerals on the jersey. The newspaper account concentrated on a report of the scoring plays, 19-13 favour of Nashua, but didnt keep tabs on the yardage by rushing because with my head down I averaged 130 out of 149 total yards for Lowell including one 60-yard run where I was caught from behind by a longlegged end but did make a 15-yard touchdown run with a pass in my arm. There were slippery fumbles on all sides, blocked kicks, sliding into the waiting arms of sideline spectators, yet this game remains in my mind the most beautiful I ever played and the most significant because I was being used (along with Bill Demmons) as a workhorse without glory and played the kind of game only a professional watcher could have applauded, a lonely secret backbone game piledriving through the murk with mud-blooded lips, the dream that goes back to old Gipper and Albie Booth games on old rainy newsreels.

With the regular team of course we could have won this one, nobody's a one-man team, but no, the heroes didnt like rainy mud.

That night at home I woke up in the middle of sleep with bunched cramp muscles called Charlie Horses that made me scream: yet no one had offered me a Turkish bath at the Rex after all that insane piledriving slippery plowing and bashing with mostly children on my side.

(But was somebody trying to raise the odds on the big Thanksgiving football game coming up next in ten days?)

VII

Okay, but comes the big Thanksgiving Day football game, the hallowed enemies are to meet, Lowell vs. Lawrence, in a zero weather field so hard it was like ice. Now the 'heroes' were ready and started without me. The heroes had to have their day on radio with eighteen thousand watching. I'm sitting in the straw at the foot of the bench, with, as they say in French, *mon derrière dans paille* ('my arse in the straw'). Comes the end of the first half, no score whatever. Second half they figure they might need me and put me in. (Maybe they figure I looked awful bad in that Nashua game and nobody'll care.) At one point I am almost loose, but some kid from Lawrence just barely trips me with a meaty Italian hand. But a few plays later Kelakis flips me a 3-yard lob over the outside end's hands and I take this ball and turn down the sidelines and bash and drive head down, head up, pause, move on. Downing throws a beautiful block, somebody else too, bumping I go, 18 yards, and just make it to the goal line where a Lawrence guy hits me and hangs on but I just jump out of his arms and over on my face with the game's only touchdown. The score is 8-0 because Harry Kiner has already blocked a Lawrence punt and jumped on it in the end zone for a 2-point safety. We could have won 2-0 anyway. Some line we had. But as the game ends, pandemonium and et cetera, I run immediately into the locker rooms in front of everybody else on the field so I can change fast for Thanksgiving Dinner at home and who's in the locker room of Lowell High cursing and kicking his helmet around, but Pie Menelakos, as though we'd lost, and cursing because it was I and not himself who scored the only touchdown of the game?

So there you have it.

He gets an offer from Norwich in Vermont while Francis Fahey comes to my house followed by Lu Libble's men a few days later.

So in this case, wifey, I could be bitter, I am bitter, but God gave my chance to help myself.

Poor Pa meanwhile, at home, turkey, cherry pies, free bowling in the alleys, hooray, my dream of going to college was in like Flynn.

Still I say, what means it? You may say I'm a braggart about football, although all these records are available in the newspaper files called morgue, I admit I'm a braggart, but I'm not calling it thus because what was the use of it all anyway, for as the Preacher sayeth: 'Vanity of vanities . . . all is vanity.' You kill yourself to get to the grave. Especially you kill yourself to get to grave before you even die, and the name of that grave is 'success', the name of that grave is hullaballoo boomboom horseshit.

BOOK TWO

1

Bragging still, but telling the truth still, during all this time I was getting A's and B's in high school, mainly because I used to cut classes at least once a week, to play hookey that is, just so I could go to the Lowell Public Library and study by myself at leisure such things as old chess books with their fragrance of scholarly thought, their old bindings, leading me to investigate other fragrant old books like Goethe, Hugo, of all things the *Maxims* of William Penn, just reading to show off to myself that I was reading. Yet this led the way to actual interest in reading. Led to a careful reading of H. G. Wells' *Outline of History*, stupid examinations of the Harvard Classics, and deep awe in the tiny print on onionskinned pages white as snow as found in the Eleventh Edition of the *Encyclopaedia Britannica* (Ency. Brit. XI Ed.) with its detailed record of all that ever happened until 1910 as compiled for the last time in copious happy terms by Oxford and Cambridge scholars – loving books and the smell of the old library and always reading in the rotunda part of the back where was a bust of Caesar in the bright morning sun and the entire range of cyclopedias in semicircle shelves. What even actually furthered my education there was that, at about 11 A.M., I'd saunter out of the library, cut through the Dutton Street tracks near the Y.M.C.A. so as not to be seen out the window maybe by Joe Maple my English teacher, cut across the railroad bridge near the Giant Store, over tracks that ran over naked crossties through which you could see that whirling deep canal with its plop of floating snows, then down Middlesex to the Rialto Theater, where I'd sit and study the old 1930's movies in careful detail. Well of course most of us have done this anyway but not when playing hookey at eight fifteen and after reading at leisure in library till eleven, hey?

Not only that, but that winter I was high scorer on the Lowell High track team and even had time to have my first love affair with Maggie Cassidy, said story recorded in novel of same name in detail.

Being a football and track star, a highgrade scholar, independent, nutty with independence in fact so that when blizzards broke out in Lowell it was only I by myself and nobody in sight out there in the woods of Dracut hiking kneedeep with a hockey stick, just to get an appetite for Sunday dinner and to pause under pines to hear the crazy crows go 'Yak.' Being also goodlooking and strong I'm sure a lot of people hated my guts then, even you, wifey, when you let slip last fall 'Well I was never popular like you were,' Fact was, I wasnt popular at all but hated by most, really, because after all that's going a little too far, trying to outdo everybody in everything except of course being invited to the Girl Officers' Ball and having my picture on the society page. Time enough for that, even, ha ha, as if I cared, or care now. That was vanity too, including that last remark, to make such an effort to cut everybody down. You'll be glad to know I got my comeuppance, so dont worry.

The next step was to pick a college. My mother insisted on Columbia because she eventually wanted to move there to New York City and see the big town. My father wanted me to go to Boston College because his employers, Callahan Printers of Lowell, were promising him a promotion if he could persuade me to go there and play under Francis Fahey. They also hinted he'd be fired if I went to any other college. Fahey, as I say, was at the house, and I have in my possession today a postcard he wrote Callahan saying: 'Get Jack to Boston College at all costs.' (More or less.) But I wanted to go to New York City too and see the big town, what on earth was I expected to learn from Newton Heights or South Bend Indiana on Saturday nights and besides I'd seen so many movies about New York I was . . . well no need to go into that, the waterfront, Central Park, Fifth Avenue, Don Ameche on the sidewalk, Hedy Lamarr on my arm at the Ritz. I agreed my mother was right as usual. She not only told me to leave Maggie Cassidy at home and go on to New York to school, but rushed to McQuade's and bought big sports jacket and ties and shirts out of her pitiful shoeshop savings that she kept in her corset, and arranged for me to board with her stepmother in Brooklyn in a nice big room with high ceiling and privacy so I could study and make good grades and get my sleep for the big football games. There were big arguments in the kitchen. My father was fired. He went downtrodden to work in places out of town, always riding sooty old trains back to Lowell on weekends. His only happiness in life now, in a way, considering the hissing old radiators in old cockroach hotel rooms of New England in the winter, was that I make good and justify him anyway.

That he was fired is of course a scandal and something about Callahan Printers I havent forgotten and is another black plume in my hat of 'success.' For after all what is success? You kill yourself and a few others to get to the top of your profession, so to speak, so that when you reach middle age or a little later you can stay home and cultivate your own garden in bliss: but by that time, because you've invented some kind of better mousetrap, mobs come rushing across your garden and trampling all your flowers. What's with that?

II

First, Columbia arranged to have me go to prep school in New York to make up credits in math and French, subjects overlooked by myself at Lowell High School. Big deal, I couldnt speak anything but French till I was six, so naturally I was in for an A right there. Math was basic, a Canuck can always count. The prep school was really an advanced high school called Horace Mann School for Boys, founded I s'pose by odd old Horace Mann, and a fine school it was, with ivy on granite walls, swards, running tracks, tennis courts, gyms, jolly principals and teachers, all on a high hill overlooking Van Cortlandt Park in New York City upper Manhattan. Well, since you've never been there why bother with the details except to say, it was at 246th Street in New York City and I was living with my stepgrandmother in Brooklyn New York, a daily trip of two hours and a half by subway each way.

Nothing deters young punk kids, not even today, here's how I managed it: a typical day:

First evening before first day of school I'm sitting at my large table set in the middle of my high-ceilinged room, stately erect in the chair, with pen in hand, books ranged before me and held up by noble bronze bookends found in the cellar. It is completely formal beginning of my search for success. I write: 'Journal. Fall, 1939. Sept. 21. My name is John L. Duluoz, regardless of how little that may matter to the casual reader. However, I find it necessary to give some pretense of explanation for the material existence of this Journal' and other such schoolboy stuff, followed by 'And I will give some sort of apology for using pen and ink.' ('Harrumph!' I'm thinking. 'Egad! Zounds, Pembroke!") And then I add in ink: 'It seems that such men as Thackeray, Johnson, Dickens, and others had to compile vast volumes in pen and ink, and despite the fact that I not modestly admit some degree of proficiency in typewriting, I feel that I should not proceed in my literary ventures with such ease as would befit a typewriter. I feel that a recurrence to the old method would sort of leave a silent tribute to those old gladiators, those immortal souls of journalism. Stay! I am not in any way suggesting that I am included in their fold, but that what was good enough for them, should by all means suit me.'

This done, I go downstairs to the basement where my great-stepmother Aunt Ti Ma has fixed up her place like a combination of gypsy with drapes and hanging beads in doorways, and lace doilies Victorian style, a thousand dolls, comfort, beautiful, clean, neat chairs, reading her paper, big fat happy Ti Ma. Her husband is Nick the Greek, Evangelakis, whom she met and married in Nashua N.H. after the death of my own mother's Pa. Her daughter Yvonne, blue-eyed, companion of her mother, married to Joey Robert who comes home every night at eleven with the *Daily News* from a trucking warehouse job and gets in his T-shirt at the kitchen table and reads. Down there they have for me all the time great vast glasses of milk and beautiful Sand Tart cakes from Cushman's of Brooklyn. They say 'Go to bed early now, Jacky, school and practice tomorrow. You know what your Mama said, gotta make good.' But before I go to bed, full of cake and ice cream, I make my lunch for the next day: always the same: I butter one sandwich plain and the other peanut butter and jam, and throw in a fruit, either apple or banana, and wrap it up nice and put it in bag. Then Nick, Uncle Nick, takes me by the arm and says: 'When you have more time I tell you some more about Father Coughlin. If you want some more books, there are many more in the cellar. Look this one.' He hands me a dusty old Jules Romain novel called *Ecstasy*, no I think it was *Rapture*. I take it upstairs and add it to my library. My room is separated from Aunt Yvonne's by nothing but a huge double glass door but the gypsy drapes are there. My own room has a disusable marble fireplace, a little sink in an alcove, and a huge bed. Out the vast Brooklyn Thomas Wolfe windows I see exactly what Wolfe always saw, even in that very month: old red light falling on Brooklyn warehouse windows where men lean out on sills in undershirts chewing on toothpicks while taking a break.

I set up my neatly pressed pants, sports jacket, schoolbooks, shoes in place together neatly, socks over that, wash and go to bed. I set the alarm clock for, listen to this, 6 A.M.

At 6 A.M. I groan and get out, wash, dress, go downstairs, take that lunchbag and rush out into the pippin red nippy streets of Brooklyn and go three blocks to the IRT subway at the El on Fulton Street. Down I go and push into the subway with hundreds of people carrying newspapers and lunchbags. I stand all the way to Times Square, threequarter solid hour, every blessed morning. But what does young dughead do about it? I whip out my math book and do all me homework while standing, lunch between feet. I always find a corner where I can sorta guard my lunch between feet and where I can lean and turn and study with face to lurching car wall. What a stink in there, of hundreds of mouths breathing and no air coming in; the sickening perfume of women; the well-known garlic breath of Old New York; old men coughing and secretly spitting between their feet. Who lived through it?

Everybody.

By the time we're at Times Square, or maybe Penn Station at 34th just before that, most people rush out, to midtown work, and Ah, I get the usual corner seat and start in on the physics studies. Now it's easy sailing. At 72nd Street we pick up another slue of workers headed for uptown Manhattan and Bronx work but I dont care anymore: I've got a seat. I turn to the French book and read all those funny French words we never speak in Canadian French, I have to consult and look them up in the glossary in back, I think with anticipation how Professor Carton of French class will laugh at my accent this morning as he asks me to get up and read a spate of prose. The other kids however read French like Spanish cows and he actually uses me to teach them the true accent. Now you'd think I'm close to school but from 96th Street we go past Columbia College, we go into Harlem, past Harlem, way up, another hour, till the subway emerges from the tunnel (as tho by nature it was impossible for it to go underground so long) and goes soaring to the very end of the line in Yonkers practically.

Near school? No, because there I have to go down the elevated steps and then start up a steep hill about as steep as 45 degrees or a little less, a tremendous climb. By now all the other kids are with me, puffing, blowing steam of morning, so that from 6 A.M. when I got up in Brooklyn, till now, 8:30, it's been two and a half hours of negotiating my way to actual class. A chore I found a thousand times more difficult than when we used to walk that mile and a half to Bartlett Junior High School from Pawtucketville and Rosemont.

III

I dont understand why, except it must be an exceptional school; but 96 percent of the students are Jewish kids and most of them are very rich: sons of furriers, famous realtors, thissa and thatta and here come mobs of them in big black limousines driven by chauffeurs in visored hats, carrying large lunchboxes full of turkey sandwiches and Napoleons and chocolate milk in thermos bottles. Some of them, like students of the first form, are only ten years old and 4 feet tall; some of them are funny little fat tubs of lard, I guess because they didnt have to climb that hill. But most of the rich Jewish kids took the subway from apartments on Central Park West, Park Avenue, Riverside Drive. The other 4 percent or so of the students were from prominent Irish and other families, such as Mike Hennessey whose father was the basketball coach of Columbia, or Bing Rohr a German boy whose father had been a big contractor connected with building the gym. Then came the 1 percent to which I belonged, called ringers, B or A average students who were also athletes, from all over, New Jersey, Massachusetts, Connecticut, Pennsy, who had been given partial financial scholarship arrangements to come to Horace Mann, get their credits for college, and make the joint the Number One high school football team in New York City, which we did that year.

But first, 8:45 or so, we all had to sit in the auditorium and be led in the singing of 'Onward Christian Soldiers' by English Professor Christopher Smart, followed by 'Lord Jeffrey Amherst' which was a song no more appropriate for me to sing (as descendant of French and Indian) than it was appropriate for the Jewish kids to sing 'Onward Christian Soldiers.' It was fun no less.

Then the classes began. History class with Professor Albert which bored me because this was the only classroom that faced east-northeast across the dim trees of Van Cortlandt Park and therefore faced toward Lowell, in fact the trees had the dim Indian look of Masschusetts trees, so I sat there not really listening to Albert and pondering my own history: Maggie Cassidy foremost, as would all seventeen-year-old reveries, but also my Pa, proud by now, my Ma (at the very moment seeing that my typewriter was being mailed and would arrive that very afternoon in Brooklyn, for instance), and my sister. A welling of tears almost to remember the boyhood friends waiting back there for me. Had the idea history would never interest me anyway, and besides Professor Albert was dull on the subject, accurate yes, I s'pose, but history is best explained dramatically, because for God's sake nobody's going to tell me that massive Homeric War so to speak, between the Achaeans and the Iliums was caused merely by some economic factor concerning trade, what about the trade in Helen's chastity belt? Or the belt in the eye Paris was about to get from Philoctetes? Anyway, this was the class that I spent mooning and viewing the window vistas especially on cloudy days when the trees held that sad New England non-New Yorkish deep gray knighthood look. Directly across the hall it was then physics class with sprightly little Billy Wine explaining Archimedes' bathtub, or Ohm's law which I never could figure, where in fact I was really the dunce of the class but caught on later and made a fair mark (B-minus). I'd never fiddled with the mechanics of an auto, for instance, like all the other football players in the class; they laughed at me because I didnt know the essentials of a battery. I was about to show em a battery out on the field.

Next class was English with Professor Christopher Smart; now what better name should your English teacher have unless it be William Blake or Robert Herrick or Lord Geoffrey Chaucer? And from him I always got an A-plus, old Joe Maple of Lowell High School had done me well teaching to appreciate not only Walt Whitman but Emily Dickinson and letting the other kids moon over Ernest Henley's 'My head is bloody, but unbowed.' In English class it developed that I had to write a half-dozen term papers for some of the wealthy Jewish kids, at two dollars a throw, and for the football ringers for free or else. Easy, with my typewriter in my Brooklyn quarters. You may say this was bad but what about Deni Bleu selling daggers behind the lockers to little tubby kids for a fin?

Lunch was where everybody removed their lunchbags from their lockers and rushed into the cafeteria type dining room to grab the milk or soft drinks or coffee. Here I ate my humble awful lunch among fragrant turkey sandwiches, it wasnt the first time I was about to eat worse than everybody in sight, and later, with success assured at last, as they say, lost my appetite anyway. Sometimes a rich kid would give me a delicious fresh juicy chicken sandwich, ah wow, especially Jonathan Miller who got to really like me and was the first to invite me home for dinner and finally for whole weekends where, on Friday mornings, say, after some holiday dance, his rich Wall Street financier father would get up and sit at a grand mahogany table in the diningroom, in this seventeenth-floor apartment on West End Avenue right across from the Schwab Mansion (still standing then), and out of the kitchen would come out a sweet Negro butler bringing him his grapefruit. Which the old man would proceed to dig into with a spoon, and just like in the movies the spurt of grapefruit juice would hit me in the eye across the tablecloth. Then he'd have one simple softboiled egg in an eggcup, neatly whack it, eat out of it with a silver spoon, adjust his spectacles, say over the New York *Times* to his son Jonathan: 'Jonathan, why arent you like your friend Jack here? He is, as we say in Latin, *mens sana et mens corpora*, healthy mind and healthy body. He combines all the excellence of a Greek, that is, the brain of an Athenian and the brawn of a Spartan. And you, look at you.' This was awful. Because poor old Jonathan was the first guy to get me interested in formal literature apart from the Sherlock Holmes interests I'd had so far in my kid compositions, got me to understand Hemingway and try to write like him, and showed me a thing or two around town later in the way of avant-garde movies, and manners, and mores, and Dixieland jazz. Anyway sometimes at lunch, seeing my awful peanut butter sandwiches, he'd offer me some of his chicken sandwiches beautifully prepared by his maid, and the football team would guffaw. I was not popular with the other members of the football team because they thought I was hanging around with the nonathletic Jewish kids and snubbing the athletes, for sandwiches, favors, dinners, two-dollar term papers, and they were right I guess. But I was fascinated by Jewish kids because I'd never met any in my life, especially these well-bred, rather fawncy dressers, tho they all had the ugliest faces I ever saw and awful pimples. I had pimples too, tho.

Sometimes lunch, in good weather, would then spill out into

the green lawns and we'd all stand around having soft drinks in the sun, if it was a snow thaw there'd be snowball fights and snowballs thrown against the Tom Brown plaque on the ivied walls that said: 'Horace Mann School for Boys.' It's only today I found out Horace Mann's son once went on a trip to Minnesota with Henry David Thoreau, a neighbor of mine at Walden Pond near Concord, trees of which I can see on clear days from this present upstairs bedroom where I'm writing this *Vanity of Duluoz*.

IV

After lunch it was the French class, mentioned before, Professor Carton of Georgia actually a sickly but sweet old Southerner who liked me and wrote letters to me later and I think was a bit on the gay side, in the best sense. In this class I got to sit next to Lionel Smart, who became my really best friend, Liverpool Jew of some sort from London whose father, a renowned chemist, had sent him and brother and mother to the United States to avoid the London blitz: also rich: but who taught me jazz by taking me down to the Apollo Theater in Harlem after the football season where we sat in the front row and had our eyes and ears blasted out by the full great Jimmy Lunceford band and later Count Basie.

He was funny, Lionel. In the following class, math, he was called 'Nutso' by Professor Kerwick. Professor Kerwick says: 'Now boys, smart are ye? I'll give you a number series and I want you to tell me what the relation is' (or words to that effect, I'm no calculus-iser). He said: 'Are you ready? Here it is: 14, 34, 42, 72, 96, 103, 110, 116, 125.' Nobody could figure out but it rang a strange familiar tune in my noodle and I almost was about to jump up and announce what it 'sounded' like at least but was afraid of our football quarterback, Biff Quinlan, who kept giving me wry looks because I hung around with Lionel and Jonathan Miller and the other Jewish kids instead of him and his bunch of thugs you might say (today Biff however is beloved respected old football coach at Horace Mann School for Boys, so of course he was no thug, nobody was), but I was afraid of being laughed at. As for Nutso everybody laughed at him anyway. 'All right, Nutso Smart, get up and tell me what that is.'

'I don't knaow," he says with his London accent, blushing as usual, slouching like a hepcat or like Lester Young the jazz tenorman on a street corner, in loose-fitting beautiful sports coats one different every day of the month practically.

Prof Kerwick glared at all of us, eyes popping, face red, glasses glinting, 'Ha ha ha, it's the express stops on the Seventh Avenue Subway, you bunch of plob heads.'

Finally, end of day, with the same guy we had to endure geometry. The only thing I remember learning there was that if you stick a ruler in the ground next to a tall tree, and measure the shadow of the ruler and the shadow of the tree, you can get the height of the tree without having to climb it like Tarzan. I can measure the circumference of a circle? I can draw a circle in the earth and call Mephistopheles, or do ring-around-the-rosy, but can never also figure what's inside of it. Again the football boys excelled me in this.

V

Ah, but now the football field. Practice. We don our regalia, as Don Regalia the sportswriter always says in the New York *Sun*, and we come out. Of all things and lo and behold, the coach of Horace Mann, Ump Mayhew, is going to let me start every game and is going to let me do the punting and even a little passing. It seems he thinks I'm okay. I start practicing my kicking and by God after a few days I've got some spiraling kicks soaring into the blue and landing sometimes 65 yards away (with the wind behind me). But in cases where the wind is against me, he tells me to spiral em off low, like bullets, which I learn to do off the right part of my turned-in right foot, boom. And further, he teaches me to quick-kick, which means, you're lined up as tho ready to receive the ball and run with it. You make a step as tho you're going to plunge into the line. Instead you take one quick step back, still bending low, and just plunk the ball on a low line drive over everybody's head out over the safety man's head because in this case he's running up anyway to catch you running. Result: the ball goes belumping back 30 or 40 yards and everybody runs after it and sometimes we recover it ourselves and that's one of the tricks that made our team not only the high school champs of New York City that year but what they called in the paper 'the mythical prep school champs' of New York City.

Which is no mean achievement for a high school team.

Reason why is Biff Quinlan, aforementioned quarterback and present-day coach now, who was a bull of a boy, about my size but with a bigger neck and even bigger calf muscles, and brains, I mean football brains, what you call a field general: the guy who examines the situation and decides what to do next. Then there was the other back, Bud Heilbroner, rangy, fast and wiry somewhat like Kiner of Lowell High School, who was a good blocker and a tough competitor tho he had mainly come to Horace Mann for baseball reasons (a big league prospect). Then we had a nifty little Italian passer Rico Corelli from New Jersey (all these other guys were from New Jersey practically) who had, however, the same flair for dramatisation and iddly-piddly that Menelakos had at Lowell. In any case, we didnt need him much, because Quinlan could pass just as well in a pinch.

It was the line, really, as usual, that made us something to watch. It was the wiry little center, Hunk Lebreon, a blue-eyed black-haired Breton like me (tho he didnt know it or care to know it), who was so ferocious on defense and downfield blocking he had everybody scattering everywhichaway. He was small, but big Ray DeLucia of the Bronx was big, and even with early hurt collarbone, at his end of the defensive line not much got through. Then there was this sort of waterfront tough, a big blond Forrest Tucker-looking type tho not as big, who was scary just to look at and just as strong, Roy Hartmann. There were other good boys, two Germans who came from rich families (not Jews but real Germans), not necessarily real pro type football players but very good. I think the key to our football team was really Gus Bath, who, when you looked at him, looked like a slim lounger around poolhalls, who moved lazy, had no strength it seemed, gazelle sort of, but was all over the place like horse manure, which is another way of saying 'ubiquitous,' when the chips were down. He was the other end. With Bath and DeLucia on each end, and Lebreon in the middle at center, and Hartmann the blond bull at tackle, and a quiet fellow called Art Theodore mild as spring's first muddy moon, and Ollie Masterson (really a basketball star but a competitor, and a competitor who got all shot up in World War II later), we had a line that could allow me and Quinlan to roll.

VI

Now the typical first day was over: we showered after practice, dressed up and went our various ways, me down the hill to the subway with my books, bone-weary of course, dark over the roofs of upper Manhattan, the long El ride dipping down into the subway, zoom down thru old Manhattoes, me thinking 'What's up there above this hole? Why, it's sparkling Manhattan, shows, restaurants, newspaper scoops. Time Square, Wall Street, Edward G. Robinson chomping on a cigar in Chinatown.' But I had to stick to my guns and ride all the way to Brooklyn and get off there, trudge to Ma's roominghouse (we called her Ti Ma) and there was my huge steaming supper, eight thirty, almost time for bed already, barely time to talk to old Nick about Father Coughlin or Greek pastries and of course no time to do any homework in my room.

I went up to my room and looked sighing at that first entry I'd made the night before, the big 'opening night,' which ended: 'I am now making elaborate preparations for tomorrow. I've set the clock, gotten my clothes ready, etc. Tonight I evolved a plan of self-tutoring which I commenced officially. The subjects are five in number and I shall take one per evening, with a subsequent self-examination for the week after. The subjects are Mythology, Latin, Spanish, Literature, and History. As if I didn't have enough studies coming up from the ivy halls of Horace Mann. However, my motto is "The more you study, the more you subsequently know; naturally, the more you know, the nearer you get to perfection as a journalist." ' So then.

So now, Sept. 25, 1939, I write wearily: 'Today was very hectic. Opening of school, practice, arrival of mail and typewriter, and all the subsequent excitement and work render me incapable of record.'

And so the Journal ended there.

Time enough to get around to that later, them thar journals and stuff, as you'll see.

VII

After a few minutes of dozing at my great bookish table I just got up and went to bed, first making my lunch downstairs and kissing Ma and Yvonne goodnight and listening to Joey in his undershirt explain to me what's happened in New York today.

In the morning at six I get up, take lunch, but no books, I've made up my mind. I ride the subway standing up all the way to Times Square but instead of doing my homework I'm watching the faces of New York at leisure. It's just like in Lowell again, I'm playing hookey to study other facets of life. It's like, I could have called this book 'The Adventurous Education of Jack Duluoz.'

I get off at Times Square all tingling with excitement, come out on a sparkling fall day, and go down to the Paramount Theater which I know at this time wont be crowded, wait around wandering the theater marquee streets till the doors open, go into the huge carpeted movie palace and sit right down in tenth row front to watch the huge neat screen and the stage show that follows.

Then I come out, hungry, eat my lunch at a counter with milk shakes, outdoor counters of Times Square, as thousands of junkies and criminals and whores and working people and what-not rush by, my what a sight for a smalltown boy, and then, idly and almost suavely, knowing exactly where to go, I saunter to yon Apollo Theater where it says on the marquee: 'Jean Gabin in *The Lower Depths*, Also Louis Jouvet in *Bizarre, Bizarre*.' . . . French movies! And in those days they were presented in French soundtrack, as originally made, but with English subtitles below, so that if Professor Carton missed me that day in HM French class, he shoulda been with me to watch them eyes of mine dart from subtitle to face of actor, to mouth of actor, as, innocently, I tried to figure out why these people of Paris spoke so much through their throat, spitting like Arabs, instead of on their tongues, frankly, that is, *franchement*, one of the many things to say the least I was going to learn out of school. (Gabin spoke good French.) (As for the film at the Paramount, it was probably Alice Faye in the rain with a spaghetti signboard because she failed to pay her restaurant bill.)

Now, midafternoon, I came out of the French theater, knew it was impossible to go to football practice two hours away and uptown, and could not attend anyway from stiff muscles, so I looked around for still another movie, across the street from the Apollo, say, where was Errol Flynn and Miriam Hopkins in *Virginia City* and boy what fun, emerging in the glittering lights of autumn dusk and all set to go home to Brooklyn with a whole day's different kind of learning in my belly. The New York Public Library was only two blocks away but since I had the choice of more than just the Lowell Rialto . . . and anyway time enough for that too.

The moral of what I'm saying is, as when I said 'Adventurous Education,' let a kid learn his own way, see what happens. You cant lead a horse to water. Just as I'm writing exactly what I remember according to the way that I want to remember in order, and not pile the reader with too much extraneous junk, so, let a kid pick out exactly what he wants to do in order not to grow up into a big bore rattling off the zoological or botanical or whatever names of butterflies, or telling Professor Flipplehead the entire history of the Thuringian Flagellants in Middle German on past midnight by the blackboard.

In these cases, the mind knows what it's doing better than the guile, because the mind flows, the guile dams up, that is, the mind strides but the guile limps. And that's no guileless statement, however, and that's no Harvard lie, as M.I.T. will measure soon with computers and docks of Martian data.

VIII

The first game of the year we had to face a powerful team called Blair, undefeated, and we were not ready for them mainly I think because we'd just met anyway and came from all over the eastern map. We had a couple of school frumps in the lineup anyway that we weeded out later. In the first part of the game we almost went all the way for the first touchdown but the big Blair boys stopped us and rolled us back and went over us 13-0 so everybody figured HM was a frump team as usual.

They werent reckoning with that core lineup of tought eggs of ours. In fact, on the basis of that first seasonal loss, Columbia, which had probably intended to send the Columbia freshman team to play us the following week as per schedule, simply sent up the Columbia freshman *seconds*. It was a sin. By that time we had practiced all week and got our signals straight and in a pouring rain clobbered them 20-0. In this game, as against Blair, I got off those pesky quick kicks, and then, from deep punt formation received the long pass from Lebreon at center, pretended to punt, but ran, through the open sieve of defenses, and went all the way. Quinlan also scored, and Heilbroner. Another long run I made and a longlegged fellow came up behind me in the mud and caught me right near the goal line from the back, just as in the Nashua game, recall, but this time he had me by the scruff of the shoulderpad neck and just dumped me down on my noggin. I was knocked out. Good enough, getting it back after that Halmalo incident in sandlot Lowell.

Funny, too, that after I regained consciousness, and they figured I could go on, it happened to be the moment of the change of quarters, so we had to line up going in the opposite directions. What they didn't know was that I was still dotty and woozy. In fact I leaned there in the huddle with my mates in the rain and was asking myself, 'What are we doing on this rainy field that tilts over in the earth, the earth is crooked, where am I? Who am I? What's that?'

'I said four, seven, three on the scobbish' (the more-or-less quarterback instructions as I registered them).

'O yeah?'

'Whatsa matter you dotty Dulouse?'

'He oughta be, he just got knocked out.'

"'Well just stand there, or run, or fall down, let's go, boys.' And they all ran back to assume their positions and I stood there in the rain watching them, watching the tilted earth, with a goonybird look (maybe I'm crazy and my parts are scattered still), and bang, the play develops, I just stand there watching it. It was the first time I was ever knocked out, except for a childhood tumble in Massachusetts, when I felt it had all happened before in exactly the same way. I've heard of men dying saying 'I remember this' and in fact up ahead in the story is just that. . . .

But we won that game easily, 20-0, and after the game we all ran into the gym and I felt sufficiently recovered to accept Jonathan Miller's challenge to a wrestling match in the regular ring they had there near the lockers, little Jonathan Miller (on the wrestling team) wearing full wrestling regalia: me in my jockstrap only, I'm afraid, fall down on my back, grab his legs with my feet squeezing, turn him over to his belly, jump on his back and pull out an arm (not hurting him) and bend it, put my other arm through the bend, and fold a knee over the whole shebang and give him the old whango bango, holding him locked there like a lobster claw as the football players, watching me wrestling a goon, yell 'Hey the great Dulouse, look at him go.' But I'll bet you, nobody on that team challenged me to wrestle, that was a fast move, faster than that when you consider I didnt hurt him. As you know, wifey, wrestling used to be a big art in Lowell and at one time I was the Masked Marvel of Pawtucketville, as my older cousin Edgar was, and my father used to promote wrestling matches from Lowell to There.

What annoyed me was the way the football team, that is, the other ringers from New Jersey, looked down on me for playing around with the Jewish kids. It wasnt that they were anti-Semitic, they were just disdainful I think of the fact these Jewish kids had money and ate good lunches, or came to school some of em in limousines, or maybe, just as in Lowell, they considered them too vainglorious to think about seriously. Okay. Okay. Because now the big game was coming up against St John's Prep which we were s'posed to lose 100 to 0.

IX

That was the following Saturday, sunny cold day, beautiful for football, Uncle Nick saw to it I went to bed early Friday night and in the morning I told him I'd take a walk first and then together we would ride the subway to HM and he was going to see me play for the first time. I went out, got a haircut on Schermerhorn Street, staring at my ugly face (I thought) in the mirror, then went down to the local soda parlor and ate two huge hot fudge sundaes. A dim figure lurked back and forth on the sidewalk with gray felt hat, hands clasped at back, sneaking, stalking, but I never noticed it. Full of hot fudge sundaes I went back to Ma's house, picked up Nick, we got on the subway and rode those hours up along the rib of Manhattan reading the *Daily News*.

At the HM field the big day, the maroon-clad St John's Prep team, undefeated, proud, jumping around and ready for a cinch. Out come me and Biff Quinlan and the gang and get out on that field. I remember at one point a St Johnner getting loose and going up the sidelines by the crowd. I was playing safety, that is, in the position to catch punts and run em back. But in this game, full of good hot fudge sundaes, I was hot to be a defensive player too, just for once. In fact all my football life I only played wild determined defense when I felt like it. I came up on that guy as fast as I'd come up on Halmalo that day in Lowell at age thirteen, actually went past him out of bounds into the crowd, but just stuck my right arm out and took him with me 10 feet into the mob.

Standing there in that yelling scattered mob (some of them on the ground) was the assistant backfield freshman coach of Columbia, McQuade, who later told me he never saw such a terrifying tackle in his life. 'How come you're not hot on defense anymore?' And nobody was hurt, either, that's the point of the terror of that tackle. That poor St John runner thought the Lord God himself had swept him off to Heaven, I'm telling you, that's how swift and easy it was.

'Attaboy Jack' yelled the team beginning to like me. We buckled down to give the favorites hell. Biff Quinlan drilled a pass right into waiting Ray DeLucia's arms in the end zone, and we won 6-0. All we have to do for the rest of the game is smear St John's and push em back. It was the biggest upset of the season in New York City. We were actually the mythical, that is, the unofficial champions of prep school football in New York City, and such a scandal! That night in the *World Telegram* a big story told how HM had cheated and brought in bruisers all over from New Jersey, Bronx, Pennsy, Mass. as 'ringers' and that it wasnt kosher to do so. But there wasnt one large-sized 'bruiser' among us. We were all little guys, relatively, except De Lucia. The reporters were in the showers looking at us and shaking their heads. Who the hell could beat St John's?

Why, St John Duluoz and the boys, naturally, and this may sound funny but this was the second time that on a high school team I had participated in the defeat of St John's Prep. You see, a prep school is a step up over a high school. That other time, written about in *Maggie Cassidy*, was when me with the leadoff stick, then Joe Melis, the Mickey Maguire, then Johnny Kazarakis, actually defeated St John's Prep relay team in the Boston Garden in another unbelievable upset (not that I contributed so much in either case, it's just that you've got to have old St John aboard).

Joking aside, after that game everybody was afraid of us.

X

On Armistice Day, next game, my Pop Emil Duluoz came down all the way from Lowell just to see me play against Garden City, in Long Island, and also to check on how my studies were going, how the situation was in the boardinghouse in Brooklyn, go see a few shows, eat a few New York steaks, take me out to see the town and generally amuse himself. Naturally I wanted to show off for Pop. Funny man that he is, and used to locker rooms as a former wrestling *and* boxing promoter around Lowell, he hung around as we changed and joked with us and the coaches didnt mind one bit: and my father's presence amused the rest of the team. 'That kooky Dulouse's got a hell of a nice father.' None of their own fathers ever dared to come in the locker room. We went out and took the field against poor Garden City and somewhat hurt them, if you ask me. For instance at one point, after throwing a block for Biff Quinlan I look up from the ground and see his big feet plowing onward about 20 yards with his head down, over the goal line, knocking kids aside in every direction. And a few plays later, to show off to my father and remind him again, some poor Garden City kid is waltzing around his left end precisely as Halmalo had done, but he a stranger in this case, I pull the same trick, come up full speed, low, get inside his interference and hit him head on in a legitimate and clean tackle at the knees that knocks him back 10 feet. Off the field on a stretcher.

Now I begin to feel bad about football and war. And showing off. But after the game (HM 27, Garden City 0) my father is beaming and all delighted as we shower. 'Come on Jacky me boy, we're going out and hit the town tonight.' So we go down to Jack Delaney's steak restaurant on Sheridan Square, myself little knowing how much time I was destined to spend around that square, in Greenwich Village, in darker years, but tenderer years, to come.

Ah it's Good Friday night and I'm going to write what I want.

XI

In a way, tho, I was paying back my father in good kind for the humiliation of his being fired because I had not wanted (had not wanted?), hadnae wanted to go to a Jesuit school, let's put it flatly. Not only did I want to go to Columbia College in New York City so I could dig the city instead of, say, South Bend, or Boston, or Durham N.C., but I didnt like the idea of being told what to think by professors in big black robes and end up . . . well, I dont know where I got the idea that Jesuits are not to be trusted, but I've been reading about that in history these past years, the only hitch being, lo and bingo, I'm now one of the world's worst secret Jesuits, everything I do is based on some kind of proselytisation, everything I've written, just take a close look. 'I got this position where the Jesuits aint got no right to be sore at me and where the non-Jesuits may sigh and rest,' I'm sayin to myself tonight. To each his own.

What do the Jesuits really say? That everybody's got to be a Catholic because there's no other way out of the impasse of medieval theology. But if like Pascal, Blaise Pascal, their 'enemy' in the seventeenth century, they simply should say that Christ is the Son of God because nobody can *prove* otherwise, I should have bought them. Yet I'm a Jesuit today, secret General of the Order, like Ulysses S. Grant the general that rocks in the rocking chair with a bottle . . . but more of this later when I get into the history of the vanity of what resulted from the football and the college studies that led to the writing and the thinking, wifey dear.

So here comes the game against Tome. Tome is an undefeated team (prep school) from Maryland and has absolutely no regard for our awesome reputation now in New York City. Here they are all lined up. I've again had my two hot fudge sundaes in Brooklyn that morning, that 'shadow' has twice passed the windows of the ice cream parlor, again I ride uptown with Uncle Nick. This time he's looking at me funny.

A cold sunny day, all the gang from the school yelling on the sidelines, and midway in the first quarter I get a punt spiraling down to me from the blue and hope to God I wont drop it because I'm not going to raise my hand and ask for a fair catch, which would mean, catch it and touch it down to the ground meekly. I know they'll be right on me when I catch it. But once it's in my breadbasket and there they are looming over me, the Tome ends who've come barreling down the field to nab me, I dart to the right laughing and go scooting along past their outstretched hands and come up to the sidelines where I see my chums cheering: Bill Keresky, Gene Mackstoll, Jimmy Winchel (more about them later) and I yell: 'Hey Bill! Hey Gene!' and seeing a guy from Tome is coming up to bump me into the crowd I reverse, that is, *reverse* is too slow a word, I *jack off* to the left, leaving everybody ('Jack be Nimble, Jack be Quick!' said the little picture Ma had hung on my bedroom wall in Lowell) and there I am sweeping into the whole gang in midfield. I've caught the punt on my own 28-yard line, I'm now at midfield. They're all there. Lebreon throws a block across a Tome guy so I jack right again and sprint to the sidelines again. Once again a Tome guy. I jack off left again, leave him there, another downfield block by Hartmann, another by De Lucia, another by Theodore, even Quiffy Quinlan is rolling around some guy's legs; I see that all I have to do is keep my eyes open and slant right in another 30 yards as fast as I can. I get to the 5-yard line, am in trouble with a cluster of three Tome men, come right up on them staring right at them like I'm going to try to bust head on into their midst and scatter them, which they laugh to think is impossible, being big, but brainy suddenly jacks off right again, leaving them there doing the minuet, and we win the game 6-0, another big upset in the prep school east in 1939.

In this game, too, somewhere in the third quarter, I let loose a quick kick I'll never forget. (Now if Quinlan, Corelli *et al.* want to reminisce about their great play in that game and the others, let them, but this is my turn.) I actually squatted down as if to catch the center pass and run, back up, plunked the ball, just right off my twisted-in foot, and spiraled through the air a 55-yard punt that then proceeded to roll another 30 yards or so in the wind and ended up resting on the Tome two or some such awful development for them. And I even threw a pass, I think my second pass of the year, an idea by Ump Mayhew as element of surprise, and completed it, to Quinlan, who caught it and ran a first down out the sidelines.

Mainly, you might say, it was myself that gazed on our coach Mayhew with amazement, more than the amazement with which he gazed at me, because for the first time in my official football career a coach had actually let me play every minute of every game in exactly the manner I was born to play.

And my Paw wrote him that.

And after the Tome game was over and we were the heroes of New York City prep football, up comes that 'shadow' behind me, touches me on the shoulder, it's Uncle Nick, he says to me: 'If you not eat so many hot fudge sundaes this morning, you score six more touchdowns.'

BOOK THREE

I

After that it was the usual resting on laurels, waiting to go to Columbia the following autumn, casual movies, casual love affairs (?) (no such thing), casualties not crass, in any case, in other words, since I didnt play basketball (too short) and didnt want to run outdoor track I had nothing to do all winter but enjoy my new friends, the classes too, a whole mess of idle stuff that can be summed up in a few succinct cameo sentences in a paragraph: as wit:

Weekends at Ray Olmsted's apartment with his parents and kid brother, in Yonkers, the affair with Betty there, skating on the Yonkers pond and a few kisses here and there. Sharpy Gimbel yelling 'Hi' from his convertible at the dance. Excited talks over scores with Izzy Carson in his West End Avenue apartment. A cigar given to me by a cigar manufacturer. New York Giants football games at Polo Grounds with Gene and his father. Central Park at dawn. Chuck Derounian the Armenian kid playing me old Bix records in Washington Heights. Hors d'oeuvres at Jake Kraft's on Fifth Avenue, incredibly thick rugs and huge marble statuettes and fragrance of coats in the hall. Walks in the blizzard across the Brooklyn Bridge, alone. Running down Fifth Avenue downtown pellmell with a small paralysed man in my arms, with . . . wait a minute, pushing a small paralysed man down lower Fifth Avenue in his wheelchair, taking him in my arms, putting him in the cab, folding in his wheelchair, he saying 'Thanks, that was a great run! I'm a music publisher, my name is Porter.'

(True.) (Cole Porter on a secret spree?)

Everybody sighing to kiss Babsy Schler who must be the ugliest bat on earth today by now. Interviewing Glenn Miller backstage at the Paramount Theater for the school paper, Glenn Miller saying 'Shit ' Interviewing Count Basie in the Savoy Ballroom in Harlem, for the school paper, Count saying: 'I want quiet brass.' Hanging around lunchcarts hoping to meet Hemingway heroes. Lounging around with the Irish gang of Horace Mann, Hennessey, Gully Swift, O'Grady, with feet slightly stuck out and a certain accent. Same gang on street corner on Columbia campus when I visit Hennessey for weekends there, now with Jacky Cabot and others including one silent slender lad: William F. Buckley, Jr! Sunday mornings on Park Avenue looking out the Venetian blinds of David Knowles' bedroom, his parents away, his maid coming in with breakfast. Every one of them I went to their house. Dean John Goldthwaite introducing his son to me in front of the rose-covered granite cottage on HM campus, son turns out to be president of a giant airline today. Everybody in the school wants the two pretty girls in the office staff down in the lockers. Class photo Duluoz fails to show up, too busy somewhere. At a school play the Gerson twins come out of both ends of a box: both look alike: one of them later saw 'insects in the snow' in Red China. Jimmy Winchel, pimply, playing the violin and chasing after girls all the way to the Riviera, it turned out, after which he had to charge to Brazil with two million. Jonathan Miller looking at me thru slitted eyes because of what his father said. Gully Swift playing pingpong. Reginald W. Klein putting on an English accent, saying he's going to be a poet. Mike Hennessey looking at me and saying 'Flazm.' Marty Churchill making extra money, tho rich, by walking an old invalid down upper Broadway every night at eight. Ray Olmsted combing his hair with Tyrone Power eyebrows. Jacob U. Gelsenheimer serious on the viola. S. Martin Gerber looking thru a microscope. Ern Salter patting his belly like comedian Jack E. Leonard. Biff Quinlan shaking his head at me. Irv Berg on the microphone. Joe A. Gold, later to be killed in the war, having me for weekend at his apartment on Riverside Drive, his two small older brothers discussing silk stocks. Bill Keresky looking at me and saying 'Schlazm.' Gene Mackstoll jerking down Broadway as tho being yanked at by the Invisible Man. Also looking at me and saying, 'Frazm.' Lionel Smart, eyes shining bright, making me listen to Lester Young on clarinet playing 'Way Down Yonder in New Orleans' and the other side, 'I Want a Little Girl.' Cy Zukove swimming in the pool with great athletic forward drive.

II

Not such a hot cameo. How about this? (I want to give you an exact but short picture of what it was like at that really remarkable school.) Because they were a bunch of wits. Now wits abound in Lowell too, wifey, like you know, but these are big-town New York wits and to explain it:

Say, I do, that among the fantastic wits of this school Jimmy Winchel ranked practically number one. I was just an innocent New England athlete (well not so innocent, but of wit in the witty sense, yes) but I was suddenly thrown into what amounted to an academy of incunabular Milton Berles hundreds of them wisecracking and ad libbing on all sides, in the classroom when possible, on the field, at recess, in the subway going home into downtown Manhattan, proper, over the phone at night, even years later in letters exchanged from college to college. We were all in stitches all the time. The chief claque of official huge wits was led by Bill Keresky, Gene Mackstoll, Marty Churchill (né Bernstein), Mike Hennessey, Gully Swift, Paul O'Grady and Ern Salter but when mention of Jimmy Winchel was made there fell a kind of stricken convulsion just at the thought of him. He was insanely witty. So much so that now, today, as I read about his recent escapade with the two million dollars I mentioned, I laugh, not because I think it's funny (and anyway Jimmy's paid it all back honestly, or tried), but because Jimmy is so funny, it's almost as tho he'd pulled this last fantastic joke to tear the funny-guys of HM apart for once and for all (in some dim way at the back of his mind when he absconded to Brazil I do seriously believe this to be true, God bless child even when he get old).

Prep school humor is always a little bit insular. At HM in that year there were three elements mainly involved: (1) A kind of Al Kelly doubletalk, 'Flazm,' 'Schmazm,' etc. (as I showed) used when you couldnt find the right word, the humour coming mainly from the particular adolescence of lip delivery (kid humor), and (2) saying 'mine' instead of 'me,' 'yours' instead of 'you,' 'his' instead of 'he,' 'His is going to write mine a letter' etc. in a completely madcap extension of phallic reference common among kids, and (3) using the names of classmates who were not 'wits' and were not 'athletes' but were rather obscure serious scholars behind their spectacles studying about Hérault de Séchelles and the Hortus Siccus and the Hindu Kush and the Manoeuvres Military and Louise de Quéroualles and the neuro-pathological *Spirochae pallidum* with Professor Lionel Greeting at dusk, and whose names, altho almost invariably hilarious in themselves (Bruno Golemus, Melvin Mandel, Otis Zimmerman, Randall Garstein, Matthew Gdansk), were infinitely more hilarious when you thought of their shabby pitiful demeanors and ridiculous obscurities about the campus and so amenably given to goof-off putdowns (sometimes little tiny weird fourth-formers with undeveloped masculinities, naturally, say, but already *strange*). So later I get letters at Columbia from Jimmy at Cornell in 1940 that go like this: 'Dear F—— face, after all my flasimode talking to you etc. you must call her tonight and ask her when Dick's is coming into the city again and leap up to mine. So I'll see yours Saturday's. I'm coming into its this week's load . . . or in other words Dear Wang Load, how do you like this paper, I got so much of the Wang Load stuff that I will probably have to give it to my grandchildren to use for toilet paper. I'm really terribly sorry that I didnt write to yours sooner but mine was a little tired from overwork and I knew that yours wasnt so tired as mine so that if mine overexerted while writing to yours, yours might have to also overexert and write to mine. Does yours get it? Mine does. How're Gussie Resbin, Minnie Donoff, Kittie Kolpitz, Mordecai Letterhandler, Ishmael Communevisch, Downey Coucle the Irish Tenor, and all the boys getting along? I heard that Gabe Irrgang, Andrew Lawrence Goldstein, Ted Dressman, Ray Flamm and you were really tearing your sphe-roids off playing football for Coach Lu Libble at Columbia, and that you and Mel Mandel and the Gerson brothers were really going to town' (these all scholars I'd never talked to, even, sort of expertise secret technicians studying in lower labs). 'Did you hear about the fellow who went to the doctor and said "Doctor please look at my kidley" and the doctor said "You mean your kidney dont you?" then the man said "That's what I said diddle I?" . . . P.S. By the way, S. Martin Gerber sends his regards to all the boys back at HM including Joe Rappaport and Axel Finnkin.' And the letter's signed: 'J. Winchel, Alias Christian Goldberg.'

But just to show yours further, wifey, what it's like to be in that school, Bill Keresky was a classmate of Jimmy's at Cornell at the time (this is a year later but relevant to explaining the school in 1939) and tried to outdo Jimmy with the following letter: 'Dear Jack, how's everything at Columbia's? Have Hennessey and Mandel made the basketball team yet? Jerkit Winchel trades his '31 Chevy in for a '32 Windslammer so we've been riding ours around It's'hacas in style of late. It's been snowing up here and is as cold as a date in midwinter in Flushing. The seniors of the house had us shoveling snow and I almost froze it, I think next week might be initiation and mine is already begging for mercy's. We had our ends pounded off last week for excessive dubbing during the meal, without our frosh things on. It's so cold here I thought we could get out of wearing our frosh caps but I found out they have special winter fresh pulloffers that you must wear in winter. They probably even make you wear frosh things underneath when you have an affair with a coed's. Give my best to Flavius Fondle, Otis Outhouse, Duke Douche, Ann Enema, Schuyler Scrotum, Venus Venereal, Wanda Wantit, Schuyler Scuttle, Stephen Straddle, Scrag Scrotum, Terrence Tinkleman, Rod Railspitter, Flogg Itt, Vera Vajj, Pauline Partutient, Nessie Nightsoil, Messy Mingle, Olga Orgy and Phyllis Straddler. Write! Dont miss The Importance of Being Ernest's starring Reggie Klein and Irvie Sklar. P.S. Livia Lips, Tina Tip, Chad Chaff, Marmaduke Modess, Manny Monthly, Monty Mound, Bea Between, Pierpont Pussnblood, Staunton Sterile, Charlotte Shriveled, Hank Hang, Eunice Underslung, Forrest Fieldcookie, Meadow Waffle, Terrence Tonguebath, Ray Roundtheworld and Flavious Fecal were all asking for you. P.P. S.S. Dont forget to drop a note to Apollo Goldfarb and Arapahoe Rappaport.' It was all moonlight on the lawn, J. D. Salinger middleclass Jewish livingrooms with the lights out and the futile teenage doubledate blind smooching in the park, all these kids who became financial wizards, restaurateurs of great renown, realtors, department store tycoons, scientists, here they are stalking around the halls of the school with incredible leers waiting like tigers to pounce on someone with a sleering joke, the latest, an academy of wits finally as I say.

III

Anyway you get an idea, just from this mosaic, what it was like after the football season was over, and then, come graduation time I had no money to buy a white suit so I just sat in the grass in back of the gym and read Walt Whitman with a leaf of grass in my mouth while the ceremonies were going on in the field, with flags. Then when it was over I came over and joined everybody, shook hands all around, graduated with a 92 average, and rode downtown with Mike Hennessey and his mother to his apartment on the Columbia campus, 116th and Broadway, which was going to be my campus in the fall after a summer in Lowell. (Played on the baseball team for HM that spring but not well: I batted about .197, ugh.)

BOOK FOUR

I

It's one goddamn crisis after a friggin other. Dont have to print that. But will. It's English. It's the daily newspaper.

Did I come into this world thru the womb of my mother the earth just so I could talk and write like everybody else?

Because this is the part that will interest you, wifey. It was the summer of 1940 and I had nothing to do but sleep at home in my bedroom on Gershom Avenue now, go swimming when I felt like it, go beering on Saturday nights with G.J. and Lousy and Scotcho and the boys on Moody Street, hang around reading Jack London's life and pin up long words I couldnt memorize, write them down in big letters on slips of paper and pin them all over my bedroom wall so's in the morning when I woke up there it would be staring me in the face: the bunch of words on the wall: 'Ubiquitous,' 'Surreptitious,' 'Demonological,' 'Business,' 'Urine.' Just kidding. Just light my lamp at midnight in the cool Lowell summernights and read Thomas Hardy. And under the influence of Jonathan Miller start writing my own brand of serious 'Hemingway' stories, later . . . later a voice was calling me from Gershom Avenue, which, as you may know, is the street where is located the Pawtucketville Social Club that my father used to run, the bowling alley and poolroom. Pa still bowled and played pool there but was no longer the manager. Nevertheless in the company of old Joe Fortier, Sr, he could be heard yelling across the echoey neighborhood and you could hear old Joe swearing up a storm that had the Merrimack River bored in her rocks. Great fat stars gloomy with fat stared down at me, putting men now in the mind of what Thoreau said about the little blisters that appear on good autumn pears when you look at em close with a magnifying glass: he said the blisters 'they whisper of the happy stars,' whilst russet red McIntosh apples only yell of the sun and its redness. I'm hanging around and there's the call 'Jack-eeee' out on Gershom Avenue. I go out, look down the long fifteen steps of the street porch and there stands a curly black-haired boy strangely familiar. 'Aint you the guy called me from the street when I was twelve on Sarah Avenue?'

'Yeh, Sabby Savakis.'

'Didnt I know you on the sandbank?'

'Yes.'

'Whattaya want?'

'Just wanta see you, talk to you. Always wanted to.'

'What the hell you want to see me for?'

'No particular reason. Been watching you.'

'Oh now I remember you, Greek kid, used to hang around, ah, with Tsotakos or sumptin, on the sandbank, come from Rosemont.'

'Since the river flooded in 1936, we've moved to Stevens Street.'

'Oh, yass,' I said like W. C. Fields, thinking, inside, 'So . . . *nu*?'

He says 'They call me Sabby but my name is really Sabbas . . . in fact it's Sabbas the Prince of Crete.'

'The Prince of Crete?'

'Aye, and I know you, you're Baron Jean Louis Duluoz.'

'Who told you that?'

'O I went down to, ah, Phoebe Avenue and talked to Gussie Rigolopoulos and some of your other friends, it's just a joke, I just want to talk to you, always wanted to.' We sat on the doorstep. 'Do you read Saroyan?' he says. 'Thomas Wolfe?'

'No, who are they?'

He says: 'I want to write plays, produce, direct, and act in them: I want to wear a white Russian tunic with a blood red heart sewn on the part over my heart. I'm going to be a student at a Boston dramatic school this summer. You could write plays.'

'Who told you I wrote?'

'Gussie told me you wrote a beautiful song about a girl at a carnival, and O he says also, I mean, he says your letters are like poems. He says you say his letters are good too.'

'Yeh I've got em all here.'

'Why dont we go out and have a few sundaes, or beer if you want, and just talk about things? You know I used to go to Bartlett School too and I knew Miss Wakefield too. We could go see Miss Wakefield in fact if you'd like to, and do you know Ronnie Ryan and Arch MacDougald, they all want to meet you too, and you ran track with my best friend John Kazarakis and he told me about you too, how you used to walk around Boston after the races and eat hamburgers in the Greek joint near the El and had nothing to do. . . . Have you been reading, what do you read?'

'Well I've been reading Hardy, Thoreau, Emily Dickinson, Whitman. . . .'

Sabby: 'Pretty solid so far.'

I said to myself: 'O well I'll humor this crazy Greek and go see what he's like.' Out loud: 'I'll put on my gear and we'll go walkin downtown, see if there's any quiff around.'

'Quiff? what's that?'

'Girls, you dumpling,' I shoulda said, but I said nothing, because after all who knows even to this day what 'quiff' is, even in Lowell, Lawrence, Haverhill, Concord, Manchester, Laconia, Franconia, St Johnsbury, St Magog or Hundson's Bay or in any direction south or west, or, should I dare say it, east?

II

Anyway, wifey, that's how I finally started to talk to your brother Sabbas, who said he was the Prince of Crete, which he probably was once, but only recently of Spartan, or Maniatti, descent.

Big curly-haired guy, thought he was a poet, and was, and as we got to be friendly began to instruct me in the arts of being interested (as they say in Mexico, *interesa*) in literature and the arts of kindness. I put him in this chapter (say I archly) about Columbia, because he really belongs to that period which followed the adolescnce of the prep school and introduces the serious business.

Among my souvenirs, by God, is the friendship of Sabbas Savakis.

And I'll tell you why in plain English poesy: he'd sing me 'Begin the Beguine' in a big voice whether we were crossing the bridge, sitting in saloons or just on my doorstep or his own father's doorstep in the Lower Highlands. He'd yell Byron at me: 'So we'll go no more a-roving/So late into the night. . . .' It's not because he died in the war, on the beachhead at Anzio wounded, died in an Algiers North Africa hospital of gangrene, or probably broken heart, because a lot of other guys died in World War II including some I've already mentioned in this book (Kazarakis, Gold, Hampshire,) others I dont even know what happened), but because the memorabilia of my knit just knits a knight in my night's mind. *That's* plain English poesy? Because, okay, he was a great kid, knightlike, *i.e.*, noble, a poet, goodlooking, crazy, sweet, sad, everything a man should want as a friend.

III

Actually I didnt see much of Sabbas that summer, it was mainly the old gang and a lot of swimming at Pine Brook, to which we walked 2½ miles to our own special 'Bareass Beach' as 'twas called, where, once when I was eleven years old, basking nekkid in the sun with the gang, here comes my Marist brother who taught me fifth grade at St Joseph's Parochial School, all dressed in black, plowing across the furzy brush of the woods as tho he was coming to chastise me: but instead he whips off his robes and runs yelling and diving into the brook in his shorts. Girls had to make a detour around this beach. By the time I went to Columbia in early September for the beginning of football training I was as brown as Muhammad Mayi.

In fact that was the summer, too, when Pa unexpectedly joined me and the boys on the 2½-mile walk on a particularly hot evening and he too, whipping off his clothes, yipped and ran in his shorts to the edge of the brook and jumped in feet first. But he weighed 250 pounds and the weather'd been dry all August and he landed standing in 3 feet of water and almost broke his ankle. It really almost broke my heart, to see him so happy in his yipping leap and end up toppling over in that little fetid pint of water.

The time for Pine Brook was always dawn, when the water was cool, especially June, July, when we used to have underwater distance contests and go considerable distances flapping low among the white stones below. Over 100 feet sometimes I'd go, this was before we all started smoking. Gene Plouffe used to do the double donut flopflop right off a 30-foot perch in a tree. Lousy used to slip right into 6 feet of water and come up as if skimming the surface. When I tried this too (off the 30-foot perch) I always hit the sandy bottom with my hands. It was just a case of hanging around in the grass and suddenly saying 'Ah hell it's hot' and jumping in. We also played a lot of baseball in Dracut Tigers field, scrub it's called, where you get to bat and get ten whacks out, if you keep hitting singles or homeruns you keep going till you're out ten times, either from fly ball or thrown out at first, though none of us bothered to run them out. Then you go into right field and work your way back. This was the way we worked out our occasional night-before beerfests. The first night we all got drunk, a brawling hot night on Moody Street, we were all so exhilarated we kept grabbing everybody in the street and telling them they were God, old men, other guys, everybody, even one another. This ended up in a puking wrestling match under the stars by the moaning river with mobs of home-going drunks watching saying 'Looka those crazy kids, drunk for the first time, d'jever see the likes of such slobs?' This was when I was beginning to gain my reputation as 'Zagg,' which was the name of the Pawtucketville town drunk who kept throwing up his hands like Hugh Herbert and saying 'Woo Woo.' I was at bat in a twilight game of baseball, the pitcher chewing his cud was examining the catcher's sign, I waved the bat, I was barechested because lobster red from a sunburn caught the day in the hot haze at Lakeview, suddenly as the pitcher winds up and I 'coil' to get ready, that crazy G.J. yells out 'That's what we'll call him . . . ZAGG!' And I watched a strike go by under my chest.

Of Sabby Savakis more anon, it was the following summer, 1941, we ran around more and went into the study of poetry and plays and did some hitchhiking and cemented our friendship.

IV

But now some old buddies, the Ladeau brothers, proposed to drive me to New York for my school year because they were going to see the World's Fair at Flushing Meadows and might as well take me along for the ride and I could help with the gas instead of taking a bus. And who comes along, riding in the rumbleseat in back of the old 1935 coupe, hair blowing in the wind, singing, 'Whoooeee, here we come New York!' if it wasn't my old Pop himself, Emil? Me and 350 pounds of Pop and baggage in a rumbleseat, all the way with the car veering here, veering there. I guess from the unsuitable disposition of weight in the back, all the way to Manhattan, 116th Street, Columbia campus, where me and Pa got out with my gear and went into my dormitory, Hartley Hall.

What dreams you get when you think you're going to go to college! Here we stood in this sort of drear room overlooking Amsterdam Avenue, a wooden desk, bed, chairs, bare walls, and one huge cockroach suddenly rushing off. Furthermore in walks a little kid with glasses wearing a blue skullcap and announces he will be my roommate for the year and that he is a pledge with the Wi Delta Woowoo fraternity and that's the skullcap. 'When they rush you you'll have to wear one too.' But I was already devising means of changing my room on account of that cockroach and others I saw later, bigger.

Pa and I then went out on the town, to the World's Fair too, restaurants, the usual, and when he left he said, as usual: 'Now study, play good ball, pay attention to what the coach and the profs tell you and see if you cant make your old man proud and maybe be an all-America.' Fat chance, with the war a year away and England already under blitz.

It seems I had chosen football and come to the brim of the top of it just at that time when it would no longer matter to anybody or his uncle.

There were always tears in my Pa's eyes when he said goodbye to me, always tears in his eyes those latter years, he was, as my mother often said, '*Un vrai Duluoz, ils font ainque braillez pi's lamentez* (A real Duluoz, all they do is cry and lament).' And rage too, b'God, as you'll see later when my Pa finally got to meet Coach Lu Libble of Columbia.

Because from the start I saw that the same old boloney was going to be pulled on me as in Lowell High School. In the freshman backfield there was a good blocking boy called Humphrey Wheeler, but slow, and a slow plodding fullback called Runstedt, and that's about it. Absolutely nobody of any real ability and nothing like the gang at HM. In fact one of the boys was small, slow, weak, nothing at all in particular, and yet they started him instead of me and later on I talk to him and discover he's the son of the police chief of Scranton. Never in my life have I ever seen such a bum team. The freshman coach was Rolfe Firney who had made his mark at Columbia as a very good back who'd made a sensational run against Navy that won the game in 1934 or so. He was a good man, I liked Rolfe, but he seemed to keep warning me about something all the time and whenever the big coach, famous Lu Libble went by, all sartorial in one of his 100 suits, he never even gave me the once-over.

The fact of the matter is, Lu Libble was very famous because in his very first year as coach at Columbia, using a system of his own devised at his alma mater, Georgetown, he won the bloody Rose Bowl against Stanford. It was such a sensational smash in the eye all over football America nobody ever got over it, but that was 1934, and here it was 1940 and he hadnt done anything noteworthy since with his team and went clear into the 1950's doing nothing further either. I think it was that bunch of players he had in 1934 who carried him over: Cliff Montgomery, Al Barábas, *et al.*, and the surprise of that crazy KT-79 play of his that took everybody a year to understand. It was simply . . . well I had to run it, anyway, and you'll understand it when we run it.

So here I am out with the Columbia freshman team and I see I'm not going to be a starter. Will admit one thing, I wasnt being encouraged, as I'd been by Coach Ump Mayhew at HM, and psychologically this made me feel lackadaisical and my punting, for instance, fell off. I couldnt get off a good kick anymore and they didnt believe in the quick kick. I guess they didnt believe in touchdowns either. We practiced at Baker Field in the one field in back. At dusk you could see the lights of New York across the Harlem River, it was right smack in the middle of New York City, even tugboats went by in the Harlem River, a great bridge crossed it full of cars, I couldnt understand what had gone wrong.

One great move I made was to switch my dormitory room from Hartley Hall to Livingston Hall where there were no cockroaches and where b'God I had a room all to myself, on the second floor, overlooking the beautiful trees and walkways of the campus and overlooking, to my greatest delight, besides the Van Am Quadrangle, the library itself, the new one, with its stone frieze running around entire with the names engraved in stone forever: 'Goethe . . . Voltaire . . . Shakespeare . . . Molière . . . Dante.' That was more like it. Lighting my fragrant pipe at 8 P.M., I'd open the pages of my homework, turn on station WQXR for the continual classical music, and sit there, in the golden glow of my lamp, in a sweater, sigh and say 'Well now I'm a collegian at last.'

V

Only trouble is, the first week of school my job began as a dishwasher in the diningroom cafeteria sinks: this was to pay for my meals. Secondly, classes. Thirdly, homework: *i.e.*, read Homer's *Iliad* in three days and then the *Odyssey* in three more. Finally, go to football practice at four in the afternoon and return to my room at eight, eating voracious suppers right after at the training table in John Jay Hall upstairs. (Plenty of milk, plenty of meat, dry toast, that was good.)

But who on earth in his right mind can think that anybody can do all these things in one week? And get some sleep? And rest war-torn muscles? 'Well,' said they, 'this is the Ivy League son, this is no college or group of colleges where you get a Cadillac and some money just because you play football, and remember you're on a Columbia University Club scholarship and you've got to get good marks. They cant feed you free, it's against the Ivy League rules against preference for athletes.' In fact, tho, the entire Columbia football gang, both varsity and freshmen, had B averages. It was true. We had to work like Trojans to get our education and the old white-haired trainer used to intone, 'All for glory, me boys, all for glory.'

It was the work in the cafeteria that bothered me: because on Sundays it was closed and nobody who worked got to eat anything. I s'pose in this case we were s'posed to eat at the homes of friends in New York City or New Jersey or get food money for home. Some scholarship.

I did get invited to dinner, formally with a big formal card, by the dean of Columbia College, old Dean Hawkes, in the house on Morningside Drive or thereabouts right near the house of Nicholas Murray Butler, the president of Columbia. Here, all dressed up in Ma's best McQuade-Lowell-selected sports coat, with white shirt and tie and pressed slacks (the cleaner was on Amsterdam across the street), I sat and ate my soup by gently lifting the saucer away from me, spooning away from me, smiled politely, hair perfectly combed, showed suave interest in jokes and awe in the dean's serious moments. The entrée was meat but I cut it delicately. I had the best table manners in those days because my sister Ti Nin had trained me back in Lowell for these past several years; she was a fan of Emily Post's. When, after dinner, the dean got up and showed me (and the three other special lads) his prized Dinosaur Egg I registered actual amazement; whoever thought I'd get to see a billion-year-old egg in the house of an old distinguished dean? I say house, it was a sumptuous apartment. He thereupon wrote a note to my mother saying: 'Your son, John L. Duluoz, may I say with pride, Mrs Duluoz, has absolutely the best and most charming table manners it has ever been my pleasure to enjoy at my dinner table.' (Something like that.) She never forgot that. She told Pa. He said 'Good boy,' tho when Pa and I used to eat late-night snacks in Lowell it was eggs this way, butter that way, hell be damned, up on the ceiling, EAT.

But I loved Dean Hawkes, everybody did, he was an old, short bespectacled old fud with glee in his eyes. Him and his egg . . .

VI

The opening game of the season the freshman team traveled to New Brunswick N.J. for a game against Rutgers' freshmen. This was Saturday Oct. 12, 1940, and as our varsity defeated Dartmouth 20-6, we went down there and I sat on the bench and we lost 18-7. The little daily paper of the college said: FRESHMEN DROP GRID OPENER TO RUTGERS YEARLINGS BY 18-7 COUNT. It doesnt mention that I only got in the game in the second half, just like at Lowell High, and the article concludes with: 'The Morningsiders showed a fairly good running attack at times with Jack Duluoz showing up well . . . Outstanding in the backfield for the Columbia Frosh were Marsden (police chief's son), Runstedt and Duluoz, who was probably the best back on the field.'

So that in the following game, against St Benedict's Prep, okay, now they started me.

But you remember what I boasted about how, to beat St John's, you gotta have old St John on the team. Well I have a medal, as you know, over my backyard door. It's the medal of St Benedict. An Irish girl once told me: 'Whenever you move into a new house two things you must do according to your blood as an ancient Gael: you buy a new broom, and you pins a St Benedict medal over the kitchen door.' That's not the reason why I've got that medal now but here's what happened:

After the Rutgers game, and Coach Libble'd heard about my running, and now his backfield coach Cliff Battles was interested, everybody came down to Baker Field to see the new nut run.

Cliff Battles was one of the greatest football players who ever lived, in a class with Red Grange and the others, one of the greatest runners anyway. I remember as a kid, when I was nine, Pa saying suddenly one Sunday 'Come on Angie, Ti Nin, Ti Jean, let's all get in the car and drive down to Boston and watch the Boston Redskins play pro football, the great Cliff Battles is running today.' Because of traffic we never made it, or we were waylaid by ice cream and apples in Chelmsford, Dunstable or someplace and wound up in New Hampshire visiting Grandmère Jean. And in those days I kept elaborate clippings of all sports and pasted them carefully, among my own sports writings, in my notebooks, and I knew very well about Cliff Battles. Now here all of a sudden the night before the game with St Benedict and we freshmen are practicing, here comes Cliff Battles and up to me and says 'So you're the great Dulouse that ran so good at Rutgers. Let's see how fast you can go.'

'What do you mean?'

'I'll race you to the showers; practice is over.' He stood there, 6 foot 3, smiling, in his coach pants and cleated shoes and sweat jacket.

'Okay,' says I and I take off like a little bird. By God I've got him by 5 yards as we head for the sidelines at the end of the field, but here he comes with his long antelope legs behind me and just passes me under the goalposts and goes ahead 5 yards and stops at the shower doors, arms akimbo, saying:

'Well cant you run?'

'Ah heck your legs are longer than mine.'

'You'll do allright kid,' he says, pats me, and goes off laughing. 'See you tomorrow,' he throws back.

This made me happier than anything that had happened so far at Columbia, because also I certainly wasn't happy that I hadnt yet read the *Iliad* or the *Odyssey*, John Stuart Mill, Aeschylus, Plato, Horace and everything else they were throwing at us with the dishes.

VII

Comes the St Benedict game, and what a big bunch of lugs you never saw, they reminded me of that awful Blair team a year ago, and the Malden team in high school, big, mean-looking, with grease under their eyes to shield the glare of the sun, wearing mean-looking brown-red uniforms against our sort of silly-looking (if you ask me) light-blue uniforms with dark-blue numerals. ('Sans Souci' is the name of the Columbia alma mater song, means 'without care,' humph.) (And the football rallying song is 'Roar Lion Roar,' sounds more like it.) Here we go, lined up on the field, on the sidelines I see that Coach Lu Libble is finally there to give me the personal once-over. He's heard about the Rutgers game naturally and he's got to think of next year's backfield. He'd heard, I s'pose, that I was a kind of nutty French kid from Massachusetts with no particular football savvy like his great Italian favorites from Manhattan that were now starring on the varsity (Lu Libble's real name is Guido Pistola, he's from Massachusetts).

St Benedict was to kick off. They lined up, I went deep into safety near the goal line as ordered, and said to myself 'Screw, I'm going to show these bums how a French boy from Lowell runs, Cliff Battles and the whole bunch, and who's that old bum standing next to him? Hey Runstedt, who's that guy in the coat next to Cliff Battles there near the water can?'

'They tell me that's the coach of Army, Earl Blaik, he's just whiling away an afternoon.'

Whistle blows and St Benedict kicks off. The ball comes wobbling over and over in the air into my arms. I got it secure and head straight down the field in the direction an arrow takes, no dodging, no looking, no head down either but just straight ahead at everybody. They're all converging there in midfield in smashing blocks and pushings so they can get through one way or the other. A few of the red Benedicts get through and are coming straight at me from three angles but the angles are narrow because I've made sure of that by coming in straight as an arrow down the very middle of the field. So that by the time I reach midfield where I'm going to be clobbered and smothered by eleven giants I give them no look at all, still, but head right into them: they gather up arms to smother me: it's psychological. They never dream I'm really roosting up in my head the plan to suddenly (as I do) dart, or jack off, bang to the right, leaving them all there bumbling for air. I run as fast as I can, which I could do very well with a heavy football uniform, as I say, because of thick legs, and had trackman speed, and before you know it I'm going down the sidelines all alone with the whole twenty-one other guys of the ball game all befuddling around in midfield and turning to follow me. I hear whoops from the sidelines. I go and I go. I'm down to the 30, the 20, the 10, I hear huffing and puffing behind me, I look behind me and there's that selfsame old long-legged end catchin up on me, like Cliff Battles done, like the guy last year, like the guy in the Nashua game, and by the time I'm over the 5 he lays a big hand on the scruff of my neck and lays me down on the ground. A 90-yard runback.

I see Lu Libble and Cliff Battles, and Rolfe Firney our coach too, rubbing their hands with zeal and dancing little Hitler dances on the sidelines. But St John ain't got a chance against St Benedict, it appears, because anyway naturally by now I'm out of breath and that dopey quarterback wants me to make my own touchdown. I just cant make it. I want to controvert his order, but you're not supposed to. I puff into the line and get buried on the 5. Then he, Runstedt, tries it, and the big St Ben's line buries him, and then we miss the last down too and are down on the 3 and have to fall back for the St Benedict punt.

By now I've got my wind again and I'm ready for another go. But the punt that's sent to me is so high, spirally, perfect, I see it's going to take an hour for it to fall down in my arms and I should really raise my arm for a fair catch and touch it down to the ground and start our team from there. But no, vain Jack, even tho I hear the huffing and puffing of the two downfield men practically on my toes I catch the ball free catch and practically say 'Alley Oop' as I feel their four big hands squeeze like vises around my ankles, two on each, and puffing with pride I do the complete vicious twist of my whole body so that I can undo their grip and move on. But their St Benedict grips have me rooted to where I am as if I was a tree, or an iron pole stuck to the ground, I do the complete turnaround twist and hear a loud crack and it's my leg breaking. They let me fall back deposited gently on the turf and look at me and say to each other 'The only way to get *him*, don't *miss*' (more or less).

I'm helped off the field limping.

I go into the showers and undress and the trainer massages my right calf and says 'O a little sprain wont hurt you, next week it's Princeton and we'll give them the old one-two again Jacky boy.'

VIII

But, wifey, it was a broken leg, a cracked tibia, like if you cracked a bone about the size of a pencil and the pencil was still stuck together except for that hairline crack, meaning if you wanted you could just break the pencil in half with a twist of two fingers. But nobody knew this. That entire week they told me I was a softy and to get going and run around and stop limping. They had liniments, this and that, I tried to run, I ran and practiced and ran but the limp got worse. Finally they sent me off to Columbia Medical Center, took X rays, and found out I had broken my tibia in right leg and that I had been spending a week running on a broken leg.

I'm not bitter about that, wifey, so much as that it was Coach Lu Libble who kept insisting I was putting it on and told the freshman coaches not to listen to my 'lamentings' and make me 'run it off.' You just can't run off a broken leg. I saw right then that Lu for some reason I'll never understand had some kind of bug against me. He was always hinting I was a no-good and with those big legs he ought to put me in the line and make 'a watch charm guard' out of me.

Yet (I guess I know now why) it was only that summer, I forgot to mention, Francis Fahey had me come out to Boston College field to give me a tryout for once and for all. He said 'You really must come to B.C., we've got a system here, the Notre Dame system, where we take a back like you and with a good line play spring him loose down the field. Over at Columbia with Lu Libble they'll have you come around from the wing, you'll have to run a good twenty yards before you get back to the line of scrimmage with that silly KT-79 reverse type play of his and you'll only at best manage to evade maybe the end but the secondary'll be up on yours in no time. With us, it's *boom*, right through tackle, guard, or right or left end sweep.' Then Fahey'd had me put on a uniform, got his backfield coach MacLuhan and said: 'Find out about him.' Alone in the field with Mac, facing him, Mac held the ball and said:

'Now, Jack, I'm going to throw this ball at you in the way a center does; when you get it you're off like a halfback on any kinda run you wanta try. If I touch you you're out, so to speak, and you know darn well I'm going to touch you because I used to be one of the fastest backs in the east.'

'Phooey you are,' I thought, and said 'Okay, throw it.' He centered it to me, direct, facing me, and I took off out of his sight, he had to turn his head to watch me pass around his left, and that's no Harvard lie.

'Well,' he conceded, 'you're not faster than I am but by God where'd you get that sudden takeoff? Track?'

'Yep.' So in the showers of B.C. afterward, I'm wiping up, I hear Fahey and Mac discussing me in the coaches' showers and I hear Mac say to Fahey:

'Fran, that's the best halfback I ever saw. You've got to get him to B.C.'

But I went to Columbia because I wanted to dig New York and become a big journalist in the big city beat. But what right had Lu Libble to say I was a no-good runner. And, wifey, listen to this, what about the night the winter before, at HM, when Francis Fahey had me meet him on Times Square and took me to William Saroyan's play *My Heart's in the Highlands*, and in the intermission when we went down to the toilet I'm sure I saw Rolfe Firney the Columbia man watching from behind the crowd of men? On top of which they then sent Joe Callahan to New York to take me out on the town too, to further persuade me about Boston College, and eventually Notre Dame, but here I was at Columbia, Pa had lost his job, and the coach thought I was so no-good he didnt even believe I'd broken my leg in earnest.

Years later I published a poem about this on the sports page of *Newsday*, the Long Island newspaper: fits pretty good; because it also involves the later fight my father had with Lu about his not playing me enough and some arrangement that went sour whereby Lu was s'posed to help him get a linotypist job in New York and nothing came of it:

TO LU LIBBLE

Lu, my father thought you put him down
 and said he didnt like you

He thought he was too shabby for your
 office; his coat had got so

And his hair he'd comb and come
 into an employment office with me

And have me speak alone with the man
 for the two of us, then sigh

And repented we home, to Lowell; where
 sweet mother put out the pie
  anywye.

In my first game I ran like mad
 at Rutgers, Cliff wasnt there;

He didnt believe what he read
 in the *Spectator* 'Who's that Jack'

So I come in on the St Benedicts game
  not willing to be caught by them bums

I took off the kickoff right straight at
  the gang, and lalooza'd around

To the pastafazoola five yard line,
  you were there, you remember

We didnt make first down; and I
  took the punt and broke my leg

And never said anything, and ate hot
  fudge sundaes & steaks in the
    Lion's Den.

Because that's one good thing that came of it, with my broken leg in a cast, and with two crutches under my good armpits, I hobbled every night to the Lion's Den, the Columbia fireplace-and-mahogany type restaurant, sat right in front of the fire in the place of honor, watched the boys and girls dance, ordered every blessed night the same rare filet mignon, ate it at leisure with my crutches athwart the table, then two hot fudge sundaes for dessert, that whole blessed sweet autumn.

And I never did say anything, so as to say, I never sued or made a fuss, I enjoyed the leisure, the steaks, the ice cream, the honor, and for the first time in my life at Columbia began to study at my own behest the complete awed wide-eyed world of Thomas Wolfe (not to mention the curricular work too).

For years afterward, however, Columbia still kept sending me the bill for the food I ate at training table.

I never paid it.

Why should I? My leg still hurts on damp days. Phooey.

Ivy League indeed.

If you dont say what you want, what's the sense of writing?

IX

But O that beautiful Autumn, sitting at my desk with that fragrant pipe now taped like my leg was taped, listening to the beautiful Sibelius Finnish Symphony which even to this day reminds me of fragrant old tobacco smoke and even tho I know it's all about snow, and my dim lamp, and before me laid out the immortal words of Tom Wolfe talking about the 'weathers' of

America, the pale-green flaky look of old buildings behind warehouses, the track running west, the sound of Indians in the rail, the coonskin cap in his hills of old Nawth Caliney, the river winking, the Mississippi, the Shenandoah, the Rio Grande . . . no need for me to try to imitate what he said, he just woke me up to America as a Poem instead of America as a place to struggle around and sweat in. Mainly this dark-eyed American poet made me want to prowl, and roam, and see the real America that was there and that 'had never been uttered.' They say nowadays that only adolescents appreciate Thomas Wolfe but that's easy to say after you've read him anyway because he's the kind of writer whose prose poems you can just about only read once; and deeply and slowly, discovering, and having discovered, move away. His dramatic sections you can read over and over again. Where is the seminar on Tom Wolfe today? What is this minimization of Thomas Wolfe in his own time? Because Mr Schwartz could wait.

But there I am sitting at my desk, book open, and I says to myself: 'Now it's almost seven thirty, we'll hobble down to ye olde Lion's Den, have filet mignon, hot fudge sundaes, coffee, and then hobble on down to the one hundred sixteenth subway stop [remembering Prof Kerwick and his mathematics series numbers] and ride on down to Times Square and go see a French movie, go see Jean Gabin press his lips together sayin '*Ça me navre*,' or Louis Jouvet's baggy behind going up the stairs, or that bitter lemon smile of Michele Morgan in the seaside bedroom, or Harry Bauer kneel as Handel praying for his work, or Raimu screaming at the mayor's afternoon picnic, and then after that, an American doublefeature, maybe Joel McCrea in *Union Pacific*, or see tearful clinging sweet Barbara Stanwyck grab him, or maybe go see Sherlock Holmes puffing on his pipe with long Cornish profile as Dr Watson puffs at a medical tome by the fireplace and Missus Cavendish or whatever her name was comes upstairs with cold roast beef and ale so that Sherlock can solve the latest manifestation of the malefaction of himself Dr Moriarty. . . .'

Lights of the campus, lovers arm in arm, hurrying eager students in the flying leaves of late October, the library going with glow, all the books and pleasure and the big city of the world right at my broken feet. . . .

And think of this in 1967: I even actually used to get on my crutches and go to Harlem to see what was going on, 125th Street and thereabouts, sometimes to watch spareribs turning in the spareribs shack window, or watch Negroes talk on corners; to me they were exotic people I'd never known before. I forgot to mention earlier, on my first week at HM in 1939, hands clasped behind my back I'd actually walked all over Harlem one whole warm afternoon and evening examining all this new world. Why didnt anybody hit up on me, say to sell me drugs, or hit me, or rob me: what did they see? They see a tweeded college boy studying the street. People have respect for those things. I must have been an awfully weird-looking character anyway.

So I'd go into the Lion's Den, sit in my regular chair in front of the fire, the waiters (students) would bring me the supper, I'd eat, watch the dancers (one beauty in particular, Vicki Evans, interested me, Welsh girl), and then I'd go down to Times Square for my movies. Nobody ever bothered me. I always had, of course, nothing but something like sixty cents on me anyway and must have looked like it with that innocent face.

Now also I had time to start writing big 'Wolfean' stories and journals in my room, to look at them today it's a drag but at that time, I thought I was doing allright. I had a Negro student friend who came in and boned me on chemistry, my weakness. In French I had an A. In physics a B or C-plus or so. I hobbled around the campus proud like some heroic skimaster. In my tweed coat, with crutches, I became so popular (also because of the football reputation now) that some guy from the Van Am Society actually started a campaign to have me elected vice-president of next year's sophomore class. One thing sure I had no football to play till the sophomore year, 1941. To while away the time that winter I wrote sports a little for the college newspaper, covered the track coach interviews, wrote a few term papers for boys of Horace Mann who kept coming down to visit me. Hung around with Mike Hennessey as I say on that corner in front of the candy store on 115th and Broadway with William F. Buckley Jr sometimes. Hobbled down to the Hudson River and sat on Riverside Drive benches smoking a cigar and thinking about mist on rivers, occasionally took the subway to Brooklyn to see Grandma Ti Ma and Yvonne and Uncle Nick, went home for Christmas with the crutches gone and the leg practically healed.

Sentimentally getting drunk on port wine in front of my mother's Christmas tree with G.J. and having to carry him home in the Gershom Avenue snow. Looking for Maggie Cassidy at the Commodore Ballroom, finding her, asking for a dance, falling in love again. Long talks with Pa in the eager kitchen.

Life is funny.

A cameo for size: one night in the Phi Gamma Delta fraternity house, where I was a 'pledge' but refused to wear the little blue skullcap, in fact told them to shove it and insisted instead on giving me the beer barrel, which was almost empty, and raised it above my head at dawn and drained it of its dregs . . . all alone one night, in the completely empty frat house on 114th Street, except maybe for one or two guys sleeping upstairs, completely unlighted house, I'm sitting in an easy chair in the frat lounge playing Glenn Miller records fullblast. Almost crying. Glenn Miller and Frank Sinatra with Tommy Dorsey 'The One I Love Belongs to Somebody Else' and 'Everything Happens to Me,' or Charlie Barnet's 'Cherokee.' 'This Love of Mine.' Helping paralytic or spastic Dr Philippe Claire across the campus, we've just been working on his crossword puzzles which he writes for the New York *Journal-American*, he loves me because I'm French. Old Joe Hatter coming into my dormitory room one drenching night, with battered hat all dissolved in rain, bleary-eyed, saying, 'Jesus Christ is pissing on the earth tonight.' At the West End Bar Johnny the Bartender looking over everybody's heads with his big hands on the counter. In the lending library I'm studying Jan Valtin's *Out of the Night*, still a good book today to read. I wander around the Low Library wondering about libraries, or something. Told you life was funny. Girls with galoshes in the snow. Barnard girls growing bursty like ripe cherries in April, who the hell can study French books? A tall queer approaching me on a Riverside Park bench saying 'How you hung?' and me saying 'By the neck, I hope.' Turk Tadzic, varsity end of next year, crying drunk in my room telling me how he once squatted on Main Street in a Pennsy town and shat in front of everybody, ashamed. Guys pissing outside the West End Bar right on the sidewalk. The 'lounge lizards,' guys who sit in the dormitory lounge doing nothing, with their legs up on other chairs. Big notes pinned to a board saying where you can buy a shirt, trade a radio, get a ride to Arkansas, or go drop dead more or less. My leg's better, I'm now a waiter in John Jay dining hall, that is, I'm the coffee waiter, with coffee tray balanced in left hand I go about, inquisitively, gentlemen and ladies give me the nod, I go to their left and pour delicate coffee in their cups; a guy says to me: 'You know that old geezer you just poured coffee for? Thomas Mann.' My leg's better, I saunter over Brooklyn Bridge remembering that raging blizzard in 1936 when I was fourteen years old and Ma'd brought me to Brooklyn to visit Grandma Ti Ma: I had my Lowell overshoes with me: I'd said 'I'm going out and walk over the Brooklyn Bridge and back,' 'Okay,' I go over the bridge in a howling wind with biting sleet snow in my red face, naturally not a soul in sight, except here comes this one man about 6 foot 6, with large body and small head, striding Brooklyn-ward and not looking at me, long strides and meditation. Know who that old geezer was?

Thomas Wolfe.

Go to Book Five.

BOOK FIVE

I

Late that Spring, just about when my freshman year was over and the sophomore year was on the way, I was coming out of a subway turnstile with Pa after we'd seen a French movie on Times Square and here comes Chad Stone the other way, with a bunch of Columbia footballers. Chad was destined to become captain of the Columbia varsity, later a doctor, later to die at age thirty-eight of an overworked heart, goodlooking big fellow from Leominster Mass. by the way, and he says to me: 'Well Jack, you've been elected vice-president of the sophomore class.'

'What? Me?'

'By one vote, you rat, by one vote over ME.' And it was true. My father immediately took my picture in a ratty Times Square booth but little did he dream what was about to happen to my dingblasted old sophomore year, it was now May 1941 and events were brewing indeed in the world. But this sophomore vice-president boloney has no effect on my chemistry professor, Dr So-and-So, who, puffing on his pipe, informed me that I had failed chemistry and had to make it up that summer at home in Lowell or lose my scholarship.

Thing about chemistry was, the first day I'd gone to class, or lab, that fall of 1940, and saw all those goddamned tubes and stinking pipes and saw these maniacs in aprons fiddling around with sulfur and molasses, I said to myself 'Ugh, I'm never going to attend this class again.' Dont know why, couldnt stand it. Funny too, because in my later years as more or less of a 'drug' expert I sure did get to know a lot about chemistry and the chemical balances necessary for certain advantageous elations of the mind. But no, an F in chemistry, first time I'd ever flunked a course in my life and the professor was serious. I wasnt about to plead with him. He told me where to get the necessary books and tubes and Faustian whatnots to take home for the summer.

It was a nutty summer at home, therefore, where I absolutely refused to study my chemistry. I missed my Negro friend Joey James who'd tried to bone me all year, as I say.

I went home that summer, and instead I played around with swimming, drinking beer, making huge hamburger sandwiches for me and Lousy ('Ye old Zaggo Special' he called them because they were nothing but hamburg fried in lots of real butter and put on fresh bread with ketchup), and when late August came around I still hadnt made anything up in particular. But by now they were ready to let me try the course over again, as according to Lu Libble's plan, and other friends, because now we had a football team to contend upon and anyway I was probably smart enough to make it all up. Oddly, I didnt want to.

That summer Sabbas became a regular in my old boyhood gang of G.J., Lousy, Scotcho *et al.* and we even took a crazy trip to Vermont in an old jalopy to get drunk on whiskey for the first time in the woods, at a granite quarry swimming hole. At this swimming hole I took a deep breath, drunk, and went way down about 20 feet and stayed there grinning in the goggly dark. Poor Sabbas thought I had drowned, whipped off all his clothes and dove in after me. I popped up laughing. He cried on the bank. (St Sabbas was the founder of a sixth-century monastery, Greek Orthodox, now buried in Holy Sepulcher Church in Jerusalem under the officiation of Patriarch Benedictos in 1965.) I took another shot of whiskey and grabbed a little tree about 5 feet tall, wrapped it around my bare back, and tried to rip it up by the roots from the earth. G.J. says he'll never forget it: he says I tried to pull all Vermont up from the roots. From then on he called me 'Power Mad.' As we drank the whiskey further I saw the Green Mountains move, to paraphrase Hemingway in his sleeping sack. We drove back to Lowell drunk and sick, me sleeping on Sabby's lap all the way, as he cried, then dozed, all night.

Later me and Sabby hitchhiked to Boston several times to go see movies, lounge in Boston Common watching the people go by, occasionally Sabby leaping up to make big Leninist speeches at the soapbox area where pigeons hung around watching the argufyings. There's Sabby in his blazing white shirtsleeves and with wild black curly hair haranguing everybody about the Brotherhood of Man. It was great. In those days we were all pro-Lenin, or pro-whatever, Communists, it was before we found out that Henry Fonda in *Blockade* was not such a great anti-Fascist idealist at all, just the reverse of the coin of Fascism, *i.e.*, what the hell's the difference between Fascist Hitler and anti-Fascist Stalin, or, as today, Fascist Lincoln Rockwell and anti-Fascist Ernesto Guevaro, or name your own? Besides, may I remark here in a sober mood, what did Columbia College offer me to study in the way of a course of theirs called Contemporary Civilisation but the works of Marx, Engels, Lenin, Russell and other assorted blueprintings that look good on blue paper and all the time the architect is that invisible monster known as Living Man?

Also, I hitchhiked to Boston a couple of times with Dicky Hampshire to prowl the waterfront to see if we could hop a ship for Hong Kong and become Victor McLaglen adventurers. On Fourth of July we all went to Boston and wandered around Scollay Square looking for quiff that wasnt there. I spend most of my Friday nights singing every show tune in the books under an apple tree in Centreville, Lowell, with Moe Cole: and boy could we sing: and later she sang with Benny Goodman's band awhile. She once came to see me in broad afternoon summer wearing a tightfitting fire engine red dress and high heels, whee. (I'm not mentioning love affairs much in this book because I think acquiescing to the lovin whims of girls was the least of my Vanity.)

But the summer wore on and I never got my chemistry figured out and then came the time when my father, who'd been working out of town as linotypist, sometimes at Andover Mass., sometimes Boston, sometimes Meriden Conn., now had a steady job lined up at New Haven Conn. and it was decided we move there. My sister by now was married. As we were packing, I went about and nighted the Pawtucketville stars of trees and wrote sad songs about 'picking up my stakes and rolling.' But that wasn't the point.

One night my cousin Blanche came to the house and sat in the kitchen talking to Ma among the packing boxes. I sat on the porch outside and leaned way back with feet on rail and gazed at the stars for the first time in my life. A clear August night, the stars, the Milky Way, the whole works clear. I stared and stared till they stared back at me. Where the hell was I and what was all this?

I went into the parlor and sat down in my father's old deep easy chair and fell into the wildest daydream of my life. This is important and this is the key to the story, wifey dear:

As Ma and Cousin talked in the kitchen, I daydreamed that I was now going to go back to Columbia for my sophomore year, with home in New Haven, maybe near Yale campus, with soft light in room and rain on the sill, mist on the pane, and go all the way in football and studies. I was going to be such a sensational runner that we'd win every game, against Dartmouth, Yale, Princeton, Harvard, Georgia U., Michigan U., Cornell, the bloody lot, and wind up in the Rose Bowl. In the Rose Bowl, worse even than Cliff Montgomery, I was going to run wild. Uncle Lu Libble for the first time in his life would throw his arms around me and weep. Even his wife would do so. The boys on the team would raise me up in Rose Bowl's Pasadena Stadium and march me to the showers singing. On returning to Columbia campus in January, having passed chemistry with an A, I would then idly turn my attention to winter indoor track and decide on the mile and run it in under 4 flat (that was fast in those days). So fast, indeed, that I'd be in the big meets at Madison Square Garden and beat the current great milers in final fantastic sprints bringing my time down to 3:50 flat. By this time everybody in the world is crying Duluoz! Duluoz! But, unsatisfied, I idly go out in the spring for the Columbia baseball team and bat homeruns clear over the Harlem River, one or two a game, including fast breaks from the bag to steal from first to second, from second to third, and finally, in the climactic game, from third to home, zip, slide, dust, boom. Now the New York Yankees are after me. They want me to be their next Joe DiMaggio. I idly turn that down because I want Columbia to go to the Rose Bowl again in 1943. (Hah!) But then I also, in mad midnight musings over a Faustian skull, after drawing circles in the earth, talking to God in the tower of the Gothic high steeple of Riverside Church, meeting Jesus on the Brooklyn Bridge, getting Sabby a part on Broadway as Hamlet (playing King Lear myself across the street) I become the greatest writer that ever lived and write a book so golden and so purchased with magic that everybody smacks their brows on Madison Avenue. Even Professor Claire is chasing after me on his crutches on the Columbia campus. Mike Hennessey, his father's hand in hand, comes screaming up the dorm steps to find me. All the kids of HM are singing in the field. Bravo, bravo, author, they're yelling for me in the theater where I've also presented my newest idle work. a play rivaling Eugene O'Neill and Maxwell Anderson and making Strindberg spin. Finally, a delegation of cigar-chewing guys come and get me and want to know if I want to train for the world's heavyweight boxing championship fight with Joe Louis. Okay, I train idly in the Catskills, come down on a June night, face big tall Joe as the referee gives us instructions, and then when the bell rings I rush out real fast and just pepper him real fast and so hard that he actually goes back bouncing over the ropes and into the third row and lays there knocked out.

I'm the world's heavyweight boxing champion, the greatest writer, the world's champ miler, Rose Bowl and (pro-bound with New York Giants football non pareil) now offered every job on every paper in New York, and what else? Tennis anyone?

I woke up from this daydream suddenly realising that all I had to do was go back on the porch and look at the stars again, which I did, and still they just stared at me blankly.

In other words I suddenly realised that all my ambitions, no matter how they came out, and of course as you can see from the preceding narrative, they just came our fairly ordinary, it wouldnt matter anyway in the intervening space between human breathings and the 'sigh of the happy stars,' so to speak, to quote Thoreau again.

It just didnt matter what I did, anytime, anywhere, with anyone; life is funny like I said.

I suddenly realised we were all crazy and had nothing to work for except the next meal and the next good sleep.

O God in the Heavens, what a fumbling, hand-hanging, goof world it is, that people actually think they can gain anything from either this, or that, or thissa, or thatta, and in so doing, corrupt their sacred graves in the names of sacred-grave corruption.

Chemistry shemistry . . . football, shmootball . . . the war must have been getting in my bones.

When I looked up from that crazy reverie, at the stars, heard my mother and cousin still yakking in the kitchen about tea leaves, heard in fact my father yelling across the street in the bowling alley, I realized either I was crazy or the world was crazy: and I picked on the world.

And of course I was right.

II

In any case my father had gone ahead to New Haven, started working on the job in West Haven it was, and idly, or let someone else do it, had an 'apartment' found for us in the Negro Ghetto district of New Haven. It wasnt so much that my mother or father or myself minded Negroes, God bless em, but broken glass and crap on the floor, broken windows, bottles, ruined plaster, the works. Ma and I traveled from Lowell, following the moving truck, on the New Haven Railroad, got there at dawn, a musty fust of pluck mist over the railyards at sunrise, and we walk in the hotting streets to this third story crapulous 'apartment.' 'Is that man crazy?' says Ma. Already, after having done all the packing and arrangements, and after even running downstairs after poor Ti Gris our cat and falling down the stairs after it (on Gershom Avenue) and hurting her hip and leg, here she is, hopefully perfumed, tho worn out from the all-night train from Lowell with its interminable silly stops in Worcester or someplace of all places, here she finds a place not even the cheapest landlord in Lowell or Tashkent would rent to the milkiest Kurd or horsiest Khan in Outer Twangolia, let alone French Canadians used to polished-floor tenements and Christmas cheer based on elbow grease and Hope.

So we call up Pa, he says he didnt know any better, he says he'll call a French Canadian realtor and mover of New Haven and see what we can find. Ends up, Fromage the French Canadian mover has a little cottage by the sea at West Haven not far from Savin Rock Park. Our furniture by now is in the warehouse in New Haven. My little kitty Ti Gris has jumped out of his box somewhere along the route when the truckers stopped for chow and is gone forever in the woods of New England. In the warehouse as they're shoving around I see one of Ma's dresser drawers yaw open and inside I see her bloomers, crucifixes, rosaries, rubber bands, toys; it suddenly occurs to me people are lost when they leave their homes and convey themselves to the hands of brigands good or bad as they may be. But the French Canadian man, old fellow about sixty, has that wonderful French Canadian accent on Hope and says 'Come on, cheer up, *là bas* ('there') let's get the stuff on the truck, rain or no rain' – it's raining cats and dogs – 'and let's go to your new cottage by the sea. I'll rent it to you for sixty dollars a month, is that so bad?'

We even buy a bottle to nip us along and all go on the truck, the man, then Pa, then me all huddled up against the door, and Ma between Pa and me. Off we go in the rain. We drive out to the seacoast of Long Island Sound and there's the cottage.

They park the truck, the other French Canadian movers show up, and boom, they're unloading everything and rushing into the cottage with it. It's a two-story affair with three bedrooms upstairs, kitchen, parlor, heating arrangement, what else do you want? In the glee of the situation, and a little high on the bottle, I put on my swim trunks and ran across the mud toward the strand in a lashing gale from the Sound. Ah that menace of monstrous rolling waves of gray water and spray, put me in the mind of something past and something future.

Because you know, wifey, the first time I saw the sea? I was three years old and somebody took me to Salisbury Beach, I guess, or Hampton, I remember somebody offering me five dollars if I'd get into my bathing suit and I refused. In those days I used to lock myself in the toilet. Nobody was going to see me part naked in those days. But I stood there and put my little three-year-old hands to my brow and looked deep into the horizon of the sea out there, and it seems I saw what it was like, the actual waving gray, the Noah's Ark inevitably floating on it, popping up and down, the groan and creak of it, the lash of rigs winging, the very centerfoam splowsh and lick: I said to myself then: 'Ah soliloquizer, what royal wake out there, what heave boom smack . . . etc. What pain in salt and door?'

As my poor mother huddled in the parlor of her new cottage she watched me walk right out into the sea and begin to swim. I rose high up with the crest of the waves and then sank way down into their valleys below, I tasted the salty spray, I smashed my face and eyes onward into the great sea, I could see it coming, I laughed aloud, I plowed on, bobbed up and down, got dizzy with the rise and fall of it, saw the horizon in the gray rainy distance, lost it in a monster wave, put out for a boat which was anchored there and said 'We're Here.'

Begod and BeJesus we were. I got on the boat and bobbed there awhile, side, side, stern, stern, looked back, saw my Ma waving, laughed, and jumped into the sea. Underneath I deliberately stared deepward to see the darker gray there. . . . Great day in the morning dont ever do it, during a rainstorm dont ever get down to the bottom of the sea and see what it looks like further in toward Neptune's inhappy *clous* ('nails').

Three silver nails in a blue field.

III

And the next day, to add to the woes of my mother and father, who are trying in one way or another to be happily unpacking, it's sunny, I put on my swimming trunks again and go out swimming straight a mile toward the nearest sandbar. I get out on the sandbar (having swum the Merrimack up and down along the Boulevard many times for practice), and one afternoon swam pine drunken Pine Brook about a hundred times up and down, a few miles or so, for practice, come to the sandbar and take a nap in the early September sun. Come dusk the water's lapping at me toes. I get up and swim back toward our cottage, which I can see a mile away. Slow, slow, always swim slow and let your head lean in the waves like in a pillow. There's my poor Paw out there on the seawall hands to eyes looking for his drowned son. He sees me coming. 'Whoopee!' he yells to Angie my Ma. 'Here he comes!'

'What?'

'There he is! That's him. Coming real slow!' And I pull up and go in the house and wonder what they were scared about. 'It's time tomorrow for you to go to Columbia and start your sophomore year, now stop fooling around. Go down to the corner, it's only a mile, buy the evening paper, some ice cream, cigarettes, cigars, here's the money . . . '

'We're going to have a good time here,' says Ma.

'When there's storms the sea'll be looking for your parlor,' I shoulda warned her.

It was just a summer resort, empty in fall and winter, and really that Sound can kick up in December to March. A big mansion along the rocks a half mile down the beach was the home of Helen Twelvetrees the old actress. My Ma actually talked to her later on.

Bill Keresky you remember from HM, and Gene Mackstoll, and another guy came in a sports car to fetch me to take me to New York for the new year. To pack my suitcase I went up in the attic to fetch certain things and my both feet fell down thru the phony ceiling and I landed my crotch right on a beam and cried. I got over it in a half hour. We got in the car, kissed the folks goodbye, and went to the City.

They drove me straight to Baker Field, the Columbia U. training house, and there was Lu Libble working over his plays at the blackboard in the diningroom, the footballers sitting around watching and listening, everybody giving me dirty looks because I was a day late. Upstairs, bunks. Morning, breakfasts, saltpeter so we wouldnt get horny, showers, taping, aching muscles, hot September sun tacklings of silly dummies held by assistant coaches and idiots with cameras taking our pictures dodging this way or that.

What were the chances of Columbia this year? Nothing, as far as I could see, since the only real football player on the team, Hank Full our quarterback, had joined the Marines just a day ago and was leaving. Thackeray Carr wasnt bad. Big Turk Tadzic of Pennsy was ready but they had to make contact lenses for him, an end. Big Ben Kurowsky got sore at me after scrimmage because I evaded his attempted tackle and picked me up in the showers and held me up sky high at arm's length saying 'You lil bastart.' Then he glowered at Chad Stone who was too big to pick up. It was Chad's job and mine to take out Kurowsky on what is called the 'high-low,' that is, 'you hit him high and I'll hit him low,' I hit Kurowsky low and Chad hit him high. Chad was 6 foot 3. I was 5:8½. We got Kurowsky out of there some of the time. He was 6 foot 4 and weighed 240.

They could have had a good team but the war was coming up.

And then in practice I began to see that good old Lu Libble wasnt going to start me in the starting lineup but let me sit on the bench while Liam McDiarmid and Spider Barth, who were seniors, wore out their seniority. Now they were shifty and nifty runners but not so fast or strong as I was. That didnt matter to Lu Libble. He insulted me in front of everybody again by saying 'You're not such a hot runner, you cant handle the KT-79 reverse deception' – as if I'd joined football for 'deception' for God's sake – 'first thing you know, you with your big legs' – they werent that big – 'I'm going to make you a lineman.

'Now run and do that reverse.'

With my eyes I said 'I cant run any faster these first two days, my legs are sore.'

Never mind, he said with his eyes, putting me in mind of the time he made me run on a broken leg for a week.

At night, after those meaningless big suppers of steak and milk and dry toast, I began to realise this: 'Lu Libble wont let you start this year, not even in the Army game against your great enemy Art Janur [who pushed me out of the showers when I was a kid in Lowell High but got his come-uppance from Orestes Gringas], and not even maybe next year as a junior, he wants to make a big hero out of his Italian Mike Romanino, well Mike is certainly a great passer but he runs like Pietryka like an old cow. And Hank Full's leaving. The hell with it. What'll I do?'

I stared into the darkness of the bunkrooms thinking what to do.

'Ah shucks, go into the American night, the Thomas Wolfe darkness, the hell with these bigshot gangster football coaches, go after being an American writer, tell the truth, dont be pushed around by them or anybody else or any of their goons. . . . The Ivy League is just an excuse to get football players for nothing and get them to be American cornballs enough to make America sick for a thousand years. You shoulda stuck to Francis Fahey. . . .'

Well I can't remember what I was thinking altogether but all I know is that the next night, after dinner, I packed all my gear in my suitcase and sauntered down the steps right in front of Lu Libble's table where he was sitting with his assistant coaches figuring out plays. My bones were rasping against my muscles from the overtraining, I limped. 'Where you going Dulouse?'

'Going over to my grandmother's house in Brooklyn and dump some of this clothes.'

'It's Saturday night. Be back by tomorrow at eight. You gonna sleep there?'

'Yeh.'

'Be back by eight. We're going to have a light calisthenics, you know the part where you get on your back and turn your skull to the grass and roll around so you wont get your fool neck broken in a game?'

'Yes sir.'

'Be back at eight. What you got in there?'

'Junk. Presents from home, dirty laundry. . . .'

'We got a laundry here.'

'There's presents, letters, stuff, Coach.'

'Okay, back at eight.'

And I went out and took the subway down to Brooklyn with all my gear, whipped out a few dollars from the suitcase, said goodbye to Uncle Nick saying I was going back to Baker Field, walked down the hot September streets of Brooklyn hearing Franklin Delano Roosevelt's speech about 'I hate war' coming out of every barbershop in Brooklyn, took the subway to the Eighth Avenue Greyhound bus station, and bought a ticket to the South.

I wanted to see the Southland and start my career as an American careener.

IV

This was the most important decision of my life so far. What I was doing was telling everybody to go jump in the big fat ocean of their own folly. I was also telling myself to go jump in the big fat ocean of my own folly. What a bath!

It was delightful. I was washed clean. The bus went down to Maryland and I joyed like a maniac just because I was looking at 'real Southern leaves.' A Negro from Newark kept talking to me in the seat, about how he won at pool in Newark and lost something in poker and now was going to see his dying Paw in Virginny. I wished I had enough money to go to Virginia but my ticket stopped at Washington D.C. There, on a dismal street full of mailboxes and Negroes leaning against them, I got a room full of bedbugs, heat, couldnt sleep, paced around, and in the morning took the bus back to New York, where I transferred to New Haven so I could go home and see Pa. I was on the road for the first time.

He was mad as hell but I explained to him how I wasnt supposed to start the opening game or any games as far as I could see. 'Ah,' he said, 'I saw that from the start, same thing as Lowell High. You could have been a great football player Jacky but nobody wanted to give you a chance. If I had money and could slip em a few bucks . . . '

'Never mind, the war's coming up, who cares now?'

'I care!'

'I don't . . . if all these kids I grew up with are going out there, like Dicky Hampshire, what the heck, I feel like a shit.' (In French, that word, *merde*, is never a bad word, it's just the truth.) (Buy that.)

'Well what are you gonna do now?' says Pa.

'I heard there's a job in a local rubber plant for a tire hemmer or whatever they call it . . . ' That night in my room, as Ma and Pa slept, I played Richard Wagner as I gazed at the moonlighted Sound. I little dreamed I'd be sailing that Sound one day soon. It was the 'Magic Fire Music' from *Die Walküre* but I had sinus trouble and a kind of virus and almost choked to death.

In the morning I showed up at the rubber plant, got the job, spent all morning in the noisy rubber-dust joint rolling up tires and inrimming them with some kind of gum, got disgusted at noon and walked away and never asked for any morning's pay.

I went down in the afternoon, in the lengthening shadows of Long Island Sound, saw cottages on little hills overlooking distant coves, and came to a fairyland playground where children, among autumn leaves, were riding hobbyhorses to the tune of 'In the Good Old Summertime.' Tears came into my eyes. The great American football player hero and hero miler and hero world's champ boxer and writer and playwright was just a sad young man like Saroyan with curly hair surveying child's delight in the gloaming of the sun . . .

Ah, poetic. I went home and told Pa I couldnt take that job. He said 'There's a postcard here for you, from Hartford Connecticut, from your little buddy Joe Fortier, says he can get you a job as a grease monkey there.'

'Okay I'll go tomorrow.'

'It isn't that we dont want you in the house . . . but I have to walk a mile to that printing plant every morning, your mother remember was wiping tables in the Waldorf Cafeteria in New Haven last week while you were s'posed to be making the football team. Here we whack along in the same pickle as ever. Why dont you people ever do right?'

'We'll see about that. I'll get that grease monkey job in Hartford and show you.'

'Show me what you little punk?'

'I'll show you that I'm goin to become a great writer.'

'No Duluoz was ever a great writer . . . there never was such a name in the writing game.'

'It's not a game . . . '

'It's Hugo, Balzac . . . It's not your fancypants Saroyan with his fancy titles.'

But in the morning, before breakfast, Pa was out there on the beach picking up clams and enjoying the fresh Breton air. Ma was gaily making bacon and eggs. I had my bag packed and all I had to do was walk a mile or so and take the trolley to downtown New Haven, hop the railroad, and go to Hartford. The sun shone on the seawall.

You'd think after showing them how to swim I coulda shown them how to swim all the way.

V

In Hartford I got the job, it's not an important section of the book except for the fact it was the first time I had a room of my own, in a cheap roominghouse on Main Street, Hartford, and rented an Underwood portable typewriter, and when I came home at night tired from work, after eating my nightly cheap steak in a tavern on Main Street, came in and started to write two or three fresh stories each night: the whole collection of short stories called 'Atop an Underwood,' not worth reading nowadays, or repeating here, but a great little beginning effort. Outside my room's window was nothing but a bare stone wall which later put me in the mind of Melville's 'Bartleby the Scrivener' who had a similar view out of his window and used to say 'I know where I am.' Coachroaches, too, but at least no bedbugs.

I had no money in particular till I got paid the fifteenth of the month. As a consequence I fainted of hunger one day in the Atlantic Whiteflash Station where I was greasemonkeying with a kid called Buck Shotwell. He saw me out on the floor of the garage. 'What the hell's the matter? Wake up.'

I said 'I havent eaten in two days.'

'For God's sake come to my mother's house and eat.' He drives me to his mother's house in Hartford and she, bowlegged and fat and kind by the table, gives me a quart of milk, beans, toast, hamburg, tomatoes, potatoes, the works. Buck loans me two bucks to carry me over till the fifteenth. Both of us are wearing coveralls covered with grease.

When the management of the stations discovers I'm not such a hot grease monkey, knowing nothing about the mechanics of cars, they put me on the gas pump to pump gas and wipe windows and break open oil cans and put a spout in em and pour oil into the oil hole. In those days greasers only had to lift little oilcup covers and pour in, but you had to know where all the little oilcups were located. Meanwhile, it was autumn, 'old melancholy Oktober' I called it: 'There's something olden and golden and lost/ in the strange ancestral light/ There's something tender and loving and sad/ in Oktober's copper might. . . . Missing something . . . sad, sad, sad/ End of something . . . old, old, old,/' it was beautiful with falling red leaves aching, and then old silver November moved in, bringing fainter flavors and grayer skies, snow you could smell.

I was happy in my room at night writing 'Atop an Underwood,' stories in the Saroyan-Hemingway-Wolfe style as best as I could figure it at age nineteen. . . . Tho sometimes longing for a girl. One day I was resting on the grass in front of our gas station in East Hartford and I saw a sixteen-year-old girl go by with dimples behind her knees, in the flesh where the knee bends, in back, and followed her to the lunchcart and made a date for her to meet me in the woods outside the Pratt & Whitney Plant. We just talked and watched airplanes go by. But we made the mistake of leaving the wood together at five o'clock exactly when the Pratt Whitney workers were all coming out in cars, toot toot, whoo whoo, yippeeeeeee, and all that, and we both blushed. A few nights later in her aunt's home I made the blushes worth a count. Also, at the time (no trouble), me and Shotwell were shifted to another gas station in Farmington and there came two girls across the street, he said 'Come on Jack,' jumped in the car, we chased them, picked them up, went out to a November russet meadow and made the car bounce all afternoon: the ridiculous concerns of grease monkeys, I'd say.

VI

Careening in the American night. Then comes Thanksgiving and I'm lonesome for home, turkey, kitchen table, but have to work five hours that day, but here comes a knock on my cockroach door with the stone wall view: I open it: it's big idealistic curly-haired Sabbas Savakis.

'I thought I would join you on this day which is supposed to have some kind of significance concerning thanks.'

'Very good, Sab.'

'Why did you quit Columbia?'

'I dunno, I just got sick of bumping around . . . It's allright to be an athlete if you think you're going to get something out of college but I just dont think I'll get anything out of college . . . I set a new record there cutting classes, as I wrote you . . . Phooey, I dunno . . . I wanta be a writer . . . Look at these stories I been writing.'

'It's just like a sad Burgess Meredith movie,' says Sabby, 'you and I alone for Thanksgiving Day in this room. Shall we go out and see a movie?'

'Sure, I know a good one down at the Cameo.'

'Oh I saw that one.'

'Well I didnt.'

'Which one didnt you see?'

'I didnt see the one at the Olympia.'

'Well you go to the Olympia and I'll go to the Cameo. Is that the way to abandon old Sabby on Thanksgiving Day?'

'I'm not saying that, let's go eat first . . . whatever movie you wanta see, go see it. I'm gonna see what I want.'

'O Zagg, life is sad, life is – '

' "Life is real, life is earnest," I think your Wordsworth said.'

'Guess what? My sister Stavroula has a new job, my brother Elia grew three inches this summer, my brother Pete is a sergeant in the Quartermaster Corps, my sister Sophia has a new boyfriend, my sister Xanthi got a new hand-knitted sweater from my sister-in-law, *beautiful* sweater, my father is well, my mother is making a big turkey today and gave me hell for coming to Hartford to you, and my brother Marty thinks of going in the service, and my brother Georgie is getting honors in high school, and my brother Chris is thinking of quitting the Lowell *Sun* and going in the service. Why dont you come back to Lowell and write sports for the Lowell *Sun*?'

'I want to write "Atop an Underwood." You ever hear about the old whore had a thousand spikes coming out of her like a porcupine: that's how many stories I got coming out of my ears.'

'But you've got to be selective.'

'Where shall we eat?'

'Let's go to a sad lunchcart and have the blue plate turkey special and bring pencil and paper and write a Saroyan story about it.'

'Ah Sabby, you big old Sabby. I'm glad you come to see me on Thanksgiving Day . . . '

'Something will come of it,' says he almost crying. 'Jacky you were s'posed to be a big football star and scholar or something or other at Columbia, what brings you to this sad room and with that sad typewriter, your tortured pillow, your hungers, your coveralls full of grease . . . are you really sure this is what you want to do?'

'It's not important, Sab, why didnt you bring me a cigar? It's not important because I'm going to show you that I know what I'm doing. Parents come, parents go, schools come, schools go, but what's an eager young soul going to do against the wall of what they call reality? Was Heaven based on the decisions of the aged fools? Did the elders tell the Lamb who to bless?' – I didnt speak as well as that, of course, but it fits – 'Whose eyes brood in the moot Yes? Who can tell the blooded Baron what's to be done with farted America? When does youth take No for an answer? And what is youth? A rose, a swan, a ballet, a whale, a phosphorescent little fishy children's crusade? A sumach growing by the tracks on the Boston & Maine? A tender white hand in the moonlight child? A loss of eleemosynary time? A crocka bullshit? When say the ancestors it's time for Thanks

Giving, and the turkey light is on the marsh, and the Indian corn you can smell, and smoke, ah, Sabby, write me a poem.'

'I happen to have one here; listen: "Remember, Jack, lest we/ lose/ Remember, Jack, sunsets/ that glimmered on/ two laughing, swimming/ youths/ Oh! so long ago/ Remember the mists of/ early New England/ the sun glaring thru/ the trees and chambers/ of Beauty." See? And then: "The dawn, the flowers you/ brought home to your/ mother and then back/ back to realism" . . .'

Elated we ran out of the roominghouse and went down Main Street Hartford to a 'sad lunchcart' and had the blue plate turkey special. But by God and b'Jesus if we didnt part at the monument downtown, he to the right, me to the left, because we had different movies we wanted to see.

After the show, dusk lights, he met me again on the same corner. 'How was the picture?'

'Aoh, okay.'

'I saw Victor Mature in *I Wake Up Screaming*.'

'And?'

'He's very interesting: I dont care about the plot . . .'

'Let's go down and drink beer on Main Street . . .'

In there that night a guy tried to start a fight with my old Lowell buddy Joe Fortier now a grease monkey with me. I went into the men's room, gave the men's room door a coupla whacks with my fist, came out, went up to the guy, said 'Leave Joe alone or I'll knock you across the street' and the guy left. Meanwhile Sabby was having a long talk at the bar with somebody. And two weeks later my father wrote and said 'Come on back to New Haven, we're packing and moving back to Lowell, I have a new job now in Lowell at Rolfe's.'

Then, as now, I was proud that I had written something at least. A writer's life is based on things like that. I wont bore the reader with the story of my writing development, can do that later, but this is the story of the techniques of suffering in the working world, which includes football and war.

BOOK SIX

I

The most delicious truck ride I ever had in my life was when, after the movers put all the furniture aboard and my mother went ahead in a car with sister Nin, the movers arranged my father's easy chair at the tailgate's hem of the truck and I could sit there, lean back, smoke, sing, and watch the road wind away from me at 50 miles an hour, the line on curves snaking away into the woods of Connecticut, the woods getting different and more interesting the closer we approached old Lowell in north-eastern Massachusetts. And at dusk as we're hitting thru Westford or thereabouts and my old white birch reappeared grieving in hill silhouettes, tears came to my eyes to realise I was coming back home to old Lowell. It was November, it was cold, it was woodsmoke, it was swift waters in the wink of silver glare with its rose headband out yander where Eve Star (some call it Venus, some call it Lucifer) stoppered up her drooling propensities and tried to contain itself in one delimited throb of boiling light.

Ah poetic. I keep saying 'ah poetic' because I didnt intend this to be a poetic paean of a book, in 1967 as I'm writing this what possible feeling can be left in me for an 'America' that has become such a potboiler of broken convictions, messes of rioting and fighting in streets, hoodlumism, cynical administration of cities and states, suits and neckties the only feasible subject, grandeur all gone into the mosaic mesh of Television (Mosaic indeed, with a capital *M*), where people screw their eyes at all those dots and pick out hallucinated images of their own contortion and are fed ACHTUNG! ATTENTION! ATENCIÓN! instead of Ah dreamy real wet lips beneath an old apple tree? Or that picture in *Time* Magazine a year ago showing a thousand cars parked in a redwood forest in California, all alongside similar tents with awnings and primus stoves, everybody dressed alike looking around everywhere at everybody with those curious new eyes of the second part of this century, only occasionally looking up at the trees and if so probably thinking 'O how nice that redwood would look as my lawn furniture!' Well, enough ... for now.

Main thing is, coming home, 'Farewell Song Sweet from My Trees' of the previous August was washed away in November joys.

But it's always been the case in my life that before a great catastrophe I feel unaccountably gloomy, lazy, sleepy, sick, depressed, black-souled and arm-hanged. That first week in Lowell, in a nice new clean little first floor of a two-family house on Crawford Street, after we'd unpacked and I stuck my old childhood desk near the window and the radiator, and sat there smoking on my pipe and writing a new Journal in ink, all I could do was gloom over the words and thoughts of Fyodor Dostoevsky. I happened to start up on him in one of his gloomiest works, *Notes from the Underground.* At midnight, in bright moonlight, I walked Moody Street over crunching snow and felt something awful that had not been in Lowell before. For one thing I was the 'failure back in town,' for another I had lost the glamour of New York City and the Columbia campus and the tweeded outlook of sophomores, had lost glittering Manhattan, was back trudging among the brick walls of the mills. My Pa slept next to me in his twin bed snoring like a booming wind. Ma and Nin slept together in the double bed. The parlor, with its old stuffed furniture and old squareback piano, was locked for the winter. And I had to find a job.

Then one Sunday night I came walking out of the Royal Theater all elated because I had just seen Orson Welles' *Citizen Kane* and by God, what a picture! I wanted to be a genius of poetry in film like Welles. I was rushing home to figure out a movie play. It was snowing and cold. I heard a little boy rush up with newspapers yelling: 'Japs bomb Pearl Harbor!' 'War declared on Japan and Germany!' the next day. It's as tho I'd felt it coming, just as, years later, the night before the death of my father, I had tried, or would try, to walk around the block and only ended up shuffling head down . . . more on that near the end of this.

All I was supposed to do was wait for the Navy V-2 program to call me up for an examination into whether I should be in the Naval Air Force. So, meanwhile to get that job, I went to the Lowell *Sun* and asked to see the owner of the newspaper, Jim Mayo, to see whether I could be hired as a trucker's helper delivering piiles of newspapers to the dealers. He said 'Arent you the Jack Duluoz who was a football star a few years ago in Lowell High? And in New York, at Yale it was?'

'Columbia.'

'And you were preparing for journalism? Why should you be a delivery boy? Here, you take this note to go into the sports desk and tell them I want you start right in Monday morning as a sports reporter. What the heck, boy!' – clap on the back – 'We're not all hicks around here. Fifteen dollars a week do okay as a starter.'

He didnt ask, in those days employers didnt ask, but I thrilled temporarily at the thought of whipping out my college sports coat and pants and regaining ye old necktie glamour at a desk in the bright morning of men and business things.

II

So thru January and February I was a sports writing cub for the Lowell *Sun*. My Pa was very proud. In fact, on several occasions he got a day's work running a linotype in the press room and I used to proudly bring him one of my typewritten stories (say about Lowell High basketball) and give it to him on his rack, and we'd smile. 'Stick to it kid, *découragez ons nous pas, ça va venir, ça va venir*.' (Means: 'Let's not get discouraged, it's gonna come, it's gonna come.')

It was at this time that the phrase 'Vanity of Duluoz' occurred to me and was made the title of a novel that I began writing at my sports desk at about noon every day, because from nine till noon was all it took me to do my whole day's work, I could write fast and type fast and just kept feeding that copy all over the place on fast feet. Noon, when everybody left the tacking editorial office, and I was alone, I snuck out the pages of my secret novel and continued writing it. It was the greatest fun I ever had 'writing' in my life because I had just discovered James Joyce and I was imitating *Ulysses* I thought (really imitating 'Stephen Hero' I later discovered, a real adolescent but sincere effort, with 'power' and 'promise' pronounced Arch MacDougald our local cultural mentor later). I had discovered James Joyce, the stream of consciousness, I have that whole novel right in front of me now. It was simply the day-by-day doings of nothing in particular by 'Bob' (me), Pater (my Pa), etc., etc., all the other sportswriters, all my buddies down at the theater and in the saloons at night, all the studies I had rebegun in the Lowell Public Library (on a grand scale), my afternoons of exercising in the Y.M.C.A., the girls I went out with, the movies I saw, my talks with Sabbas, with my mother and sister, an attempt to delineate all of Lowell as Joyce had done for Dublin.

Just for instance the first page went like this: 'Bob Duluoz awoke neatly, surprised at himself, swung his legs deftly from under the warm sheets. Two weeks now, doing this daily, how the hell? myself one of Earth's biggest slothards. Rose in the cold gray morning without a tremor.

'In the kitchen gruntled Pater.

' "Hurry up there, it's past nine o'clock."

'Duluoz, the crazy bastard. He sat down on the bed and thought for just a moment. How do I do it? Bleary eyes.

'Morning in America.

' "What time does the mail come?" ask gruntled Pater.

'Duluoz, the turd said: "Around nine o'clock." Ooooooaa-yaawn. He fetched up his white socks, which were none too white. He put them on. Shoes need a shine. Old socks found dusting slowly under dresser; use them. He rubbed his shoes shinewise with the old socks. Then on swung the trousers, jingling, jingling, jingling. Jingle. Chain and some money and two keys, one for home, one for Business Men's Lockers in local Y.M.C.A. Local . . . that son of a bitch of a newspaper word. Free $21 membership . . . showers, rower, basketballs, track, pool, etc., radio too. Handle I the destiny of the "Y's" press success. Handle I the. Press success. Bob Duluoz, the rovin reporter. What Socko calls him.

'Morning in America.'

(And so on.)

Get it?

That's how writers begin, by imitating the masters (without suffering like said masters), till they larn their own style, and by the time they larn their own style there's no more fun in it, because you cant imitate any other master's suffering but your own.

Most beautiful of all in those winter nights I used to leave my father snoring in his room, sneak into the kitchen, turn on the light, brew a pot of tea, put my feet in the oil stove oven, lean back that way in the rocking chair, and read the Book of Job down to its tiniest detail in its entirety, and Goethe's *Faust*, and Joyce's *Ulysses*, till daybreak. Sleep two hours and go to the Lowell *Sun*. Finish the newspaper work at noon, write a chapter of the 'novel.' Go eat two hamburgs on Kearney Square in the White Tower. Walk up to the Y, exercise, even punch the sandbag and run the 300 around the upstairs track fairly fast. Then into the library with notebook where I was reading H. G. Wells and taking down elaborate notes, right from the beginning with the Mesozoic age of reptiles, intending to work my way up to Alexander the Great before spring and actually looking up all of Wells' references that puzzled or interested me in the *Encyclopaedia Britannica* XI Ed which was right there in my old rotunda shelves. 'By the time I'm done,' I was vowing, 'I shall know everything that ever happened on earth in detail.' Not only that, but home at dusk, supper, an argument with Pa at supper table, a nap, and back to the library for a second round of 'learning everything on earth.' At nine, library closing, exhausted from this horrible schedule, old sad Sabbas was always waiting for me at the door of the library, with that melancholy smile, ready for a hot fudge sundae or a beer, anything so long as he could exchange with me some kind of bouquet of homage.

This isn't a book about Sabby proper, so I hurry along . . .

III

And who to this day can give a flinging frig for what Superintendent Orrenberger said, places that are called The Commonwealth, like Massachusetts, are usually the nesting holes of thieves.

Because, as I say Sabby and my folks aside, when winds of March began to melt the porcelain of that old winter, I got it in my head that I wanted to quit that newspaper and hit the road and go South. It's a good thing Jeb Stuart never met me in 1862, we woulda been a great team of hellions. I love the South, I dont know why, it's the people, the courtliness, the care about your own courtliness, the disregard of your *beau regard*, the love of tit for tat in a real field instead of deception, the language above all: 'Boy Ah'm a-gonna tell you naow, I'm going South.' One afternoon the Lowell *Sun* assigned me to go interview Coach Yard Parnell of the Lowell Textile Institute baseball team and instead, when I came home to get ready for this interview, just a few blocks away, I just sat in my room and stared at the wall and fluffed off and said 'Ah hell, shuck, I'm not going anywhere to interview nobody.' They called, I didnt answer the phone. I just stayed home and stared at the wall. Already Moe Cole'd been over a coupla times on the couch in everybody-working-afternoon. If Ariadne was mounted by a Ram, or wanted to mount a Ram, what difference does it make to a nineteen-year-old boy?

I am the descendant of Jean-Baptise LeBri de Duluoz an old gaffer carpenter from St-Hubert in Temiscouata County, Quebec, who built his own house in Nashua N.H. and used to curse at God swinging his kerosene lamp during thunderstorms yelling '*Varge!* [Whack!] *Frappe!* [Hit!] *Vas y!* [Go ahead!]' and 'Dont give me no back talk' and when women hit up on him in the street he told them where to get off with their bustles and bounces and desires for bracelets, he did. The Duluoz family has always been enraged. Is that a sign of bad blood? The father line of Duluoz, it isnt French, it's Cornish, it's Cornish Celtic (the name of the language is Kernuak), and they're always enraged and arguing about something, there is in them, not the 'angry young man' but the 'infuriated old man' of the sea. My father that night is saying: 'Did you go to Textile Institute and interview the baseball coach?'

'No.'

'Why not?' No answer. 'Did that Mike Hennessey have to say anything in his letter from New York about Lu Libble wants you to come back to the team?'

'All kinds of things, he's thinking of joining the Naval Reserve, he says there is a course for sophomores so I guess I might make that.' But Pa's face (Pater's face) said something sarcastic: and I say 'What's the face for? You dont think I'll ever get back to college, do you? You dont ever think I can do anything.'

Ma sighed. 'There they go again.'

'I didnt say that!' shouted Pa angrily. 'But they wont be too glad to have you after the way you let them down last fall . . . '

'I left because I wanted to help the family, that was one reason, there were many reasons . . . such as I shouldnt draw breath to explain to an old pain in the ass even if it were you yourself, ee bejesus and be goddam, I was sick of the coach, he was all over me, I was sick, I knew the war was coming, I got the hell out, I wanted to stay out for awhile and study America.'

'Study mongrel America? And the gradual Pew York? Do you think you can do what you feel like all your life?'

'Yes.'

He laughed: 'Poor kid, ha ha ha, you dont even know what you're up against, and the trouble with us Duluozes is that we're Bretons and Cornishmen and it's that we cant get along with people, maybe we were descended from pirates, or cowards, who knows, because we cant stand rats, that coach was a rat. You shoulda socked him on the banana nose instead of sneaking out like a coward.'

'O sure, suppose I woulda socked him . . . would I be getting back there?'

'Who said you're getting back there? YOU'll never see the inside of Columbia again, I don't think.'

'Dammit I will, even if you dont want me to! Just dare me! If I'da listened to your encouraging words of wisdom all my life I'da rotted in Lowell a long time ago!'

'You dont know it, but you're rotting in Lowell right now.'

'O you like that thought dont you! You'd like me to join you in rotting away in Lowell.'

'AAAh you're nothing but a little punk, you were once the finest, sweetest, most innocent kid a few years ago, now look at him.'

'Yes look at me, tell me, Pa, is the world innocent?'

Ma broke in: 'Why dont you two stop fighting all the time? I never in all my life saw such a commotion in a house, *eh maudit* why dont you leave him alone Emil, he knows what he wants to do, he's old enough to know what he wants.'

Pa rose quickly from the table and began to leave the room: 'Sure, sure' – supper unfinished – 'stick up for him, he's the only thing you got, go ahead and believe in him, but you believe me, you'll starve plenty if you do, let him have his way, but dont come crying to me when you starve. Dammit!' Pa yelled on.

'Dammit!' I yelled. 'She wont starve, maybe I'm not paying her back now but I'll pay her back some day, a million times over . . . '

'Sure,' said Pa, leaving the room to make his point dramatic, 'pay her back when she's in her grave.' And he was gone into the freezing parlor fuming, stomping, Duluoz enraged. Ma looks at me and shakes her head gravely:

'I never saw such a man. I dont know how I ever lived twenty-five years with him, if you dont know listen to me, dont listen to him, if you do, you'll be the same thing he is, he never did anything himself . . . he's jealous that you'll go out and make something of yourself, dont listen to him, dont talk to him, he'll only make you mad . . .

'He's always been that way,' adds Ma, 'his whole family is crazy, his brothers are worse than he is, they're a bunch of crazy nuts, everybody in Canada knew that . . . '

Okay, me too.

Krroooooaaaooo! I could hear the railroad calling outside, okay, I'm packing tomorrow and going South and on the road.

IV

I wrote in my resignation to the newspaper, packed my bag, bought a bus ticket, and rode straight down to Washington D.C. where G.J. my Greek boyhood buddy of Lowell had a bed for me, to share with him, while in the other double bed in the room slept an old Southern construction worker called Bone who got up in the morning and scratched his back with a Chinese backscratcher and said 'Ah shit, gotta go to work again.' To me, the scrollworks few as they are up around New Hampshire Avenue, Washington D.C., represented a kind of New Orleans romance I was getting into, and G.J. and I went out the first night and hit the bars and here's this big brunette sitting in a booth with her girlfriend and says to me: 'You goin walking?'

'Sure,' I sez, 'and buy newspapers, two of em.'

With the two newspapers laid out in the grass under an oak tree in the U.S. Soldiers' Home Park we made the newspapers pay their way.

Then the backscratcher construction worker, a Southerner, driving me the first morning down to the Pentagon construction project, eyes bleary, sees a poor Negro riding a bike on Ninth Street and says 'Hey boy, wanta Nigger?' I'd never heard such talk in my life. I said:

'What you mean, dont hit him.' He swerved real close and almost hit the workingman's bike. I didnt like old Bone too much. At the Pentagon I had to pay ten dollars to join the union and then, few days later, got a job as apprentice sheetmetal worker. Huh! First day on the job I'm with this drunken sheetmetal worker who cant even find where the sheet metal's goin, goes out to lunch or someplace, dont come back, so I find a hole in the wood and dirt and take a big nap till 5 P.M. Next day, seeing my 'master' metalworker aint here I go back to crawl into my hole to sleep and there's three big blue-gum Nigras in there snoring and I manage to crawl in with them and sleep too, till five o'clock.

So that makes me a tin-eared Canuck?

Next afternoon a Negro with a shovel over his back is singing 'St James' Infirmary' so beautiful I follow him across the entire 5-mile construction field so I can hear every note and word. (Forgot to mention that on my way down to Washington that spring, 1942, I stopped off in New York just so I could hear Frank Sinatra, and see, Frank Sinatra, sing in the Paramount Theater, waiting there in line with two thousand screaming Brooklyn Jewish and Italian girls, I'm just about, in fact, AM the only guy in the line, and when we get in the theater and skinny old Frank comes out and grabs the mike, with glamorous rings on his fingers and wearing gray sports coat, black tie, gray shirt, sings 'Mighty Like a Rose,' and 'Without a song . . . the road would never end,' oww.) Here I am following old St James across a field, and the next day I go all the way and leave the construction site and walk into the woods of Virginia and sit there all day, in what I take to be the northern part of the Wilderness of Civil War fame, and sing 'Carr-y Me Back to Old Virginny.'

Worse than that, one day I have a pint of gin in my backpocket and I hitchhike back from the Pentagon construction project over the Potomac Bridge, the guy lets me out on Pennsylvania Avenue in front of the Nation's Capitol, during the day some work's torn off the front part of my pants, I have to hold them together or my thing'll wave. As I see the Nation's Capitol, the American flag, Pennsy Avenue, I whip back for my pint in backpocket to take a nip and the thing comes out and waves at the American flag and the Capitol. Now if Jefferson, Jackson or Washington'd seen that, whoo!

I mean, the weirdest nip of gin a man ever took in old Washington D.C.

V

On top of which, I then quit the construction job on the Pentagon and get me a job as a short-order cook and soda jerk in a Northwest Washington lunchcart and one night me and my West Virginia buddy are sent down to the cellar to fetch a bag of potatoes and fall over each other and tumble down and dont break our necks. 'You all right?' I ask him.

'Yeh. I'm all right. It's just,' he says looking away dreamily west, 'it's just I mess cant go down stairs no mo without fallin, that love bug's done bit me.'

"Who?'

'The love bug's done bit me, boy, I'm in love.' I go back upstairs with the potatoes and here I am wearing this big white cook hat and two girls are at the counter and one of them, the pretty brunette, hands me a pack of pornographic playing cards:

'Bet you cant tell where that hand is? You like tham pictures?'

'Sure.'

'Well lissen, you quit this job as a soda jerk and come live with me, I'll support you, all I ask is you dont go foolin around with no Negra gals or I'll stick a nife in yore back.' So I moved in with Annie of Columbus Georgia. One night as she's moaning up to my face 'Jack you jess doin me to dayeth' we hear a great knock on the door and a great mournful voice croons out:

'Annie, it's Bing. It's only old Bing.'

'Dont answer the door,' she whispers, 'it's only old Bing.'

'Bing Crosby?'

'No it aint Bing Crosby.'

'Sounds like him.'

'Shh. He'll go away.'

'And one of these days you'll turn me back at the door too, hey Annie of Georgia?'

Meanwhile me and G.J. hung around parks looking for even more quiff, we talked about the birds at dusk in the branches over our heads, about Lowell, but later that night he got drunk and mad and pulled out his scissors and said he was going to cut a whore's breasts off. Me and Bone restrained him.

Annie found a new boyfriend, took us in her car to a drive-in, we saw Henry Fonda get drunk in the hammock during the big football game of *The Human Animal* and I got so delirious and glad I threw an empty bottle of gin clear across the trees of Virginia and yelled 'Wa-hooooo' to the moonlight, which was there too. So I'd had my Virginia.

I took a bus back to Lowell thinking with slavering thoughts of Moe Cole.

VI

That's what it's like when you're twenty and it's spring, war or no war, but the war was on . . .

So, Moe Cole and all that, and others, Marleine, etc., but now I hitchhiked to Boston with Timmy Clancy to join the United States Marines. We were examined, did a teleprogram of examinations, were passed and sworn in. That's why today people still think I'm a U.S. Marine. Officially, yes, but unofficially meanwhile I'd gotten my Coast Guard pass out of Boston, was fingerprinted, photographed and passed, hung round the National Maritime Union hall waiting for a ship and after me and Clancy were designated as Marines he hitchhiked back 24 miles to Lowell to rest and read John Adams but I went down to Scollay Square to get drunk and met some seamen, in the morning I woke up and we tottered to the seaman hall, to my surprise the union man called over the mike: 'Job for a scullion on the S.S. *Dorchester*.'

'What's scullion?'

'That's where you wash the pots and pans.'

'Where's the ship going?'

'Murmansk, boy.'

'Here we go . . . I'll be scullion.' I threw my card in and they hired me and some of those other boys and by that afternoon I was going on board the S.S. *Dorchester* with my seabag, we got drunk that night and sang in South Boston and Charlestown nightclubs and goofed around chased by cops, and at dawn troops came on board, then a lot of men, and before I knew it this big tub the S.S. *Dorchester* was steaming out of Boston Harbor for the North Pole, with destroyer escorts of the U.S. Navy on the starboard and cutters of the U.S. Coast Guard on the port, goodbye Boston, goodbye America, goodbye U.S. Marines.

It wasnt intentional. The Marines never chased me about that. Because the *Dorchester* later became an international monument ship of Merchant Marine courage, tho we could hardly guess that at the time, with all those stewpots and regular stewpots moaning in their bunks and stewpots general.

VII

The fact of the matter is, while Timmy Clancy waited in Lowell for the U.S. Marines to call him, I was sailing for the North Pole on the S.S. *Dorchester* with a bunch of drunks, Indians, Polocks, Guineas, Kikes, Micks, Puddlejumpers (Frogs, me), Svedes, Norvegians, Krauts and all the knuckleheads including Mongolian idiots and Moro sabermen and Filipinos and anything you want in a most fantastic crew. But on the ship also was the Navy gun crew in orange life belts and handling the Oerlikon antivessel guns. To get into this will get my best respects from Heaven, spelled with a capital Aitch.

Ouch. Wanta harken back just a little, Sabby Savakis'd also hitchhiked a coupla times to Boston with me, and also with Clancy, wanted to join anything I joined. Said 'I wanta sail with you on this ship.'

'Get your papers.' Went down to the Coast Guard but didnt get his papers 's fast as I did. The trouble was, he didnt look like a sailor but like a curly-haired goatsherd from Sparta. Sailors come from Cornwall I tell you.

So it was too late and he cried to see me go but I said 'I see the flowers of death in the eyes of me shipmates, it's just as well you dont come on this trip.'

'But don't you see the flowers of death in MY eyes?'

'Yes, but from where from I dont know . . . Sabby,' I added, 'I just wanta be away from you and Lowell and New York and Columbia for a long while and be alone and think about the sea . . . Please let me sail by myself for awhile.' (You Dear Man, I should have added, of course.) Before we sailed, that last morning, as I said in *On the Road* book I actually got so drunk I wrapped myself around the toilet bowl of the Scollay Square Café and got pissed and puked on all night long by a thousand sailors and seamen and when I woke up in the morning and found myself all covered and caked and unspeakably dirty I just like a good old Boston man walked down to the Atlantic Avenue docks and jumped into the sea, washed myself, grabbed a raft, came up, and walked to my ship fairly clean.

You buy sailors in wartime? Up against a monument, dearie.

BOOK SEVEN

I

Now that I look back on it, if Sabby could have got his Coast Guard papers on time and sailed on that ship with me he might have lived thru the war. It was now June 1942, with a little black bag containing rags and a collection of classical literature weighing several ounces in small print, I'd walked by a white fence near my mother's house on my way to the North Pole, to hitchhike to Boston with Timmy Clancy (later District Attorney of Essex County Massachusetts). It was, really, like Melville packing his little black bag and setting off to New Bedford to go a-whaling. If Sabby had come on board with me he might have signed off the *Dorchester* after this, her next-to-last trip, and come with me thence to Liverpool etc. But as I saw the flowers of death in the eyes of most of my shipmates I had seen the flowers of death in his eyes too. He got into the Army a few months later. Flowers of death, as Baudelaire well knew from his leaning balcony in sighin Paree, are everywhere and for all time for every-body.

We have destroyers too watching far out as we leave Boston Harbor and move north out of those waters toward the Maine waters and out to the Banks of Newfoundland where we're swallowed in fog, and the water in the scuppers, supped up from the sea to wash our buckets with, gets a-colder and a-colder. We're not in a convoy, it's only 1942, no Allied and British arrangement, just the S.S. *Dorchester* and her sister ship the S.S. *Chatham* going up north, with a freighter called the U.S. *Alcoa Pilot*, and surrounded by corvettes and cutters and destroyers and destroyer escorts and led by, my you better mind me now, the old wooden ice-cuttin ship of Admiral Byrd (the *North Star*). Five hundred civilian construction workers, carpenters, electricians, bulldoze cat men, laborers, all in Alaska boomtown wool shirts, and tho all life is but a skullbone and a rack of ribs through which we keep passing food and fuel just so's we can burn so furious (tho not so beautiful), here we went on a voyage to Greenland, 'life's delicate children' on one sea, Saturday, July 18, oil-burning transport, out Merchant Miners dock, Boston, some of the crew going about with sheathed knives and daggers more of a semiromantic fancy than a necessity, poop decks, reading the funnies on poop decks, powder and ammunition in the afterdeck storeroom not 10 feet from the foc'sle where we'uns slept, up ahead foaming main and clouds. . . .

Let's get seamenlike. A bonus for sleeping on top of a powder magazine, does that sound like Captain Blah? AGWI Lines people, own this ship, a bright and winedark sea. Anchor tied we pull out between those two lighthouses in Boston Harbor, only the *Chatham* follows us, an hour later we perceive a destroyer off our port and a light cruiser (that's right) off our starboard. A plane. Calm sea. July. Morning, a brisk sea. Off the coast of Maine. Heavy fog in the morning, misty in the afternoon. Log. All eyes peeled for the periscope. Wonderful evening spent before with the (not Navy, excuse me) Army gun crew near the big gun, playing popular records on the phonograph, the Army fellas seem much more sincere than the hardened cynical dock-rats. Here's a few notes from my own personal log: 'There are a few acceptable men here and there, like Don Gary, the new scullion, a sensible and friendly fellow. He has a wife in Scotland, joined the Merchant Marine to get back to Scotland, in fact. I met one of the passengers, or construction workers, an Arnold Gershon, an earnest youth from Brooklyn. And another fellow who works in the butcher shop. Outside of these, my acquaintances have so far been fruitless, almost foolish. I am trying hard to be sincere but the crew prefers, I suppose, embittered cursing and bawdry foolishness. Well, at least, being misunderstood is being like the hero in the movies.' (Can you imagine such crap written in a scullion's diary?) 'Sunday July 26: A beautiful day! Clear and windy, with a choppy sea that looks like a marine painting . . . long flecked billows of blue water, with the wake of our ship like a bright green road . . . Nova Scotia to larboard. We have now passed through the Cabot Straits.' (Who's Cabot? A Breton?) (Pronounced Ca-boh.) 'Up we go, to northern seas. Ah there you'll find that shrouded Arctic.' (That wash of pronounced sea-talk, that parturient snowmad ice mountain plain, that bloody Genghis Khan plain of seaweed talk broken only by uprisings of foam.)

Yessir, boy, the earth is an Indian thing but the waves are Chinese. Know what that means? Ask the guys who drew those old scrolls, or ask the old Fishermen of Cathay, and what Indian ever dared to sail to Europe or Hawaii from the salmon-tumbling streams of North America? When I say Indian, I mean Ogallag.

'As I write, tonight, we are passing thru the most dangerous phase of our journey to that mysterious northern land . . . we are steaming ahead in a choppy sea past the mouth of the St Lawrence River in a crystal clear Moonglow.' (Good enough for a Duluoz, descendant of the Gaspé and the Cape Breton.) 'This is the region where many sinkings have occurred of late.' (Keeping up with the news in New York's P.M. newspaper, I had been.) 'Death hovers over my pencil. How do I feel? I feel nothing but dim acceptance.' (O Eugene O'Neill!) 'A sort of patience that is more dreamlike than real. The great card games, the tremendous card games and crap games go on in the diningroom, Pop is there with his cigarette holder, chef's cap, mad rich rakish laugh, some of the base workers mixed in the games, the scene seasoned with impossible characters, shit language, rich warm light, all kinds of men gambling their shore pay away in a dare at Neptune . . . Sums of money changing hands with death nearby. What an immense gambling ship this is . . . and our sister ship, the *Chatham*, off our stern, same thing of course. The stake is money and the stake is life. At dusk, with long lavender sashes hovering over distant Nova Scotia, a Negro baker conducted a religious sermon on the afterdeck. He had us kneel while he prayed. He spoke of God ("We howled"), and he prayed to God for a safe journey. Then I went to the bow and spent my usual hour staring the face of the mounting northern gales. We should be off the coast of Labrador tomorrow. As I was writing just now, I heard a hissing outside my porthole, the sea is heavy, the ship just rocks and rocks real deep, and I thought: "Torpedo!" I waited for one long second. Death! Death!' (Think of your death scenes and death trips, LSD users!) 'I tell you,' sez confident young Jack London in his bunk, 'I tell you, it is NOT hard to face death' – no, sirree – 'I am patient, I shall now turn over to sleep. And the sea washes on, immense, endless, everlasting, my sweet brother [?], and sentencer [!]. In the moonlight tonight in these dangerous waters, one can see the two Navy ships that are convoying us, two tawny seacats, alert and lowslung' (O gee) . . .

Homeless waters in the North, the Aryan-Nordic up against his chappy sea-net hands.

II

But my hands werent sea-netted and chapped by rope and wire, as later the next year as deckhand, at present time I was a scullion. I'd vaguely heard of Shakespeare yelling about that, he who washes pots and scours out giant pans, with greasy apron, hair hanging in face like idiot, face splashed by dishwater, scouring not with a 'scourer' as you understand it but with a goddamned Slave chain, grouped in fist as chain, scratch, scroutch, and the whole galley heaving slowly.

Oh the pots and pans the racket of their fear, the kitchen of the sea, the Neptunes down here, the herds of sea cows wanta milk us, the sea poem I aint finished with, the fear of the Scottish laird rowing out with a nape of another fox' neck in the leeward shirsh of SHAOW yon Irish Sea! The sea of her lip! The brattle of her Boney! The crack of Noah's Ark timbers built by Mosaic Schwarts in the unconditional night of Universal death.

Short chapter.

III

None of the adolescent scribblings of that time I kept in journals'll do us now.

Here now yon breaker awash the bowsprit, 'Night aint fit for man nor dog,' and what dog, O Burns, O Hardy, O Hawkins, would go to sea except for a bone with meat on it?

In our case it meant five hundred dollars if we got back safe free and that was a lot of money in nineteen forty two-ee.

The barefooted Indian deckhand toured every foc'sle at dusk to make sure the portholes were closed and secured.

He had a dagger in his belt.

Two Negro cooks had a big fight in the galley at midnight over gambling, that I didnt see, where they swung huge butcher knives at each other.

A little Moro chieftain turned third cook, with small neck, swiveled and shriveled when he turned to see.

He had the biggest knife of them all in his belt, a first-degree Swamee machete from old Mindanao.

The pastry cook was advertised as gay and they said he belted off his gun into the mixings for all of us to enjoy.

In the steward's linen department a veteran of the Spanish Civil War, member of the Abraham Lincoln leftwing anti-Fascist Brigade, tried to make a Communist out of me.

The chief steward had no more use for me than a piece of foam of the sea hath use for him or me or anybody.

The captain, Kendrick, was hardly seen, as he was so high on the bridge and this was a big ship.

The chief cook of my galley was Old Glory.

He was 6 foot 6 and 300 pounds of Negro glory.

He said 'Everybody's puttin down a hype.' He was the one who used to pray on the poop deck at dusk . . . the real prayer.

He liked me.

Frankie Fay the Farter slept with me in the foc'sle and kept farting. Another young kid from Charlestown Mass. with curly hair tried to make fun of me 'cause I was reading books all the time. The third guy in our foc'sle said nothing, was a tall lost junky I guess.

Some ship.

Pretty soon the liquor ran out and the real drunks went down to the barbershop to get their hair cut but really only wanted a bottle of bay rum aftershave lotion.

The clever punks in the galley sent me down to the engine room to ask the chief engineer for a 'left-handed monkey wrench.' The chief yelled at me over the booming pistons that were turning the shaft of the rear screw 'There's no such-a-thing as a left-handed monkey wrench you dumbhead!'

Then they threw me a special honorary dinner and gave me the ass-hole of a duck with yams and potatoes and asparagrass. I ate it and pronounced it delicious.

They said maybe I was a fancypants football player, and a college-educated boy, but I didnt know there was no such thing as a left-handed monkey wrench or that the ass of a duck was the ass of a duck. Good enough, I could use either.

I pleased the pastry cook who gave me a brown leather jacket that hung over my wrists. He was the poop deck preacher.

I observed icebergs in my diary; the diary is really very good and I should record it here: Like, 'Incidentally, one of our two new convoy ships, a small-sized freighter converted into a sort of sub chaser and raider, carries a heroic legend. She has sunk every submarine she's found in these cold waters. She's a valiant little bitch: hits the waves briskly and carries a torpedo seaplane as well as a load of depth charges and shells.' And here's the old Aryan complaining (before we got to those icebergs): 'Fog, the *Chatham* looms astern, lowing like a mournful cow . . .'

IV

Icebergs are vast mountains of ice that float about in the North Atlantic and show themselves to be one-tenth of their whole bulk, which, hid beneath the waves, can stave a ship's hull in faster'n a black-eyed Spartan can do you in, in a Spartan provocation, only this here iceberg is white, icy, cold, dont care, and's bigger than five West St Louis Police and Fire Departments. O Budweiser, pay homage and notice.

And you see them a mile away, white ice cubes, with waves crashing against their bowsprits like in slowmotion Dinosaur movies. Splowsh, slow, the gigantic sight of great waters against a cliff, of ice in this case (not a Kern), going PLOW. You know what the name of the Cornish Celtic language is? Kernuak.

So what's Kerouac? 'Kern' being Cairn, and 'uak' language of; then, Ker, house, ouac, language of, THIS IS THE LANGUAGE OF THE HOUSE SPEAKING TO YOU IN PURE SEAMAN TONES.

Nobody on this ship of mine is going to hit an iceberg, not on your life, not with Cap'n Kendrick, and besides, we've got pork chops for supper.

V

D'jever see the eyes of the captain in the wheelroom? Did anybody bend over charts as much as that first mate? That second mate, did he have blue eyes? And the third, sharp? No ship as big as the *Dorchester* can hit disaster unless it hits into a genius.

The genius, Von Dönitz, hid under the waves in Belle Isle Strait, and we looked for his signs of foam or periscopey proppery, aye we did. Altho Hitler counseled his Naval youth to be wise and athletic you never saw better sailors than I saw in the United

States Sea. Service. Na, no Dönitz can escape the mark of a Canadian.

The usual real Canadian has blue eyes and an eye for the sea and the cove too, a real pirate, tell that to the High Command of any Navvy. He licks his lips in anticipation of any sight of breakage in the wave, whether it's a football, a turd, a dead gull, a floating happy albatross (if near enough Poles) or wavelet or sea sparrow or, really, the osprey, that do-do bird, that no go-go bird who floateth on the waves and sayeth to thee and I 'Go saileth yourselfth, I am bird what floateth on water.' Okay. Always found near land.

What land we got here? Irish Sea? Ju sea it?

VI

So I'm frying the bacon for one thousand men, that is, two thousand strips of bacon, on a vast black range, while Glory and the other assistant cooks are doing the scrambled eggs. I'm wearing a life jacket, O Baldwin apples. I hear 'Boom boom' outside. Glory is wearing a life jacket too. Boom boom. The bacon sizzles. Glory looks at me and says 'They're layin down a hipe out there.'

'Yeh.'

'Get that bacon crisp and put it in the pan, boy.'

'Yowsah,' says I, 'boss.' 'Cause he was my boss, and you buy that. 'What's goin on out there Glory?'

'There's a bunch of Canadian corvettes and American destroyer escorts layin down depth charges against a German submarine attack.'

'We're being attacked?'

'That aint no Memphis lie.'

'S-n – ucc – Q – z,' as I sneezed, 'what time is it?'

'What you wearin your life jacket for?'

'You told me to wear it, you and the chief steward.'

'Well you're makin bacon.'

'Well sure I'm makin bacon,' I said, 'but I'm thinking of that kid on that German submarine who's also makin the bacon. And who is now chokin to death in drowning. Buy that, Glory.'

'I aint layin down no hipe, you're right,' said Glory, who was real big and blues singer too but I coulda licked him in any fight because he woulda let me.

That's your American Negro man, so dont talk to me about it.

VII

The sea speaketh. Remember, why'm I a wave? Three silver nails in a blue field, turned gray by sea. Jesus, it is a Polish sea. What, Djansk? Every nobleman in Russia wore furs and gelted everybody in sight. Djanks, Skoll. Aryans.

Slaves they dared to call us.

VIII

Slaves indeed, why when you looked at the bodyguards of Khrushchev or any other regular-lookin Russian you saw some guy sellin cows in North Carolina fields at 9 A.M. . . . Aryans . . . The look where you believe that God will forgive you in Heaven . . . 'T'sa look make the whores of Amsterdam not only quake but give up their knitting . . . Ah High Germanic Nordic Aryans you brutes of my heart! . . . Kill me! . . . Crucify me! . . . Go ahead, I've got Persian friends.

And what will my Persian friends do, grow mustaches and ride jets? . . . Do you know what Jesus meant when he cried out on the cross 'Father, Father, why hast thou forsaken me?' . . . He was only quoting a Psalm of David like a poet remembering by heart: He did not repudiate His own kingdom, it's a crock to believe so, throw the Shield of David in the garbage can with the Cross of Jesus if that's what you think, let me prove it to you: Jesus was only quoting the first line of David's Psalm 22 with which he was familiar as a child even (not to mention that the sight of the Roman soldiers casting ballots for his garment reminded him of the line in the same Psalm 'They cast lots upon my vesture,' and add this too 'They pierced my hands and my feet'). PSALM 22 OF DAVID (in part): '*My God, my God, why hast thou forsaken me? Loudly I call, but my prayer cannot reach thee. Thou dost not answer, my God, when I cry out. . . . I am a by-word to all, the laughing-stock of the rabble. All those who catch sight of me fall to mocking; mouthing out insults, while they toss their heads in scorn "He committed himself to the Lord, why does not the Lord come to his rescue, and set his favourite free?" . . . I am spent as spilt water, all my bones out of joint . . . parched is my throat, like clay in the baking, and my tongue sticks fast in my mouth. . . . They have torn holes in my hands and feet . . . and they stand there watching me. . . . They divide my spoils among them, cast lots for my garments. . . .'*

He was just like a poet remembering lines of the prophecy of David.

Therefore I believe in Jesus. Tell you why if you dont know already: Jacob wrestled with his angel because he defied his own Guardian Angel. Typical.

Michael stands in my corner, 7 feet tall.

Look.

There go us.

BOOK EIGHT

I

Blaise Pascal says not to look to ourselves for the cure to misfortunes, but to God whose Providence is a fore-ordained thing in Eternity; that the foreordainment was that our lives be but sacrifices leading to purity in the after-existence in Heaven as souls disinvested of that rapish, rotten, carnal body – O the sweet beloved bodies so insulted everywhere for a million years on this strange planet. *Lacrimae rerum.* I dont get it because I look into myself for the answer. And my body is so thick and carnal I cant penetrate into the souls of others equally entrap't in trembling weak flesh, let alone penetrate into an understanding of HOW I can turn to God with effect. The situation is pronounced hopeless in the very veins of our hands, and our hands are useless in Eternity since nothing they do, even clasp, can last.

So I thought of the little German blond boy makin bacon on that underwater ship and as he stands there in his life belt trembling and sweating, nevertheless sweetly preparing breakfast for the men and officers, he hears the joints and bolts of the submarine's bulkhead hull creaking and cracking, soon water's trickling in, his bacon like the proverbial pigs who'd been handed Satan's walking papers by Jesus to go jump in the lake, is about to be wetted. Then a big close blast of depth charge and the whole ocean comes charging into his kitchen and washes round him and his stove and his humble breakfast, and him a child in

Mannerheim when the icicles were pure in the morning winter sun and Haydn was heard at the concert hall down the narrow cobblestoned streets, ah, now the water is up to his neck and he is suffocating anyway at the thought of it all: remembering his entire lifetime. The sweet blond German Billy Budd is suffocated chokingly by water in a sunken capsule. His eyes look wildly toward me in my life jacket at the black cooking range of the S.S. *Dorchester*. I cant stand it.

From that moment on I'm the only real Pacifist in the world.

I dont see it, I dont get, I dont want it. Why couldnt our two ships just meet in a cove and exchange pleasantries and phony prisoners?

Who are these smiling Satans making all the money out of this? Whether they're Russian, American, Japanese, British, French or Chinese? But wasnt Tolstoy dead right when he said in his final book, *The Kingdom of God Is Within You* (a quotation from Jesus), that the day will come when the hourglass that's sanding off war will be suddenly full? Or the day, really, when the water pendulum, having received more water on the peace bucket, will suddenly tilt to peace? All in a second it happens.

Besides, as I will show later, the Germans should not have been our 'enemies.' I say this and stake my life on it.

So Old Glory says 'Okay, boy, got the bacon ready, and I'se got the scrammed eggs, and here we go feeding one thousand men on their way to build an airbase in Greenland with muddy roads and wood shacks and mackinaw jackets, yair, 'taint been since I left St James Infirmary I felt so foolish and blue. O Lord, why hast thou forsaken me?'

On top of that I have to wash the pots and pans, mop the deck, go to bed, get woke up at noon by the second cook a Negro with a big dagger saying 'Get up you lazy bum, you're five minutes late in the galley.'

'You cant talk to me like that.'

'I've got this knife.'

'What do I care about that?'

'I'm gonna tell the captain about your back talk in the galley.'

'It's your first chance to pick on somebody aint it?' I say. Boy we didnt like each other. I went to the second mate asking to be transferred to deck but they refused. I was trapped on a steel jail floating in the icy oceans of the Arctic Circle and a slave at last.

II

Diary says: 'July 30, 1942: In the evening, a whipping wind drove in from the north and blew the fog off . . . and a cold, icy wind it was. We are really approaching the north now. This is the eighth day out of Boston, and we should be three-quarters of the way between northern Newfoundland and southern Greenland' – not yet in the Arctic Circle but a few days later – 'by now. This wind was a strange wind; it came from the far white north and it bore a message of barren desolation that murmured: "Man must not venture to me, for I am ruthless and indifferent, like the sea, and shall not be his friend and warm light. I am the north and I exist only for myself." But, off our larboard, the signal light of our new convoy ship (the Navy ships have left, and been replaced by two heavily armed trawlers) beamed across the bleak gray waters with another message . . . and this was a message of warmth and love and cheer, the message of Man . . . It was a beautiful little golden light, and it blinked the symbols of Man's language. And the thought of language, here in the bosom of a tongueless sea . . . that also was a warm golden fact.'

And: 'Prison ship! I scream to myself in the morning, heading for my pots and pans. Oh, where the Prince of Crete Sabbas, and his familiar cry: "In the morning, brothers, sympathy!" . . . about 1,800 miles astern . . . but only a feet asoul.

'But this morning, I went up on deck sleepily for a breath of air on the bow, and found myself in an enchanted Greenlandic fjord. I was literally stunned for a moment, then lapsed into boyish wonder.' – Natch – 'Eskimos in kyaks were drifting past us, smiling their strange broken-tooth smiles. And, Oh, how that line of Wolfe's came back to me in glorious triumph and truth: "Morning and new lands. . . .' For here was heavily-eyed, stupored morning, fresh and clean and strange . . . and here was a new land . . . lonely, desolated Greenland. We passed an Eskimo settlement which must have been the one on the map near Cape Farewell, Julianehaab. The American seamen were throwing oranges at the Eskimos, trying to hit them, laughing coarsely – but the little Mongolians merely smiled their idiot tender welcomes. My fellow countrymen embarrassed me no end and considerably for I know that these Eskimos are a great and hardy Indian people, that they have their gods and mythology, that they know all the secrets of this weird land, and that they have morals and an honor that far surpasses ours. The fjord is flanked' – 'fjord' means deep cliff water channel – 'on each bank by enormous brown cliffs, which are covered by some sort of heavy moss, or grass, or heather, I cant tell which. This is probably why the Northmen named the land GREEN land. And these cliffs are absolutely enchanted . . . like the dream cliffs of a child, or the place where resides the soul of Wagner's music . . . massive, fort-like, and steep; crevices considerably worn by the stream-beds of melted ice; rising in sheer tremendous beauty from the green fjord waters to a pale blue sky . . .'

And so on. I dont want to bore the reader with all this stuff about Greenland.

III

Just suffice it to say we went farther north and entered a fjord just about 100 miles latitudinally north of north tip of Iceland and went in and came to an airbase. The workers got off and went to work, bulldozers were hauled out of the *Dorchester's* cargo-hold side doors, men went ashore with saws, nails, hammer, lumber, electrical wiring, generators, whiskey, bay rum, hopeful cundroms and started to hammer off a gigantic landing field with gigantic barracks for everybody. The Coast Guard cutters, two of them that in nighttime joined us, invited us aboard to see movies. I mean the seamen of the S.S. *Dorchester*. We went on board and sat on the deck and watched Stanley meeting Livingstone in the middle of Africa, of all things. I remembered how my sister and my mother always loved the dimples of Richard Greene in that picture.

Then me and a seaman called Duke went ashore under the pretext of wanting to eat in the construction crew's mess hall, which we did, tho, but then took off to climb a nearby tall rocky mountain. We accomplished it. His name was Wayne Duke. He was a haggard youth who had been torpedoed off Cape Hatteras and who carried the shrapnel marks of the blast in his neck. He was a congenial guy but the frenzied mark of tragedy still lingered in his eyes and I doubt whether he'd ever forget the seventy-two hours he spent on the life raft and the fellow with bloody stumps at his shoulders who jumped off the raft in a fit of torture and committed suicide in the Carolinian sea . . . So one midnight, at dawn, I stood on the silent deck and gazed and thought 'What wild lusty country.' A frozen dawn rose between two cliff flanks, layers of delicate color in perfect parallel lines, reaching from rock to beetling rock and then I heard the white-gowned ladies of Greenland singing down the ice field just like in Berlioz or Sibelius or even Shostakovich . . . Haunting witches, not a woman for 1,000 miles, so me and Duke said let's go climb that sonumbitch mountain. I slept until two on that dare. When I awoke the fellas informed me one could go ashore on the launch, which went back and forth every half hour. About forty of us piled in that same kind of boat used by commandos, does fifteen knots. As we split the waves shoreward, the Army gun crew began its gunnery practice with the two-inchers on the two turrets up forward in front of the bridge. We heard the POW of the discharge, watched the geyser of sand on the distant north beach, slid swiftly past the big freighter called the *Alcoa Pilot* (carrying all that lumber and aluminium) and bumped softly in the raw new pier built by our construction five hundred drunkards, a small thing thrown up for the sake of immediate necessity, you see, and for the first time in a month, we were on land! Unfortunately I cant say that it was 'solid old earth,' it was a bed of sagging spring moss, mostly swamp and rivulet, one had to leap from moss mound to moss mound, clusters of wild flowers, however, greeted my tired sea eyes, and I thought of the Rhodora. Wayne Duke asked me if I would now consent to join him on that little mountainclimbing excursion . . . the rest of the guys were all heading over the slope of the meadow to see the lake there. There were occasional signs that the workers had begun a ditch, some boards of lumber, barrels, they were just getting started on the whiskey but let me tell you before they were done they done Spitzbergen Luftwaffe airfield in.

Duke and I headed the opposite way from the rest of the guys who were headed for the Eskimo settlement, it was not long before we had joined in a discussion on mountainclimbing as being more immediate than trying to lay some old blubber-smeared monster so we decided to go, dead serious, a peak of nice height covered with recent evidences of land and snow slides, boulders, rocks, so up we went. Straggling over rocks, walking doggedly, then resting for a smoke, and then the slope rose, steep, we had to begin to use our hands. Mountainclimbing was a difficult feat for me that day because I still had my sea legs, O Gary Snyder.

That is to say, were I to stand on level land in that condition, I would nevertheless sway as tho on deck at sea. But we made ground. The fjord just below began to diminish in size. The two ships, the *Dorch* and the *Alcoa* freighter, looked like toy ships. We climbed on, in extreme physical distress, but soon we had reached a ledge upon which rested enormous boulders in a precarious position. These we readily pushed over and watched them drop 1,000 feet and roll and thunder 1,000 more. Then we went on up, stopping several times for a drink from some virgin streamlet, then let it be remembered that Duke and I meanwhile were the first white men to climb this mountain. That's why today it's called Mount Duke-Duluoz (Mount Ford-Kerouac). The *Dorchester* and the *Alcoa Pilot* are the first ships to drop anchor in this here fjord except perhaps for some explorer ships from Eric the Red to Captain Knudsen. If they would have desired to climb a mountain they would have picked out a higher one than Mount Duke-Duluoz which is near 4,000 feet. So it is ours, because we topped it, and we did not attempt after a half hour of scrambling and dangling on promontories, perhaps 3,000 feet to a sheer drop below, to climb the last little 'flint edge' of the mountain. It was too narrow and thin, like a Sumerian tower. We had no equipment whatever except the fire of adventure in Wayne Duke's breast.

And there we were, on top of the world, not 800 miles from the North Pole of the earth's axis, surveying our dominions of sea, land, and tremendously high free sky. We discovered from away up there as we sat on strange black rocks and smoked cigarettes casually not a few inches from a drop of half mile, that there was a valley of boulders below on the other side, with a hidden lake, south of the fjord it was, seaward, which must be 1,000 feet above sea level. The Lake of Mystery we shall name it, for who knows what this lake knows, who lived on it, what's its legend? A lost race of Norse-Men? Neolithic lake-dwellers?

Stragglers of the Spaniards? Let us call it Lake of Mystery. Then Duke and I retraced our steps and almost lost our lives when I stepped on a loose boulder and began to roll off a sloping ledge with it, thus bringing an avalanche down on poor Duke below me, the boulder thundered over his head, while I, smiling with mad confidence, grabbed hold of the sliding fall with the very muscles of my buttocks and held and stopped sliding just at the edge, as Duke ducked under a leaning rock. Later both of us had further close shaves, it was definitely a matter of life and death, but we made it and went back down to the launch and on over on our boat for big supper of pork chops, potatoes, milk and butterscotch pudding.

IV

Duke was great guy. On the ship was another guy called Mike Peal who gave me my first taste of what a professional Communist agitator talks like. In my diary it says 'Mike, diminutive, intellectual, quick, clever. Communist. Fought for Loyalists in Spain, went to Russia, has met Sheean, Hemingway, Matthews, Shirer. Fought with John Lardner in Spain. Abe Lincoln Brigade. Wounded. Wife worked in Russia; in America, social work. Apartment in Greenwich Village; lived on Left Bank Paris. Art a "suppressed desire," he says. Bounced out of C.C.N.Y. in Freshman year for inciting student's union flareup. Now an N.M.U. union delegate, Seamen's Union, C.I.O. Hates Hearst, Henry Ford, DuPont, all the Fascists. Hates Jan Valtin. Worked in Soviet Union, and at the Soviet Pavilion in 1939 World's Fair. Middle height, twenty-nine, sandy hair and blue eyes. Van Dyke beard. Rings the bell over linen in the swaying linen shop.'

I showed him part of this diary I've been quoting to you and he actually censored it.

V

I dont wanta go into it too much because there's so much else and too much to tell, but our sister ship the S.S. *Chatham* was torpedoed and sunk at about this time off Belle Isle Strait, I believe, with a loss of many, many lives, about a thousand. We had steamed out of Boston Harbor together. The *Chatham* and the *Dorchester* were very valuable old tubs and finally they got the *Dorchester* too.

VI

On our return trip to Boston Harbor, without the weight of the five hundred construction workers and a lot of their earth-moving equipment in the hold, and the construction dynamite and all the stuff, we were as light as a cork and bobbed in a huge October tempest, the likes of which I only saw fifteen years later. Me god and be jesus but what a blast of wind and waves. We werent scared really, but me and some of the boys went upstairs to the old dormitories where the workers had slept and started a big pillow fight with all the pillows in sight on hundreds of bunks. Feathers flew everywhere in the dark ship as she thundered in the night. 'Night aint fit for man nor beast.' It was a walloping storm. I went out on deck and practiced the halfback jumpoff practice run so I could be ready for Columbia College football the following week. There's this nut practicing football on a bounding deck in the howling Arctic gales. But we made it to Sydney Nova Scotia where I wasnt allowed to go ashore on leave because of that mountainclimbing episode which had been officially recorded as AWOL because we were absent at noon work. Didnt bother me, but at little old Sydney everybody including Captain Kendrick went ashore on bumboats and I was left alone as 'watch' on this empty ship with a cook or two and a pilot or somebody I dunno who, I couldnt find anybody. So I went up to the captain's bridge and pulled the goddamn rope calling a bumboat from the harbor of Sydney. A little boat shining warm human lights came rushing to the ship. I ran down from the captain's bridge (where I felt as guilty, from pulling that rope, as I did later on the railroad in California pulling the engineer's rope for the crossing call, BAAA BAAA BUT BAAA). But okay, for fifty cents they took me ashore. I think the whole ship was entirely abandoned. Everybody and his uncle was drunk and got drunker.

It's a nice little town, with collieries, miners, guys with grimed faces like in Wales, they go underground, etc., with little lights on their hats, but there were also little wartime dance parties and a lot of booze and bars and I went ashore AWOL for real this time. After several whiskeys I saw thru a haze that several of my seaman buddies were sore at Wallingham because he was hiding in a shack on the pier with a big bottle of whiskey and wouldnt come out and give us any shots. 'That sonofabitch,' yelled Fugazzy, 'we'll teach him a lesson or two! Come out Wallingham or you're going to take a swim.' This was a shack sitting on the edge of the pier in Sydney Harbor. So Wallingham wouldnt come out. So we all heaved together and pushed the goddamn shack in the drink.

He swam out through the hole in the ceiling, bottle and all, and made it to the Jacob's ladder on the pier, climbed up, and walked off silent.

Only thing to do was go downtown and buy some drinks. We wrangled in alleys over dollars owed from card games and from loans and such and I wound up with two of my young buddies wandering around the dance hall and clubs, when we got sleepy we saw a nice house and went in and there were two Indian prostitutes I think you call em De Sotos. From there, satisfied, with the wind beating on old windows threatened all that gentle female warm flesh, we went to another house and I said: 'Let's go in here and sleep, looks like a mighty good blub.' We went in, found sofas and easy chairs in a front parlor type room, and went to sleep. In the morning to me utter horror I hear that there's a family of husband, wife and kiddies making breakfast in the kitchen by the hall. Husband is putting on his miner's hat, picking up his lunchpail and gloves and's saying 'Be back home Mum by five' and the kids are saying 'I'm orf to school Mum' and Mum is washing the dishes and they dont even know there's four drunken American seamen in their parlor. So I make a little noise and the old man comes out to check and sees us. He says 'Yanks a-sleeping in here? How'd you get in here?'

'Door was unlocked, we thought it was a club.'

'Well, go on sleeping boys, I'm goin' to work, and when you leave do so quietly.'

Which we did after two more hours of napping in that patriot's home.

No breakfast required.

VII

Just whiskey downtown. I got so grumbled up and bloffered I didnt even know where I was or the name of my ship, all I remember is that at some point I guess in a USO club I heard Dinah Shore beaming over from the radio in U.S.A., singing 'You'll Never Know Just How Much I Love You' and felt a languid nostalgia for good old New York and blondes. But somewhere I stumbled, and first thing I know I'm in an alley somewhere and the MP's or SP's are shooting a revolver charge over my head into the sky saying 'Halt or we'll shoot you!' So I let them arrest me and they take me to a Canadian Naval barracks and put me in a room and tell me to wait there, I'm under arrest AWOL. But I look out the window after a short nap and see all these Canadian idiots trying to play baseball with gloves, bats, balls, and I open the window of the 'barracks jail room' and jump out, grab a glove and ball and show them the way to really wind up and throw a nice sweeping curve. I even teach them batting tricks. The sun is going down cold and red in old Nova

Scotia. They're very much interested. Soon's I realise who I am and where I am I saunter away casually and go back downtown for more drinks. By now I'm broke so I'm cadging drinks off perfect strangers. Finally I wenangle my way down to the dock, call a bumboat, and go back riding sheeping to the Jacob's ladder of the S.S. *Dorchester*.

Master-at-arms or whatever you call him is glaring at me: 'He's just about the last of em, I think there's two more, and then we can sail to New York.' Sure enough, inside an hour, the last two AWOL stragglers of the *Dorchester* ship's crew come aboard from a bumboat and off we sail south.

We've had our shore leave I'll tell you.

For this I get a little onionskinned paper that says on it:

EXTRACT FROM OFFICIAL LOG.
S.S. DORCHESTER.

SEPTEMBER 27TH, 1942.—JOHN DULUOCH SCULLION ARTICLE #185 IS HEREBY FINED TWO (2) DAYS PAY FOR BEING A.W.O.L. (ASHORE WITHOUT LIBERTY) IN A FOREIGN PORT. $5.50

(A COPY OF THIS EXTRACT HAS BEEN HANDED TO JOHN DULUOCH) ————————
LBK/EGM MASTER L. B. KENDRICK.

VIII

I forgot to mention that while we were anchored in one of those fjords in Greenland an Eskimo came up in his kyak, with his big red brown face and brown teeth grinning at me, yelled 'Hey, Karyak taka yak pa ta yak ka ta pa ta fat tay ya k!' and I said 'Wha?' and he said 'Okak.' He then proceeded to take his paddle, hit it hard to the right of his sea cow-skin kyak, and did a complete underwater turn, or whirl, and came up on the other side all wet and grinning, a tremendous canoe trick. Then I began to realise he was trying to trade with me. My head was sticking out of my foc'sle porthole. So I opened my locker, after giving him the sign 'Wait a minute' and I came back and dangled by old Number 2 Horace Mann football jersey and all dem touchdowns I told you about attached to it. He nodded yes, I dropped it to him just as he handed me up a fish harpoon. It has Swedish or Danish steel on it but was connected with bone joints, and wood, and thongs.

So we sailed south from Nova Scotia and to my surprise, instead of hitting Boston Harbor we suddenly woke up one morning and saw, in the fog, the good old Statue of Liberty in New York Harbor. 'Send me your wretched' indeed. Then, after anchoring awhile, and it's October, and news of New York football and all-American football, and Fartsy Fay is laughing at me because I'm telling him I'll be in next Saturday's game against Army, we go sailing under the Brooklyn Bridge, Manhattan Bridge and Williamsburg Bridge to a great cheer of hero flag-waving crowd above. How could you believe it?

And into Long Island Sound and by God at about 8 P.M. we're steaming busily up the Sound off the shore of West Haven Connecticut where Ma and Pa and I had that cottage and where I'd swum out into the sea and they thought I was drowned, and where I'd looked inward into Neptune's heart and saw silver nails in a blue field, and the little boat called 'We're Here' . . . recall?

But what a trip, no submarine trouble, up the Sound to Cape Cod Canal, thru that canal (under the bridge) and up to Boston where we landed at before dawn and winched up, slacked in, tied up, and slept until payoff time at 9 A.M.

And what a payoff! The barefooted Indian deckhand had one of his gambling enemies in a Strangler Lewis hold and choking him to death demanding two hundred dollars, a fistfight was going on across the mess hall between so and so and such and such, and myself, here I was faced being given my pay by Gus J. Rigolopoulòs of the U.S. Coast Guard who said 'How come you didnt answer my note early this morning? Didnt you have no feeling for me?' And as I pick up my four hundred seventy dollars, there's Sabbas Savakis at the gangplank saying 'I'll ride you back on the train to Lowell, what's that you got there? A harpoon?'

'Yep, traded it to a Mexico' or some such inane reply and off we went to my Pa's house in Lowell.

IX

At home there was a telegram from Lu Libble of Columbia football team saying 'Okay Jack, now is the time to take the bull by the horns, we're waiting for you here, we expect you to make up your chemistry deficits and credits and play some ball this year.' October 1942. So all I had time to do was tell my sweet mother Ange that I had never appreciated before so much the washing of pots and pans she'd done all her life for lazy old me, that her pots and pans were infinitely cleaner and smaller than those on that hellship, and I bought a ticket on the train to New York City and went there with my college packed suitcase.

On the next run out of Boston, with me at Columbia, the S.S. *Dorchester* sailed out loaded this time with two or three thousand American soldiers of the Army and was sunk in Baffin Bay by Karl Donitz's submarine command, with a loss of most of the soldiers and most of the crew of the *Dorch*, including Glory. Later when I explained it to a writer friend, and told him what a surviving shipmate told me about it in New Orleans, that all the boys were calling for their mothers, he laughed: 'That's typical.'

And him copping out of the U.S. defense service on grounds of homo sexuality.

X

And it was also, of course, the ship that is now reverenced and made into monuments (at the Kingsbridge Veterans' Hospital in Bronx N.Y. for one) as the ship on which, or on board of which, the Four Chaplains gave up their lives and life belts to the soldiers: the Four Chaplains being two Protestants, a Catholic, and a Jew. They just went down with the ship and with Glory in those icy waters, praying.

Glory disappeared.

The steward who hated me was seen having his neck cut off by a sliced off life raft, in the waves.

The Negro gay baker I havent had exact details.

Captain Kendrick, he went down.

XI

All those pots and pans, that kitchen deck, the linen room, the butcher room, the Army guns, the steel, the scuppers, the engine room, the left-handed monkey wrench room, the German Blond Boy Waste of This World . . . There oughta be a better way to die in this world than in the service of Ammunitioneers.

XII

So Sabbas and I having disembarked from the train in Lowell railroad station, me carrying my harpoon and seabag, and having walked up School Street and over the Moody Street Bridge to my house in Pawtucketville, greeted my father, kissed him, kissed my mother, my sister, and there's that telegram from Lu Libble, I'm off in the morning.

On the campus once again I'm entrapped with this bullshit now of having to read and understand *Hamlet* by Shakespeare inside of three days while washing the dishes in the cafeteria and scrimmaging all afternoon. Lu Libble greets me accidentally on Amsterdam Avenue and says 'Well you've lost weight, them rolling waves really take the lard off you, hey? How much you weigh now?'

'One fifty-five.'

'Well I guess I cant make you a guard anymore. I think you'll run faster now.'

'My father's coming next week see if you can get him that job in Hackensack.'

'Yeh.'

Out on the field, the boys in light blue, Columbia, are all standing around in an early afternoon and here I come jogging out of the clubhouse for the first time, tightly cleated and ready. I stare at the new boys. All the good old boys are gone into the service. This is a bunch of weak-kneed punks, tall and disjointed and sorta decadent. First thing Lu Libble says, is 'We've got to teach you to do that KT-79 fake.' As I said before I didnt play football for to fake. The lights go on in the scrimmage field on Baker Field at 215th and Broadway. Who's standing watching the scrimmage? The coach of Army, Earl Blaik, and the coach of Brown, Tuss McLaughry. They say to Lu:

'Who's this Dulouse who's supposed to run so good?'

'There he is.'

'Let's see him go.'

'Okay. Duluoz, boys, come here, huddle.' Cliff Battles is there too. I have to do the little short fake steps from right wing and come around in back of the ball-receiver, fake as tho I didnt receive the ball from his handout, but actually do take it, and then start winging around left end (my wrong side), have to evade old Turk Tadzic again, who curses again, reverse my field across the line, till I come up against would-be defensive tacklers on the side there, reverse again, dodge a bit, and am all alone in the open field heading for a 190-yard run for all I know with just nobody between me and the goalpost but Lu's favorite Italian Mike Romanino, and just as Mike is getting ready to have to try to catch me and haul me down to the ground, Lu Libble blows the whistle to stop the play. Dont wanta overwork the Roman Hero too much.

But the coach of Army has seen, and the other one too, and then four days later here comes Sabbas from Lowell with his droopy big idealistic eyes wondering why I cant go out with him and study the Brooklyn Bridge, which we do anyway, tho b'now I'm supposed to write a big paper on *King Lear* and *Macbeth* too, and by this time here comes Pa, gets a room in the nearby college hotel, goes to Lu Libble's office, is turned down from a job, I hear them yelling in there, Pa comes stomping out of his office and says to me 'Come on home, these wops are just cheating you and me both.'

'What's the matter with Lu?'

'Just because he wears two-hundred-dollar suits he thinks he's Mister Banana Nose himself. The Army game is coming up Saturday, if he doesnt put you in that game then what the 'ell do you think it means?'

'*Now* coach?' I'm saying to Lu at the bench on the Army game on Saturday and he doesnt even look my way.

So the following Monday, snow in my window and Beethoven in the radio, Fifth Symphony, I say to myself 'Okay, I quit football.' I go next door to Mort Mayor's dormitory room, where he has a grand piano, and listen to him play Benny Goodman's pianist type jazz. Mel Powell. I go to Jake Fitzpatrick's room and drink whiskey while he sleeps over an unfinished short story. I go across the street to Edna Palmer's grandmother's house and lay Edna Palmer right there on the sofa. I tell the chemistry department to go tube it up. Big tackles and guards and ends of the Columbia football squad are outside my window in the snow yelling 'Hey idiot come on out have a beer.' Kurowsky is among them, Turk Tadzic, others, if they wont let me play I aint gonna hang around.

Because in the Army game I coulda gone out there and scored at least two touchdowns and made it close and incidentally I would have smeared their best runner, from Lowell, Art Janur, right smack dead ahead like I done to Halmalo when I was thirteen. If you cant be allowed to play then how can you play anything?

While Columbia varsity linemen were taking big leaks outside the West End Bar on 118th and Broadway, right in front of my little future wife Edna ('Johnnie') Palmer, who thought it was hilarious, I packed up my suitcase and my radio and went home to Lowell to wait for the Navy to call me. December 1942. (She was having an affair with another seaman who shoved her thru the subway turnstiles to save a nickel.) Chad Stone was now the captain of the team and seemed to look my way with regret. I got sick of Thackeray Carr pushing against me in scrimmage with his rocky head. It was just a great big bunch of horseshit where they dont let you prove yourself. When the chips are down. Silver nails and sawdust.

XIII

But the one thing I forgot was, when Lu Libble called me back to Columbia I rode the N.Y. N.H. and Hartford Railroad or whatever you call it, from Lowell north to Nashua and then west to Worcester, and then to Hartford, New Haven, etc., with my Pop in tow. Big old Pop had a book with him written by Willard Robertson, the old character actor in the movies, called *High Tide* or *Low Tide* or something, a story about a clam digger on the shore who saved a girl from drowning (Ida Lupino, Pop's favorite actress gal) (with Jean Gabin of France), and while Pop snored in his old railroad seat I read the entire novel for twelve hours from Lowell to New York. Now people dont do that any more. Twelve hours on a dim train with old conductors and brakemen running around yelling 'Meriden!' and me reading an entire French movie novel. Very good it was, too. To think that we werent besieged by airline hostesses with smiles of mock teeth, invitations to some kind of invisible dance, but left alone to read an entire book . . . And in the morning we went to Lu Libble's office and had that argument with Lu. But sometimes in my dreams I dream that I'm carrying too many burdens and other people are rushing along with me on the way to the terminal train station. I ask them to hold my coat, or umbrella, or cundrom, but they always politely decline and so it means that I am now going thru life carrying more burdens than I can carry. And that no one cares.

But my Pa had already read that novel and wanted me to study it in the brown lights of that old coach as it rattled thru New England . . . think of that a second when you join the Brotherhood of Railroad Trainmen. B.R.T.

Not U.R.O.C.

XIV

So me and Pa are quits with New York and I go back to Lowell to wait, as I say, for the Navy to call me, and when they do call me I've already got the German measles, I mean for real, pimples up and down my back and arms and real sick. I write a note to the Navy and they say wait two weeks. I'm at home again with Ma and I start neatly handprinting a beautiful little novel called 'The Sea Is My Brother,' which is a crock as literature but as handprinting beautiful. I'm alone in the house again with my handprint pencil and pure again but really sick from German measles. There was, in fact, an epidemic of it at that time. The Navy didnt doubt me. But the next week when I'm well again I entrain to Boston to the U.S. Naval Air Force place and they roll me around in a chair and ask me if I'm dizzy. 'I'm not daffy,' says I. But they catch me on the altitude measurement shot. 'If you're flying at eighteen thousand feet and the altitude level is on the so and such, what would you do?'

'How the screw should I know?'

So I'm washed out of my college education and assigned to have my hair shaved with the boots at Newport.

XV

Which wasnt so bad except they were all eighteen years old and here I am twenty-one.

What a bunch of bores all talking about their pimples, or girlfriends, *one*, as tho I hadnt ever had a girlfriend, and giving me these corny jokes. There's a vast difference, the service officers should know, between eighteen and twenty-one. We had to sling up our hammocks on hooks in the Newport Rhode Island barracks and every minute some eighteen-year-old nut fell out, in mid of night, plunk on the deck, and me too, while trying to turn over for more comfortable positions. Meanwhile somebody kept waking me up in my flimsy and unconditional hammock in mid of night, like 3 A.M., for to walk up and down with a flashlight and carbine (well, gat) as 'Guard' of the watch. Then in the morning they wouldnt let you smoke. And you had to duck behind boots to light your butt, boys.

The food wasnt bad. But when I had spent that month at home with German measles writing 'The Sea Is My Brother' I kept playing Shostakovich's Fifth Symphony and I was by now right spoiled. All them Cossacks riding ponies across the steppes. Instead, here I was with guys yelling in B companies 'Hi a loop, hi a loop, hup hup' and swinging by with wool caps and pea coats.

What I have to tell you about the U.S. Navy will knock your head clean off.

BOOK NINE

I

Well, I didnt mind the eighteen-year-old kids too much but I did mind the idea that I should be disciplined to death, not to smoke before breakfast, not to do this, that, or thatta. I knew the kids were stupid war fodder, as we all know, but great kids they were, as you know too, but this business of I cant smoke before breakfast and this other business of the admiral and his Friggin Train walking around telling us that the deck should be so clean that we could fry an egg on it, if it was hot enough, just killed me. Who was this gentleman who had the nerve to tell me to wipe a speck off my foot?

I am a descendant of very grand gentlemen who were in Court of King Arthur and werent told to be as clean as that, tho they were not sloppy at all, as we all know, just covered with gore (like the admiral's deck).

This antiseptic shot, and no smoking rules, and having to walk guard at night during phony air raids over Newport R.I. and with fussy lieutenants who were dentists telling you to shut up when you complained they were hurting your teeth . . . I told this Navy lieutenant, dentist, 'Hey Doc, dont hurt me' and he said 'Do you realise you're addressing a commanding officer!' Commanding indeed. And then when we all came in the first day the doc says 'Okay, pee in that tube over there' this kid said, right next to me I tell you, 'From here?' and practically nobody got the joke. That was the funniest joke from here to Chelmsford Massachusetts. The funniest part of it, the kid was serious.

That's your Navy, good men all of course.

But then these details where they get you to wash their own garbage pans, as if they couldnt hire shits to do that, or who's any kind of shit in this world eligible for garbage pan duty? I was disgusted. Then in the field, marching Army style routines, hi a loop, hi a loop, one, two, three, four, five, carrying carbines but with peacaps and blacks o' spring and the dust and the yelling drill instructors, suddenly I lay my gun down into the dust and just walked away from everybody forever more.

I went to the Naval library to read some books and take notes.

They came and got me with nets.

They said 'Are you nuts? What'd you do? You walked away from the drill field, threw your gun down, told everybody where to get off, who the devil do you think you are?'

'I am John L. Duluoz, field marshal.'

'Dont you want to go in the submarine service?'

'I've got claustrophobia.'

'They've really got you lined up for swimming ashore at night with a dagger in your teeth, Navy ranger, or commando.'

'I dont care, I aint gonna swim ashore with no dagger in my teeth for nobody. I aint,' I added, 'a frogman, I'm just a frog.'

'Your number's up.'

'Bo, go right ahead.'

'You're going to the nuthouse.'

'Okay.'

'And what's this you've been reporting to the Navy medical man that you have persistent headaches?'

'That's right.'

'Is that true?'

'Sho, who wouldnt have persistent headaches hanging around here?'

'Dont you know that your country's gotta be defended and that any national nation is not to be denied the right to defend themselves?'

'Yeh, but let me do it in the Merchant Marine as a civilian seaman.'

'What you talkin about? You're a draftee in this Navy.'

'Just put me away with all the other nuts in this here Navy. When the time comes and you have a real sea war, dont call on civilian sailors . . . '

'You're off to the nuthouse, kid.'

'Okay.'

'You're going to lose all those young buddies.'

'And they write letters home to West Virginia every night.'

'All right, here you go' so they ambulance me to the nut hatch.

Where I'm greeted by a colloquial questionnaire in which is recorded the fact that I've had the highest I.Q. intelligence rating in the history of frigging Newport R.I. Naval Base and therefore I'm suspect. As being, mind you, an 'officer in the American Communist Party.'

Naval Intelligence comes with a briefcase questioning me about that. Squads of Van Dyked bearded doctors study my eyes while stroking their chins over my handprinted novel 'The Sea Is My Brother.' What else you want a Navy man to write?

II

The first guy they introduce me to is a psychopathic maniac with long black hair on his lips. How the Navy Induction Board ever let that guy in I'll never know. His hair grows over his eyes, his lips, hips, legs and madman feet. He is the hairy madman of Heaven. He stared at me thru a wired cage googling and glibbling. I say 'What the shuck is this, a nuthouse?'

'You asked for it, you said you had perpetual headaches.'

'Yeh that's true, but what's HE got?'

'He's Roncho the Modmo.'

'Well what do I do now?'

'You go right in there with him soon as we check out your papers . . . what's the name again, John Louis Duluoz?'

'That's right . . . Louis for Lousy and Lout and Lug and John L.'

'Go right in.'

'I goes right now, Pap.' I goes in. The madman just stares at me as they assign me a bunk next to a manic depressive from West Virginia called Farty Fartington or whoever can ever remember his name, but in the bed on the other side is Andrew Jackson Holmes, which is a name everybody can remember forever from this moment on.

It's about 2 A.M. and Andrew Jackson Holmes is asleep and the other nuts (not all nuts) are snoring but the next day I go to the toilet and I'm being watched by guards, I'm wearing a bathrobe, and they say 'Okay sit there.' So I sit there. On the next bowl is sitting Andrew Jackson Holmes smoking a big cigar and looking at me bright-eyed and bushy-tailed. He says: 'I am Andrew Jackson Holmes from Ruston Louisiana, who are you boy?'

'I am John Louis Duluoz from Lowell Massachusetts.'

'I played varsity football for Luisiana State University in the line.'

'I played varsity football for Columbia in the backfield.'

'I am six foot five and weigh one hundred and ninety-nine pounds and I am a good puncher.' And he showed me his fist. Big as a nine-pound steak.

I said 'Dont ever hit that with me, what's your nickname?'

'He asks me what's my nickname, it's Big Slim from Louisiana.'

'Well Slim, what now?'

'Soon as I finish my potty I'm going back to my bed, which is next to yours, and I'm gonna show you how to cheat at cards.'

So we went back to the ward and he showed me how to mark the backs of cards with your fingernail and then showed me how that works in blackjack. Then he said 'Boy, when I was layin around in a haystack in Baltimore Maryland 'bout a year ago drinkin gin of a bottle some old boy gave me, I was thinkin of nothing . . . I was always a merchant seaman and then one day we're sailin out of Portland Maine and here comes a Coast Guard cutter with F.B.I. men aboard and drag me off telling me I'm dodgin the draft. I dont even have a mailin address. I'm big Old Slim from Louisiana and I dont know what hype they're puttin down from here to Chinatown.'

I said 'There, Big Slim, we must have a lot in common.'

'That aint no Harvard lie, boy, and no Oxford lie, nuther. Now I'm goin to show you how to cheat at poker.'

'I dont play cards, dont worry.'

'I dont know how else we can spill our time in this bizarficated ruthouse . . .'

'Well just tell me stories about your true life.'

'Well one time I flattened a cop in the Cheyenne Wyoming railyards, like this,' and this big fist like Jack Dempsey's in my face.

'Slim dont hit me with that, will ya?'

'Look, I also got, soon's the lights go out, some chewin tobacco, then, here in this paper carton we can spit . . . here's your chaw.' So we start in on chawin and spitting. The psychos were all asleep.

III

Big Slim says then 'Boy, one time I was in Atlanta Georgia and saw this burlesque gal do a show and went down to the corner bar after the show to have a short beer and whiskey, and she walked in there, ordered a drink, and I slapped her right on the rump and said "Good girl." '

'Was she mad?'

'Was she ever? But I got outa that okay.'

'What else?'

'When I was a young boy my mother put out a pie on the window in Ruston Louisiana and a hobo came by and asked her if he could have a piece. My mother said to go ahead. I said to my mother "Can I be a hobo someday Maw?" She said "It aint for the likes of the Holmeses." But I didnt take her advice and became a hobo just in love of hoboing and all that pie idea.'

'Pie Clue.'

'What?'

'Slim, have you ever hurt anybody?'

'Nossir boy, except that cop in the yards at Cheyenne.'

'What was your work?'

'East Texas oil fields boy, and bronco buster just outa there, cowboy, oil worker, hobo, tug worker in New York City Harbor, and seaman.'

'Deck?'

'What else boy, you think I'm goin to hang around in the en-gyne room with a bandana round my brow?'

'So what do we do, Slim?'

'Keep your mouth shut, we'll secure some butter knives tomorrow night supper and put em in our lockers and then we can break the locks open . . . You hear them freight trains out there bringing crap to this Naval base? We'll bust locks and go out in our pajamas and hop that freight right straight down to a haystack I told you about in Baltimore, and then we'll go to Montana, Butte, and get drunk with Mississippi Gene . . . Meanwhile,' he says, 'jist chew some of this tobacco and tell me some of yore stories.'

'Well Slim I aint as colorful as you are but I sure ben around . . . like that time in Washington when I waved my dicker at the White House, or Sydney Nova Scotia when we pushed a whole shack into the bay, or in Lowell Mass. when a guy was tryin to kill my Polish buddy against the car with a rain of killin punches, I told him to stop it, he said "What?' I said" "Stop it!" "Who are you?" "Fucketh you, man," and his father had to drag me off his back, he was really tryin to kill that poor kid.'

'Yair, you pretty strong lil ole boy but conjure up in yo mind if you will, what I would do to you with this fist?'

'Lissen Jack Dempsey that do drinketh, forget it?'

'But my Polish buddy liveth,' I said, looking Big Slim right in the eye, and he knew what I meant. (An incident I didnt throw in during the early chapters of this entire nuthouse novel.)

Slim liked me and I liked Slim, we were both strong men, and gay, independent and free-minded and the Navy I think sorta appreciated it because you'll see later.

IV

One afternoon I was smoking a butt under a bed at the end of the ward when all of a sudden the dingblasted admiral himself opened the door and ushered in two men. I blanked the butt and sneaked out looking suave. It was Leonid Kinsky and Akim Tamiroff, the Hollywood actors, coming around to entertain the entertained nuts of the huthouse ward. But it was strange. I really thought they'd seen me smoking, but no, just coincidental, Big Slim was napping, the manic depressive was napping, the hairy guy was napping, the Negro was trying to find a card game and the guy who'd shot himself thru the head was sitting glumly in a wheelchair with a bandage around his head. I go right up to Akim Tamiroff and tell him 'You were wonderful in *The General Died at Dawn.*'

'Why tank you.'

'And you, Monsieur Kinsky, how's things in the Communist Party.'

'Oh, Hokay?'

'Sorry, but, Mister Tamiroff, you were wonderful in *The General Died at Dawn* and also in *For Whom the Bell Tolls* and as the French Canadian India deadshot in De Mille's, you know, Cecil Northwest picture . . . '

'Tank you.' They had more fun than we had. I dont know what they were doing there? Dun't be silly.

V

Then here comes my Pa, father Emil A. Duluoz, fat, puffing on cigar, pushing admirals aside, comes up to my bedside and yells 'Good boy, tell that goddamn Roosevelt and his ugly wife where to get off! All a bunch of Communists. The Germans should not be our enemies but our Allies. This is a war for the Marxist Communist Jews and you are a victim of the whole plot. Would I were old enough, I would join the N.M.U. and sail with you, go down, be bombed, I dont care, I am a descendant of great seamen. You tell these emptyheaded admirals who are really stooges of the government around here that your father said you're doing the right thing,' and with this, and while being overheard by said admirals, stomped out fuming on his cigar and took the train back to Lowell.

Then in comes Sabby in a U.S. Army uniform, sad, idealistic, crewcutted now, but dream-minded, trying to talk to me, 'I have remembered, Jack, I have kept faith,' but the nutty manic depressive from West Virginny shoves him in a corner and grabs him by the private's sleeves and yells 'Wabash Cannonball' and poor Sabby's eyes are misting and looking at me saying, 'I came here to talk to you, I only have twenty minutes, what a house of suffering, what now?'

I say 'Come in the toilet.' West Virginia follows us yelling, it was one of his good days. I said 'Sabby dont worry, the kid's okay, everybody's okay . . . Besides,' I added, 'there's nothing for me or you to say . . . Except, I s'pose, that time when Bartlett Junior High School was burning down and my train was taking me back to New York prep school and you ran alongside, remember? in the snowstorm singing "I'll See You Again" . . . huh?'

And that was the last time I saw Sabby. He was fatally wounded on Anzio beachhead after that. He was a medical corpsman.

VI

Anzio: that was, as we say nowadays, Churchill's goof. How can you have a bunch of men wait ashore under hill-protected fire? Right down on them. And after that Mark Clark had the nerve to march on Rome when everybody in his right mind knew that he should have marched to the Adriatic and cut off the Germans in half? No, he wanted to be laureled in Rome. This is my laurel wreath: he may be damned for the dead of Salerno too.

But you cant court-martial the troubles of war.

I didnt add that last sentence because I'm yellow but because a general cant keep track of everything any more than I can.

VII

I sat in the window staring out at the spring trees with a kind kid from Athol Massachusetts who didnt talk to me any more after our initial night of harmonizing on 'Shine On Harvest Moon' . . . He was dying of what I dont know . . He stopped talking to me. . . . The sailor corpsmen came around to console him, bring him trays of food, he threw it right back at them . . . I said 'Why dont you sing?' . . . He answered not . . . Finally, after me and him spent a week looking out the window in absolute silence, they took him away and I never saw him again . . . They say he just died there in his padded cell. He sure could sing. French kid from Mass.

The guy with the bandage around his head had shot himself clean thru with a pistol, the bullet went in one way and came out the other, poor man wasnt even dead as he'd wished, and sat there glooming in a chair with a woeful blue-eyed stare under white shroudy bandages, like some kind of inverted-for-real Genet Hero. In one channel and out the other. A kind of corridor in the brain. Empty heads abound everywhere. Try it sometime. Dont be too sure.

But what inordinate gloom possessed him to try that? Like when the Navy discovered that me and Big Slim were hiding butter knives in our drawers, they order two big husky Navy corpsmen with straitjackets to come over and take us into control and into an ambulance and over to the train and down to Bethesda Naval Hospital in Maryland, just the state where Slim wanted to go. As I was standing around doing nothing, the two big Naval corpsmen with straitjackets were saying 'I'm not worried about the little guy Dulouse, but what about that big sonumbitch Holmes? He's six foot five.'

'Keep an eye on them.'

'What they do?'

'Hid butter knives to break open the locks and break out.'

'Sweet Navy men.'

'We gotta conduct em all the way down to Bethesda so take it easy.'

'Big boy be all right,' I said to them.

So here we go leaving Newport Naval Base under the conduction of two big Navy corpsmen with straitjackets, in an ambulance, and to the train to Washington, and Slim is in front of me, 'cause he's so big, and he keeps yelling back to me 'You still there Jack?'

'Still with you Slim.'

'You really still with me?'

'Cant you hear my voice?'

That night on the train trip to Washington we were left alone in separate sleeping compartments, while the corspmen waited outside, and I took the opportunity to fantasise, or that is, to relieve myself of the horror of masculinity. 'Heart' and 'Kiss' is only something's sung by gals.

VIII

Down there at Bethesda me and Slim was put first in the real nut ward with guys howling like coyotes in the mid of night and big guys in white suits had to come out and wrap them in wet sheets to calm them down. Me 'n' Slim looked at each other, two merchant seamen, 'Shucks boy, I wish I was back in the East Texas oil field.'

But the doctor was Dr Ginsberg and had me interviewed, read that half-written novel they'd all puzzled over in Newport R.I., and said in a grand tone. 'Well, allright, what do you really think you are.'

'I, sir?'

'Yes.'

'I'm only old Samuel Johnson, I was the nut of the Columbia campus, everybody knew it, elected me vice-president of the sophomore class and said I was a man of letters. No, Dr Ginsberg, a man of letters is a man of independence.'

'Yes, and what does that mean?'

'It means, sire, independent thought . . . now go ahead and put me up against a wall and shoot me, but I stand by that or stand by nothing but my toilet bowl, and furthermore, it's not that I refuse Naval discipline, not that I WONT take it, but that I CANNOT. This is about all I have to say about my aberration. Not that I wont, but that I cant.'

'And why did you consider yourself some kind of Samuel Johnson on the Columbia campus?'

'Well, talked to everybody about everything in literate detail.'

'And this is the image of yourself?'

'This is what I am, was, and will be! Not a warrior, Doctor, please, but a coward intellectual . . . but only in the sense that I feel I have to defend a certain portion of Athenian ethos, as might we say, and not because I'm yellow, because certainly, I AM yellow, but I just cant take that business of telling me how to be day in and day out. If you want a war, let the men run wild, if you want. Again I've failed in explaining myself. I cannot accept, or that is, I cannot live with your idea of discipline, I'm too much of a nut, and a man of letters, and besides, let me go and I'll go right back on that North Atlantic as a civilian seaman . . . '

Honorable discharge, indifferent character.

IX

No pension. No pea cap even. It was that Navy dentist who really turned me off. Who was he anyway? Some schmuck from Richmond Hill Center?

X

So I had a week left before I was to be discharged. It was May and now we were wearing our Navy whites. I was thereupon called 'Johnny Greensleeves' but not because my elbows were lying around girls' flanks but because I was hanging around drunk drinking out of bottles with a Marine called Bill McCoy, of Lexington Kentucky, in the grass parks of Washington.

Ole Bill was okay.

He used to give a sharp salute to officers in the streets of Washington while I stared at him in amazement.

I was just about the least military guy you ever saw and shoulda been shot against a Cuban wall. But you'll see later on how I saved a U.S. ship from bombardment. Two months later.

XI

So I go out and take a nap after a big drinking spree with Bill McCoy the Marine, in my Navy whites, and the workmen find me there lying on the green grass bankside, and say 'Are you alive?'

I say 'What you mean, am I alive? What's all this shit?'

They say 'We just thought you were dead. We honestly thought you were dead.'

I say 'Go droppeth a turd.' And besides, when a sailor in whites cant take a nap on a green bankside then what's painting gonna go to? Green and white, look.

Old Bill McCoy the Marine had a friend who was a sailor who was an ex-cabdriver who looked out the window with me in his bathrobe and said 'It's real cock weather out thar, wish I was out thar.' Easy does it.

Meanwhile, as I was sticking it up my ass with Mobilgas, a nut came to me and said I was not allowed on earth: I said 'Do you mean that Stan Satan walks the earth today?'

He said, 'Man he comes outa manhole covers every day in revolutionary holes in New York.'

I said I saw that down by that phony Parthenon by Wall Street. 'Steam comin outa holes.' He asked me how come I knew so much about hell, not being a denizen. I said 'Dante has apprised me of his heroes. And Goethe laid the path out. Pascal wept it thru. And the good gray poet Whitman outlined, Melville poeticized it, and my friends discussed it at night.'

He said 'Who are you?'

I said 'Little Pete.'

He said 'Do you want to shoot pool?'

I said 'After I make my break, and may not sink anything, and you miss some dumb choice, I'll slice that first ball into the corner with a little scythe, as soft as your Devil.'

'And therefore you're the Devil.'

'No, I'm his wind. And I'm gone as much from his influence, as this ungraspable handshake.'

This is where the book, the story, pivots.

This is known by Massachusetts Yankees as 'deep form.'

Funny halfbacks dont have to sell Pepsi-Cola.

BOOK TEN

I

Tho sometimes I'd just look out the window of the mad ward and watch a little dirt road that wound westward into the woods of Maryland leading to Kentucky and the rest, on misty days it had a particularly nostalgic look that reminded me of a boyhood dream of being a real 'Arkansas Railbird' with father and brothers on a horse ranch, myself a jockey, none of this drunken sailor shot and especially none of this cute and wise guy attitude toward the Navy, even the writing I've just used to describe the U.S. Navy in last few chapters has been cute and wise guy. At the age of twenty-one I could have gained a lot out of loyal membership to that outfit, learned a trade maybe, gotten out of the stupid 'literary' deadend I find myself trapped in now, especially the 'loyalty' part of it: for tho I'm a loyal person I've got nothing left to be loyal about, or for. Does it matter to five thousand sneering college writing instructors that I wrote seventeen novels after a youth of solitary practice amounting to over two million words, by the window with the star in it at night, the bedroom window, the cheap room window, the nut ward window, the porthole window, eventually the jail window? I saw that little winding dirt road going west to my lost dream of being a real American Man . . .

Of course Big Slim he woulda laughed at me hearing me talk this way and woulda said 'Name your windows, boy!'

I was discharged, made to sign my name to a form assuring that I could never file for a bonus, wasnt even given my Navy clothes (nice big pea coat, pea cap, whites, darks, etc.) but just given fifteen dollars to go downtown in my whites and buy me a going-home outfit. It was June so I bought sports shirt and slacks and shoes.

In the mess hall during the last few days at Bethesda I looked at all those guys eating that good food and yelling and talking and I felt I had betrayed not so much 'my country,' which I havent as you know, but this here United States Navy. If it hadnt been for that stupid dentist in Newport making me sick at the thought of being demeaned by a guy just because he has a higher rank. Isnt it true that the greatest admirals are the 'bulliest' and most intimate characters, 'one of the boys,' off their high horse?

Aw well, it was time for me to hit that old drunken waterfront seaman and eventual road hobo trail and at the same time keep up my studies and solitary writings. I hadnt learned anything in college that was going to help me to be a writer anyway and the only place to learn was in my own mind in my own real adventures: an adventurous education, an educational adventuresomeness, name it.

I took a few walks around lilac evening fields of Bethesda Md. with WAVES and such the last week and then went home in the choo choo train.

II

Big Slim wasnt discharged till a week later. He too went back to the Merchant Marine. He said he'd look me up in New York.

New York, that is, Ozone Park, Long Island, Queens, was where Ma and Pa had now moved, from Lowell, bringing the old piano only worth five dollars even, and all the old Lowell furniture, to begin a gay new life in the big city. Because they figured if Nin was in the WACS now (which she was), and I either in the Navy or in the Merchant Marine, we'd be more or less routing and rerouting in and through New York City. I came home in civvies to their new apartment over a drugstore in Ozone Park on a hot June morning.

But we had a gay party of it. Pa had a job on Canal Street in New York City as a linotypist and Ma had a job in Brooklyn as a skiver in a shoe factory making Army shoes, between the two of them they were socking money away in the bank, wartime wages, and living cheap, and splurging only on Saturday nights when they went out to Manhattan via the Jamaica El, the BMT subway and the rest and wound up roaming arm in arm around New York visiting interesting-looking restaurants and going to big Roxy and Paramount and Radio City movies and later, French movies, and coming home with shopping bags full of junk and toys that hit their fancy such as Chinese cigarette holders from Chinatown, or toy cameras from Times Square, or doodad figurines for shelves. This was, by the way, the happiest time of their entire married life. Their children were on their own and they began to realise they liked each other as persons. Ma even let Pa go down to the corner on Cross Bay Boulevard and make his bets with the big fat woman bookie who ran the candy store.

III

I remember the morning my father got up and found some baby mice in the closet at Ozone Park apartment and there was nothing else to do but throw them down the toilet. Red sun in June, the cars shizzing by on the boulevard, the smell of exhaust but a nice wind all the time from the nearby sea immediately blowing it away and also nice trees around.

'Poor little beasts,' he said, 'but you gotta do it.' But as soon as he'd done it he almost cried. 'The poor little dolls, it's a pity.'

'They were so cute,' said Ma in a little baby voice that would have sounded silly in English but in French Canadian only made you see what kind of little girl she'd been in her New Hampshire days, the emphasis on the word 'cute,' the English word itself used, but in French context and pronunciation, carrying in it infinite and genuine child regret that such little creatures with their tittery noses and mustaches carried such a heavy weight of diseasing filth . . . yea the little helpless white bellies, the hairs streaming back from scrawny necks in the water . . .

The other night, now (1967), when my cat died, I saw his face in Heaven just like old Harry Carey saw the face of his loyal Negro porter in Heaven at the end of the picture *Trader Horn.* I dont care who the person is you love: you love the loyal, the helpless, the trusting.

In night, my bed by the boulevard window, I thrashed in a thousand twenty-one-year-old agonies at the horror of all this world.

When I went out and signed on the S.S. *George Weems* via the union hall, and saw the paintings of three airplanes on its stack at the docks in Brooklyn, meaning they had shot down three planes in the Atlantic, I felt the same way . . .

When you're twenty-one you run to your girl. I ran up to Columbia campus to look up Johnnie, caught up with her at Asbury Park where she was living the summer with her grandmother, she put earrings on my ears and when we went to the sands all afternoon in the crowd a bunch of girls said 'What is it, a gypsy?' But this is a gypsy who doesnt eat up others as he goes along.

'I'll get a ship and come back around October and we'll live together in an apartment in New York City, right on the campus, with your friend June.'

'You're a rat but I love you.'

'Who cares?'

IV

Getting my gear ready to ship out in about a week, at my parents' apartment in Ozone Park, all of a sudden the door knocks at 8 A.M. and it's Big Slim in the door. 'Come on boy let's go out and git drunk and play the horses.'

'There's a bar right across the street to start with. As for the horses, Slim, let's wait till my Pa gets home from work at noon, he loves to go to Jamaica.' Which we did. Me, Big Slim and Pa went to Jamaica and in the first race Slim secretly laid twenty to win on the favorite while Pa put five to place on some dog he'd figured all night before in the *Morning Telegraph* form charts. Both lost. Slim had a pint of whiskey in his backpocket, me too. It was wartime, there were a million things to do. My Pa just loved Slim. B'God we went out to New York City after the races, on the train that runs back to Penn Station, and went out to hit the Bowery. Sawdust saloons and raucous big fat dames in Sammy's Bowery Follies singing 'My Gal Sal' and one old Tugboat Annie even sat on Pa's big fat lap and said he was a cute kid and buy me a beer. Pa went home exhausted and I went on with Slim into the night . . . He ended up, the last time I ever saw him, with his head in his hands howling loud and sad 'O I'm sick, I'm sick!' and bumping into lamp poles on the waterfront near the Seamen's Union. Everybody hiding in the alleys to see *him* carry on like that, big 6 foot 5 and 200-pound muscle and bones. They were building a Seaman's Chapel out of the Seamen's Union at the time, under the direction of Reverend Nordgren whom I met many years later in retirement in Florida, but it wasnt for Slim to go to a chapel. Where he ever went I'll never know. Last I heard he was punching cows in East Texas, probably not true. Where is he tonight? Where am I? Where are you?

Because when I saw the face of my beloved dead cat Timmy in the Heavens, and heard him mew like he used to do in a little voice, it surprised me to realize he wasnt even born when World War II was on, and therefore at this moment, how can he even be dead? If he wasnt born, how can he be dead? So just an apparition in molecular form for awhile, to haunt our souls with similarities to God's perfection, in Timmy's case the perfection was when he'd sit like a lion on the kitchen table, paws straight out, head erect and full-jowled, and God's imperfection when he was dying and his back was a skeletal run of ribs and spinal joints and his fur falling off and his eyes looking at me: 'I may have loved you, I may love you now, but it's too late . . . ' Pascal says it better than I do when he says: 'WHAT SHALL WE GATHER FROM ALL OUR DARKNESS, IF NOT A CONVICTION OF OUR UNWORTHINESS?' And he adds, to show you right path:

'There are perfections in Nature which demonstrate that She is the image of God' – Timmy sittin like a lion, Big Slim in his prime, Pop in his prime, me in my careless 1943 youth, you, all – 'and imperfections' – our decay and going-down, all of us – 'to assure us that She is no more than His image.' I believe that.

'God is Dead' made everybody sick to their stomachs because they all know what I just said, and Pascal said, and Paschal means Resurrection.

V

An amazing seven hours, that hot day in late June 1943, when I was sweating water through my shirt pushed up against hundreds of people in the subway, en route downtown to get my boarding papers at the National Maritime Union, cursing (because I cant stand the heat at all my blood is thick and hot as molasses), and then, seven hours later, I'm standing bow watch in the windy dark sea under stars in a big jacket as we round Nantucket and head for England, wow.

This was the aforementioned S.S. *George Weems*, I was signed on as an ordinary seaman on the four-to-eight watch, my first job on deck. I had to learn from the other fellows about picking up those fist-thick ropes and winding them about giant bits while the guy at the steam-driven winch ground up those rope cables on a big spool as big as your bedroom, or bed thereof, and all the jazz about learning to lower away lifeboats, with drills and everything at any moment's notice. All Greek to me. The bosun said I was the stupidest deckhand of all time.

'Especially,' says he, 'at nine o'clock in the evening an hour before we sail, he's complaining it's too hot in New York Harbor, he goes up on the poop deck and dives off, how many feet is that? Right into the harbor waters in the dark? How does he know there aint a big plank or something floating there preferably with nails in it to make more holes in his head? Then he comes climbing up the Jacob's ladder all drippin wet and expects the guard watch to think he's an ordinary Joe who jumped off for a coolin swim . . . how did they know you werent a German spy you dughead?'

'It was hot.'

'I'll show you some hot. And on top of that,' he later complains, 'guy never says anything to anybody and just lays in his bunk reading, mind ya, READING . . . But kid you coulda hit somethin in that water in the dark and that's a very high deck up there.'

'We did it in Nova Scotia off the *Dorchester* in the afternoons.'

'Sure, when you could see the water was clear below . . . '

On top of that, the ship is carrying 500-pound bombs in all its holds and is flying the dynamite flag, red, going to Liverpool.

VI

Flying the red dynamite flag is a warning to everybody including tugboats not to bump us too hard. If we get hit by a torpedo we all go up in a gigantic mass of shrapnel, men, pots, pans, bosuns, books, bunks, the works. Today I cant imagine how the hell I slept so well.

But here it is, seven hours after I'd cursed and sweated in the human subway in the June heat of Manhattan, ah, boy, cold winds, Atlantic again, night, stars, I turn around and look back at the bridge: little blue dim light indicates where the able-bodied seaman's got the wheel with eye on compass, where the first mate or captain stands thinking, or looking thru binoculars into the dark, off our both sides you see other ships puffing up smoke, it's a big A-Number-One convoy.

Boys in the galley stalk about and talk about a legendary German battleship that, if it finds us, can stand out there a million yards and just hammer us with longdistance shells and we cant even reach them with our protective cruisers' guns (you see the cruisers out there pitching and biting right into the wave). Morning and new seas.

Four-to-eight watch is best watch on any ship. Day's deck work ends at four thirty. Usually at seven thirty in the morning I'm on the bow watch, just standing at the front tip of the ship (bow) and looking at the water and the horizons for signs of mines or wakes of periscopes or anything suspicious. What a horizon! The sea is my brother . . . People who've never been to sea dont know that when you're out over the real deeps the water is pure blue, not a speck of green, deep blue, on choppy days with white foam, the colors of the Virgin Mary. Maybe it's not surprising the Portuguese and Mediterranean fishermen pray to Mary and by night call her the Star of the Sea, or Stella Maris. Could Roger Maris hit a homerun over the sea? Wasnt Jude a duck when he said the waves of the sea foam 'out their own shame'? (Jude 13.) Not really, considering Nature and her borning and dying. What connection is there between human shame and all that splendid PHOOEY of an ever cackling old man like that brother my sea, even tho the worms eat away and the worry warts'll win? Who put the plug in the bottomroom floor of *THAT* tub? What a round goiter of disjointed flecks, such a Slavic plain nevertheless with uprisings of white foam, some of them veritable Genghis Khans of curling trouble off the port bow . . . Who but a bow watchman standing there staring for hours at his job, at nothing but the sea, can tell you this, and better yet (as sometimes) as crow's nest watch who can spot stuff on the water miles away? The wind sometimes making a choppy wave giving off a mountain of floss sprays and letting them dissolve back in the farmless huff of waters. Little uprisings, big uprisings, phooey, the sea is like a log fire ever fascinating to watch, even intrinsically a bore, as I must be now, ever a lesson of some dumb universal kind, wisdom and all that, 'the burning away' and 'the ever shifting' horse manure of it all, the sea and all, it makes you wanta go down to the mess hall and drink three cops of coffee, or three policemen, *one*, and say goodbye to aimless universe which is after all the only brother we've got, placid or otherwise his face will frown or soothe. What can I do with those meandering lines of foam? Being a descendant of Cornish sea-mongers and Breton after that means nothing in the face of all that crop of salt and shite out cropping all over like flowers, Lord, Wolfdog Sea.

Off the coast of the Firth of Clyde the dotty pomerancy pack of it. Surprising, tho, the Irish Sea IS green.

Thank God the sea isnt my mother and never pecks at me, nor my wife and never hens at me, the sea is my brother and can either eat me plain (without apologies or tricks) or leave me alone to sway and dip and sleep and dream, on the crow's nest, like Pip up on the masthead, boy. The dangling legs of Buddy Bill from the yardarm of the British Navvy . . .

Phiddlephuck with the See, holy or otherwise, the SEA, what's below it we'll never see except with Coral Gable eyes, Israel Hands, Phineas Feet and fine tentricles in our vestibules, vestigitabbibles at least.

What a crocka horsewater.

VII

Rooming in my foc'sle with me are two seventy-year-old seadogs from the old World War I days and even before, my God, one of them, a Swede, is even still sewing canvas with a big needle. They hate me because I lie in bed and just read and refuse to learn how to sew canvas in lieu of reading and also going out at midnight to use the purser's typewriter in his little cubicle office where I'm trying to finish 'The Sea Is My Brother.' By now I've changed the names and my feeling is different. In my bunk I read, of all things, the entire Galsworthy *Forsyte Saga*, which not only gives me a view of British life before I get there (we're headed for Liverpool as I say) but gives me an idea about sagas, or legends, novels connecting into one grand tale.

Every night at five or six I'm like that barefooted Indian on the *Dorch* now, I have to cover the entire ship, all the foc'sles and staterooms, and make sure the portholes are closed and secured. It's wartime blackout regulations. So I not only have to go into the thirty-one-year-old captain's room and check his porthole as he's taking a five-minute captain's nap (poor kid never slept, I promise you), but have to brave the foc'sle of the eight-to-ten deck watch which is three nutty kids with muscles and tattoos who spend all their time practicing knife throwing against the door. When you're about to open the door (bulkhead) you hear 'Slowm,' a knife's just missed sticking in it, then you hear 'Struck!' and a knife has. Then you have to knock. Mostly rainy weather this run over, I had to wear my sou'wester all the time, you know the outfit, the Gloucester fishermen wear with rubber big hat and shroudy rubber coat, in all pictures you've seen of storms at sea of the nineteenth century, so in this outfit I have to knock and they say 'Come in, Spencer Tracy!' I'm not sure they're not going to throw another knife but it's my duty to come in and check their portholes. They hold their knives up. I never even said a word to one of them. That whole trip I didnt say more than a dozen words on board.

Then around six I was on bow watch, in the gathering sea dusk and groomus gray Atlantic spray, and that was, of course, best of all. And one night at about this time I saw an oil barrel floating on the waves at 33 degrees and picked up the telephone there in the bulkhead and called the bridge. They went carefully to the portside, a good ways away from it, called our U.S. Navy convoying ships, and later we heard the explosion of the destruction of that mine. Right in the middle of the ocean, too.

VIII

But nothing, and not even this, could satisfy the chief mate who hated my guts I'll never know why except perhaps I didnt talk to him enough, I dont know. He was a German with a big scar down his cheek and very mean. At the switch of watch duties when I was supposed to leave the bow and go down and make coffee, he was never satisfied with it, altho I made coffee better'n anybody on the ship except the chef and that's why they kept having me make the coffee. I knew how to clean out the silver urn, the cloth bucket, even how to change it, etc., had learned all this on the *Dorchester* with Glory and the other cooks, but no, this chief mate had it in for me. One morning there was a fantastic squall with waves very high, rain, thunder, even a rainbow, black cloud there, something else there, the ship pitching like mad but nevertheless the idiot first mate sends me up the iron ladder to the crow's nest. To do this I had to hang on with my hands just as hard as I ever had to hang on years later on the iron rungs of the railroad just when a jolt ran along the cars (a slack). I'm hanging upside down, I'm hanging on leaning over on the mast, that's the way the mast was waving side to side. But I made the crow's nest, closed the little door, went 'Oh aaah sigh,' but suddenly a rainbow rushed up inside of a black cloud and hit the ship head on, with it a gigantic smashing of rains, and the mast went over to starboard so far I thought my nest would touch the waves, at worst go right in with the ship foundered. But the big keel underneath creaked her arounds, oops, way way over now to the port, me up there getting this big carnival ride for free and I'm yelling 'O my God!'

Thereupon, the members of the deck crew, all N.M.U., held a meeting and denounced the first mate for sending an ordinary seaman up to the crow's nest during a serious squall. It was decided he could never do this again. 'He's trying to kill you,' the union delegate told me briefly.

Sure enough, during another rough morning, the chief mate with his scar and his unwanted coffee spits at me in Germanic accent to go out and bail the outswung life boats. To do this I have to jump over 4 feet of water or less, that is, from the ship itself and into the life boat suspended over the rushing waters, rushing from the forward momentum of the ship and also crashing from the storm. Using my hands again, I made it, bucket in hand, wearing sou'wester (but yelling 'Whoooeee!' as I'd done when I threw that empty gin bottle across the moony trees of Virginia with Annie), and I bailed and bailed. Nothing much to bail out, it was just another trick by the chief mate to get rid of me and overboard. Why, I'll never know. 'You oughta grab that guy on the dock when we get back to Brooklyn,' said a guy to me. In those days I never entertained any such thoughts. My secret thought was: 'I can do anything he wants and I wont fall off nothin.' All I wanted to do was get to my bunk and get on with my reading of the *Saga*.

It should have been the Norse Saga but anyway it kept me busy and then sleepy. I think after I spotted that mine, and after I did what the first mate wanted without a word, the crew began to respect me, because after that they let me sleep even till five fifteen, fifteen minutes after my watch had begun, not needing me right away anyhow, and woke me gently in bed: 'Come on, Dulouse, time to get up, you've slept enough.'

'The sleeping beauty,' announced the bosun as I'd walk in for coffee.

They were good boys and we had a good trip. I for one never did figure what was wrong with that chief mate. It was close to being a Billy Budd and Master-at-arms Claggart situation because he was always fuming with rage and I was always sleeping, which explains Claggart and Billy pretty well, the guilty and the innocent soul side by side in the same ship.

I thought, for instance, I heard a big fistfight and wrestling rough-and-tumble on the steel deck right over my pillow one morning, fifty guys fighting, with clubs and sledgehammers, but it was 'Pueee puee pueee' the scream of the 'All hands on deck' attack warning, and I realised I was listening to depth charges going off in a submarine attack. I just turned over and went back to sleep. Not because we had 500-pound bombs and couldnt do anything about anything anyhow, but because I was just naturally sleepy and I had figured out in the Navy nuthouse: 'I could get killed walking across the street, if Supreme Reality's arranged it, so why not go to sea?' And besides, ding-blast it, I WAS just simply sleepy all the time. They called me 'Sleepy DuLouse.' Like Beetle Bailey, you might say . . . ZZZZZ.

IX

The N.M.U. delegate at the meeting, with the approval of the members, also denounced the chief mate for the lifeboat bailing-out incident. I dont quite remember where I was during these meetings, either in the back making coffee in the big fifty-cup urn, or sleeping, or reading, or standing bow watch and dreaming, but it all worked out.

I mention all this to redeem myself from the curse of being accused of slacking in the U.S. war effort.

The looseness of discipline in the Merchant Marine, which incidentally now I remember was the big complaint the chief mate kept screaming at everybody, was what made me love it and accept it and the danger with it. Sometimes I'd think 'O boy would Pa love this, to be on this ship, with me, maybe he could have been dishwasher, nah, his legs wouldnt stand it, well, purser, with typewriter . . . but those waves, those storms, these guys.' Everything is romantic when you're twenty-one in 1943.

The war brought people closer together, no matter what you can say about the rest of it.

The thirty-one-year-old captain was constantly looking thru binoculars, having the Navy boys signal the rest of the convoy with their blinkers, drinking coffee, trying to catch nine winks. He looked like a worried executive Johnny Carson at a desk but he was a real captain. He paid no attention to the first mate. He didnt drink, like other captains I've known, seemed to be worried I think about his family. There's always something mysterious about the captain of your ship, the 'Old Man' he's called, as tho he was other than human, as everybody knows, and of course I couldnt get over those first twenty days of the voyage of the *Pequod* in *Moby Dick* when nobody even got to see Ahab but just heard his stump up and down, stump, stump, in the captain's stateroom as he brooded on the whale, that damned white whale, that damned white whale whose eyes I see right now in the Heavens (looking one this-a-way, the other that-a-way, if you know what I mean).

X

But now that I'm forty-five years old and in a continual rage myself, I can understand and sympathize with that chief mate, at last, and I know what way the salmon jump up that river of bitter time and pain, wifey . . .

And lo! one morning the sun rose plaintiff to the accusing mists of the Firth of Clyde and the ships came into a bright part of sea where on the left you could see cliffs of Scotland, on the right flat green meadows of Ireland itself with thatched huts and cows. Imagine having a thatched hut right by the sea! A farm by the sea! I stood there crying, my eyes were pouring tears, I said to myself 'Ireland? Can it be? James Joyce's country?' But also way back I remembered what my father and my uncles had always told me, that we were descendants of Cornish Celts who had come to Cornwall from Ireland in the olden days long before Jesus and the calendar they start Him from, Kerouac'h ('Duluoz') being, they said, an ancient Gaelic name. The cry was always 'Cornwall, Cornwall, from Ireland, and then Brittany.' No secret to that, all these places being tided up by the Irish Sea more or less, including Wales and Scotland over there on the portside with her lairdy cliffs. But the bosum rasps at me:

'Come on, Du Louse, aint you ever seen Ireland, get busy with these hawsers you doodle brain!' ('Ker Roach' they really called me.)

Still with tears in my eyes, I worked on, but can anybody tell me why? It was just the sight of the little thatched huts on the green meadows by the softly breaking waves, and the cows lending their long shadows to early morning sun, and the wind at my back I guess . . .

XI

Then we sailed down into the Irish Sea, laid anchor off Belfast, waited there for some British convoy boats, and crossed the Irish Sea that afternoon and night straight for Liverpool. 1943. The year the Beatles were born there, ha ha ha.

And the year some little bum in a derby hat took my advice and lived with his legs whole. As we came up the Mersey River, all mud brown, and turned in to an old wooden dock, there was a little fellow of Great Britain waving a newspaper at me and yelling, about 100 yards ahead as we bore directly on him. He had his bicycle beside him. Finally I could see he was yelling something about 'Yank! Hey Yank! There's been a great Allied victory in Salerno! Did ye know that?'

'I dont know, Mr English, but please get off that pier, from what I can tell we're going to ram it down head on . . .' But he couldnt hear me because of the wind and the tide and the noise of cranes and winches unloading other ships nearby on the Merseyside docks.

'Yank! Yank!'

'But, mon' – I think the captain'd gotten drunk at last for the first time and the chief mate maybe too on Schnapps – 'but please turn around and start running as fast as you can, this ship is not going to touch at that dock, it's going to ram it! The bridge is drunk!'

'Hey? Hey what? Salerno!'

I kept waving him away. I pointed at the bow, the bridge, the dock, at him, I said 'Run run run . . . away!' He took off his derby and ran back with his bike he was pushing, and sure enough, the bow of the S.S. *George Weems* carrying 500-pound bombs and flying the red dynamite flag rammed right into that rotten old wood wharf and completely demolished it, ce-rack-ke-rack-crack, timbers, wood planks, nails, old rat nests, a mess of junk all upended like with a bulldozer and we came to a stop in Great Britain.

'This sceptred isle.'

Now, if it had been a modern concrete job, goodbye Du Louse, this book, the whole crew and nothing but the crew, and 'alf and 'alf of Liverpool.

XII

Where does a Captain go when his ship's finally docked and here he comes out after supper all decked out in his best suit, with epaulets and all, and steps down the gangplank carefully to a waiting cab or limousine? And in this here wartime Liverpool, was he about to go have dinner (cocktails first) in a castle over a sea-crashin cliff? Or a lounge somewhere? In fact, and where does the scarred first mate go with his snarling smear of thoughts, to weirder friends somewhere? In fact, and where, even, the bosun, the lowest Portuguese ordinary, the engine room, where do they go? They're all togged out and stepping out? They amaze me as I watch them go. Because I've agreed to work the whole weekend for the Portuguese ordinary so that when he comes back, I myself can have two straight days in a row. Anybody wondering what *I'm* going to do? But where do captains go? It's like wondering about where elephants go when they die, with their tusks. Some hidden blonde? Some old fishy Britisher seadog friend who taught him to read maps in Magellan rooms? I dont care if the port's Norfolk Virginia or Liverpool or Hong Kong they must surely go to strange places. So I'm there watching everybody going ashore, I have to stay aboard two days and fiddle with the loading spotlights and the wires that feed them the electricity, make coffee for the gangplank watch, and in the morning watch all those crazy little Liverpudlian longshoremen come rushing up on their bicycles with their lunches and their thermos bottles of 'tay' as they eagerly get down to the 'job' of unloading those awesome big 500-pound bombs destined for poor old sweet Dresden or someplace or Hamburg.

But that first night, a Friday, practically the whole crew gone, I wheedled the lines around, put up rat guards extra against the original ones, pointed the spotlights right, made coffee and mostly spent most of my time rearranging things on deck and saying to myself 'Aye saye, Mayeteee' in imitation of the Lancashire accents of the longshoremen. My nose was sniffling in the riverside cool, I was having fun, all alone practically on one big ship, and suddenly it began to occur to me that someday I would become a real serious writer with no time to fool around with poetry or form or style. Besides, at dusk, red on the Mersey liquid belly, here goes this oldest and littlest freighter I ever saw in my life with old fellas sitting on the afterdeck in old chairs smoking out of pipes, the S.S. *Long Voyage Home*, bound for Bangkok I guess for the thousandth time, the ship just slipping past me at my rail, the old men not looking up, just a touch away, by pole anyway, into the sinking sun they go on long voyages to the Pacific: and I'm wondering 'Joseph Conrad wasnt wrong, there *are* old seadogs who've been to everywhere from Bombay to British Columbia smoking their pipes on poops of old sea vessels, practically born at sea they are, and die at sea, and dont even look up . . . Even have cats down below for the rats, and sometimes a dog . . . What tobacco they smoke? What they do, where they go when they put on their glad rags in Macao, to do what? What a vast crock it all is for me to even dare to think of anything when all is said and done, Mayetey, I saye, get those lines wound right . . .' Talking to myself, I laughed all night. Not even a drink since Brooklyn . . . Who needs it?

Maybe at noon I'd slip off down the cobblestoned Merseyside streets and try the pub, it was always closed, not alone they didnt have any sausage in wartime England except was made with sawdust, but no beer proper either. And always closed. Some bold old bum in a bar complained that the poor of Liverpool were using their bathtubs to put coal in.

But when my weekend was over and Portugee came back to take over my duties for two days, I put on MY glad rags, which was a shiny oiled black leather jacket, khaki shirt, black tie, Merchant Marine Army Navy Store phony goldbraid hat with visor, black shined shoes, black socks, and stepped down the gangplank leaving all the returned crew's hangovers behind me and to go buy a ticket to London England on the Midland Railway. Even the captain was now back, disappointed I'm sure.

I got a haircut downtown Liverpool, hung around the rail station, the USO club looking at magazines and pingpong players, rain, the rimed old monuments by the quai, pigeons, and the train across strange smokepots of Birkenhead and into the heart of *La Grande Bretagne* ('the Great Britain').

BOOK ELEVEN

I

When the sun came out and our train rattle-tootled across your most beautiful green countryside, England in September, early September, haystacks, fellas on bicycles waiting at the crossings as our train smashed thru, dreamy little narrow rivers that apparently feed the cottages they fell through as tho they contained the waters of Manna, hedges, old ladies with Walter Pidgeon hats clipping at half-timbered cottage hedgerows, the whole shot of England as I'd always wanted to see it only to see it I had to stand there at the door window of the mail car and look eagerly because three hundred Aussies were sitting on the floor smoking and yelling and shooting craps, soldiers. No room anywhere on that train. Boom we go into the night lights of England, bang, Birmingham, Manchester, call it what you will and in the morning I'm asleep on the floor all dirty and disheveled like all the other soldiers but we dont all care because we're in London town on leave.

In those days I used to know subways pretty well so I took a subway straight from the railroad station to Trafalgar Square which I knew was near Piccadilly Circus but I wanted to see pigeons, Trafalgar's statue of Nelson for some reason, and anyway a kid gave me a shoeshine, and I spruced up in a USO club and started wandering around in the warm city day well pleased, even went into an avant-garde painting exhibit and listened to the local contemporary intellectuals carry on as they've done before, during and after any war on your bloody history map.

Then I doodled around looking at posters and decided to try Royal Albert Hall for that evening for a performance of Tschaikowsky by the people there with Barbirolli conducting. This took me to Hyde Park and kept wondering if it was named after Mr Hyde and where was Dr Jekyll? It's fun when you're a young kid in a foreign country, especially England, after all those movies you've seen in the Rialto.

As the concert was going on, and I sat in the balcony next to an English soldier, he whipped out a volume of verse by T. S. Eliot called *Four Quartets* and said they were magnificent. Lot I cared. On my right was an American soldier who had a flask. In the midst of the performance (God knows how I managed to sit thru concerts in those days without a trip to the toilet, a sandwich or a drink or a snip of the stars) when Barbirolli announced 'As you can hear from the air raid sirens out there, London is being raided this evening by the German Luftwaffe. Shall we continue on with concert or go downstairs to our shelters?' Applause, 'No! Concert!' So they continue with the concert. But I was lucky. This was just after the real Battle of Britain in the Air, after the R.A.F. and the Canadians had clobbered Göring's Luftwaffe, and, mind ye, just before the beginning of the next nemesis: the rocket-powered super bombs of the V-1, not to mention the V-2 a little later. It was a lull in the air war in Britain when I got there.

Funny, in fact, how I never got to see a bombing raid anywhere, not even on the S.S. *George Weems* with its three strikes painted on the stack, or from Spitzbergen in 1942 Greenland. I guess that was why I was washed out of the U.S. Naval Air Force.

Anyway after the concert we all piled out of Royal Albert Hall into the pitch blackness of blacked-out London, the raid was still continuing in the suburbs I guess, and me and the *Four Quartets* soldier, and the drinking soldier, bumped on down the road together straight for Piccadilly Circus bars and late Scotch. We got plowed and stupefied in there till the very end when by God the host did actually yell out over the yells of airmen and soldiers and seamen '*Hurry up please gentlemen it's time.*' We spilled out of there into the darkness of Piccadilly, fur coats of whores kept bumping up agin ye, 'Ducks, I saye!' and, 'Hey, where?' I lost everybody and finally one fur coat said its name was 'Lillian' and so we went off together into a little cozy inn.

II

In the morning they brought us breakfast, it was gray and misty outside with coalsmoke pouring out of William Blake's chimney pots, and Lillian said 'One more time ducks and then I gets ready for tonight's duty.' So I afterward say goodbye to her, pay for the room, and go down to smoke and relax in the inn's, or hotel's, fireplace reading lounge. In there is a big fat ruddy Englishman in a tweed coat smoking a big pipe and speaking in loud and sincerely grandiose tones to an old crone in a tweed suit drinking tea out of Cheshire cups, whatever they are. The fire roars and twinkles and crackles like the big Englishman's eyes. With my own eyes I saw they were on their guard to keep England to themselves indeed. I wanted to talk to that man but I was afraid of him, Colonel Blimp and the whip hand and the hauteur and all that, but you know as well as I do what would have happened: Scotch, drinks, trips around town. Americans were naively in awe of dear auld England in those days. I've lost my awe of England today in that they've tried too much to become like 'us'. That's true. And that's no Cambridge lie.

III

Well, morning and a few cold beers with American airforcemen in Piccadilly beer bars, where they chill the beer for American tastes, a walk around, even a nap in a park during an air raid, and then I have to find my way to Threadneedle Street because Lillian or something or somebody took most of my money away: I think it fell out of my pocket in Piccadilly dark: to borrow money for the train back to my ship in Liverpool from an American shipping office. An old man carrying an umbrella and wearing a homburg hat comes up to me and says imperiously, tapping me on the shoulder, 'I say, which way to Threadneedle Street?' Why its the bloody Bank of England street, haint it? Anyway I get my money, back to the train, back to Liverpool arriving in dark late night now, and as I'm trying to wend my way back to my ship at the docks I'm stopped at the monument near the river by another bag like Lillian saying 'I saye, Ducks' and so as I said earlier in the story, up against monuments. But on my way home to the ship. I know the way, there's another air raid blackout and b'God do you think for one minute I was afraid of those possible German bombs? No, in the very middle of the cobblestoned streets of that waterfront, with my money from Threadneedle Street in one hand and a bloody cobble in the other, I stalked soft as a Canadian Indian because I could hear them breathing in those doorways of the blackout dark; the thugs and muggers who give birth to beats on piles of bitumen in bathtubs and dont pay the rent.

IV

And it was that last morning before we got ready to sail to Brooklyn that I devised the idea of 'The Duluoz Legend,' it was a gray rainy morning and I sat in the purser's office over his typewriter, he was having his last drink I guess, and I saw it: a lifetime of writing about what I'd seen with my own eyes, told in my own words, according to the style I decided on at whether twenty-one years old or thirty or forty or whatever later age, and put it all together as a contemporary history record for future times to see what really happened and what people really thought.

Naturally, it was a good thing I wasnt chosen to give the valedictory speech at Lowell High School when I graduated from that other mill.

So we lift anchor and sail out, across the Irish Sea, in a storm now, she's as green as snot God help me just like Joyce said, and then around that firth again, and out into the Atlantic with nothing between us and Great Britain but the B.B.C. coming over faintly on the radio.

And a giant storm hits up, 'huee huee' the submarines are attacking, the waves are smashing against the side of the *Weems* so strong we dont know what can ever be done about lowering away our life boats. We're empty of bombs now, light, bobbing around up and down, but it's too rough to survive if our ship gets hit in the poor almost human iron bulkheads and a virile German torpedo enters her and sinks her, us bobbing corks will freeze to death anyway (far north our route) so we just sit glumly in the galley, the whole deck and steward's crew, wearing our life belts, sucking on coffee, playing checkers, making cocoa, and the Negro second cook whips on an extra life jacket and yells 'Well, I dont know about you fellas but I'M gettin outa here' and he runs out on deck alone.

'Where's he gonna go?' says the bosun moving a checker which slides with the ship's pitch.

'There aint no place to go,' I say, adding my last six words to the four I'd already put in on the trip out.

Nobody even looks up.

Du Louse picked a wrong time to talk.

But we got outa that okay, took a left at Iceland, and got back to Brooklyn, the Moore-McCormack piers at the foot of Joralemon Street where you can see the towers of Manhattan right across the river all lit up at dusk and all those narrow byways among the canyons of concrete that show you the way to restaurants, blondes, fathers and mothers, friends, lovers, warmth, city, weddings, parades, flags, beery saloons . . .

V

And bang, we all get paid in little brown envelopes and I unloose about a hundred thousand words on all those poor shipmates of mine because somebody's brought beer aboard and I'm drunk and they complain 'That goddam Du Louse aint said ten words on the whole trip now listen to him!'

'I'm going to see my baby!' I yell and rush off across the unroasted coffee sour sweet smell of the wharf and into the streets and up to Borough Hall and into the cinnamon-smelling subway and up thru Times Square and up to Columbia campus, in a mist of rains, and run to the pad Johnnie's already sharing with June and jump in, now it's raining dogs, and not seadogs either, and there she is, radiant and happy to see me and young and she was the wife of my youth.

And that old seadog June had already been instructing her all summer, while I was at sea, how to please me at love.

So we pull the shade down on the rain and retire by candlelight after our favorite snack of cold asparagus with mayonnaise and ripe olives.

VI

Then I went home to Ozone Park to see ma and pa, at the time the song was 'People Will Say We're in Love,' it was cold October in Brooklyn as Ma had me wait in the corner as she ran in to shop for something in Abraham & Straus, and to get Barricini candy for Pa, we took the joyous Els, subways, somehow things were grand and forward-looking. Pa was in high spirits and said he still had his sea legs. I brought Johnnie home to meet them and we had beers in the German tavern on Liberty Avenue and Cross Bay Boulevard and then walked home all four, the two couples arm in arm, under the October moon and mild falling leaves.

Allegro, the composer should write here.

My next plan was to take a bus to New Orleans and sail out of there, in a few months, but during the winter I intended to commute back and forth from Johnnie's to Ma's, at Johnnie's I wrote a lot, at Ma's house too, and also get the fill of life.

Johnnie and I took a train to Grosse Pointe Michigan to meet her aunt and her father, who was a widower, but when I saw this old bum in a battered coat and battered hat coming up the street I thought 'No wonder, Missus Palmer married an old bum.' But he said 'Come on' to me and Johnnie and we followed him to his car, where he took off his battered coat and underneath it he had a tuxedo and drove us to a steamed clam dinner on the Lake St Clair shore. Then he took us yatching on his motor-driven yatch (35 feet long I forget the make or type) to Ontario across Lake St Clair where we went ashore and picked fresh mint to sprinkle on our steak in the galley that night. He had his mistress with him. We had Hudson Bay blankets to wrap up in our separate foc'sles. One time he'd got drunk with his best friend the mogul or magnate of the hotel system very famous then, but they were drunk, alone, no women, just bottles, so they ordered some mannikins from a Detroit department store and took the models' legs and had them sticking out of the portholes of the yatch and went sailing like that, putt putt putt, in front of everybody's horrified eyes, out to water clear.

And there were big wild parties of the teenage troupes of that time in various houses around Grosse Pointe, the doorbell rings and a guy yells 'Hey a beer wants to come out of the ice-box,' I went backstage to the backyard through the screen door and looked at the stars and listened to the revelry and shure did love American AS America in those days.

VII

I'm not talking in detail about my women, or ex-women, in this book, because it's about football and war, but when I say 'football and war' I have to go a step further now and add: 'Murder.' One step leads to another in a way but I had nothing to do with this murder. Or did I?

It's just that a very strange screw of events began to turn in early 1944.

To get to it, I'll just preamble by saying that in the month of May 1944 I did take a bus to New Orleans, went down to the N.M.U. hall to sign on for a ship, had no luck, hung around the seaman's club, at one point got drunk with a drunken seaman who used to be the Governor of the State of Florida (we drank under rotating ceiling fans) and walked up and down Magazine Street to make a lunchcart waitress, wrote notes to Johnnie telling her I was starving and send money, wrote home, became completely disgusted and decided to go back to New York to ship out from there as usual, or Boston. It was just a nutty subliminal desire to see New Orleans and the South, Mississippi and Alabama and all that, which I saw out the window, the cotton-pickin shacks miles and miles of em across those flats. I also got drunk in Asheville North Carolina with Tom Wolfe's drunken older brother right there in the parlor of Tom Wolfe's Asheville home with the picture of Tom and of his brother 'Ben' right there on top of the squareback piano, and spent that night mooning around with a recalcitrant or miscreant miss on a porch in the Smokies foothill night right there by the Broad River mists. (French Broad, that is.) And skirmishes with women in Raleigh, etc., and another trip in Washington D.C. and same parks, etc., but the main point is, the whole trip was foolish and I came back real quick and took off my black leather jacket in Johnnie's bedroom while she was still at art class studying with the famous George Grosz, and just went to bed. When she got home she whooped when she saw my jacket on the back of the chair.

She hadnt ever read Ovid but she sure knew all his advice about riding that pony. (Ovid, *Art of Love*, Bk. III.)

And then sad nights, rain drumming on the roof, six flights up, on 118th Street and Amsterdam just about, and in start coming the new characters of my future 'life.'

VIII

There was this kid from New Orleans called Claude de Maubris who was born in England of a French viscount now in the consular service, and of an English mother, and who now lived with his grandmother in a Louisiana estate whenever he was there, which was seldom, blond, eighteen, of fantastic male beauty like a blond Tyrone Power with slanted green eyes and the same look, voice, words and build, I mean by words he expressed his words with the same forcefulness, a little more like Alan Ladd actually, actually like Oscar Wilde's model male heroes I s'pose but anyway he showed up on the Columbia campus at this time followed by a tall man of 6 foot 3 with a huge flowing red beard who looked like Swinburne.

I forgot to mention that during the winter of 1943 and 1944 I had worked at odd jobs for extry money, including of all things a job as switchboard operator in the little local campus hotels, then later as script synopsizer for Columbia Pictures on Seventh Avenue downtown, so on my return trip from New Orleans I was planning to get one of these jobs back while waiting for a ship. It so happened that this Claude got a room in Dalton Hall, small campus hotel, so did Swinburne, I knew the management there, and that was to be the focal point of most of these events.

Well, turns out Claude arrives on the campus one warm afternoon for the second semester as freshman at Columbia and immediately runs into the library so he can play some Brahms record free in the listening booth. Swinburne's right behind him but Angel Boy tells him to wait outside so he can listen to the music undisturbed with his earphones and think. Very intelligent kid of an order you'll see later. But point is, the professor of French Classics at Columbia University at the time, Ronald Mugwump I guess he was, a little fud of some kind I never saw, or cared to look at, ran into the booth where Claude was and said something like 'Where did you come from, you marvelous boy?' You can see what was happening to this kid. And the scene.

Because talk about your Folies Bergère late 1890's *fin de siècle* dray-mas, this was the yellow pages of not only Tristan de Peradventure (whoever he was or will be) but the very yellow decadence of Beardsley, Dowson. Aleister Crowley and the rest. I knew nothing of this at the time. It just turned out that my Johnnie's apartment became the focal point of meetings for the wild *outré* gang of Columbia campus. First she tells me there's this wild new young kid hanging around the West End Bar called Claude who is blond and beautiful and strong and intelligent and comes over to her place to take showers but doesnt try to make her. Strangely, I believe her, and turns out it's true. He's just chased so much he has to hide somewhere, and being a Southern 'scion' of rich family, as she is, and needing the hearty companionship of a good gal protector, he comes there. He finally starts bringing around his girl the rich girl from Westport, Cecily.

Finally I first see him in the West End Bar after waking up from my long nap.

'There he is, there's that marvelous Claude.'

'Looks to me like a mischievous little prick,' I said to Johnnie, and I still think so. But he was okay. He wanted to ship out again, had been a seaman out of New Orleans, maybe ship out with me. He was no fairy and he was strong and wiry and that first night we got really drunk and I dont know whether it was that first night or not, it was, when he told me to get into an empty barrel and then proceeded to roll the barrel down the sidewalks of upper Broadway. A few nights later I do remember we sat in puddles of rain together in a crashing downpour and poured black ink over our hair . . . yelling folk songs and all kindsa songs. I got to like him more and more.

His 'Swinburne' had been a boy scout master in Texas, name of Franz Mueller, who first saw Claude when he joined the boy scouts innocently, wanted to go out in the woods and have fun with camps and scout knives and something to do, fourteen. The scoutmaster fell in love with the boy scout, as usual. Now I'm not a queer, and neither is Claude, but I've got to expand this queer tale. Franz, not a bad guy in himself by the way, had first spent several years in Paris in about 1936 or so and met a young fourteen-year-old French boy who looked exactly like Claude, had fallen in love with him, tried to make him, or corrupt him, or whatever the French or Greeks say, and was deported from France outright, after some kind of investigation. Coming back to America and getting a job as a scoutmaster on weekends, while during the week an instructor in a Louisiana college, who does he see but the same kid, only not French but Anjou French aristocrat boy? He goes crazy. Claude is sent by his rich grandmother to prep school at Andover School right outside Lowell Mass., is followed by red-bearded Swinburne, they throw big parties, Claude is ejected from Andover and doomed forever from going to Yale. He then tries another school. Franz follows him. It isn't that Claude wants Franz to follow him, or that he wants to turn him away, it's just a lot of fun, like one night in Bangor Maine Claude gets aboard the Whitlaw yatch with Kenny Whitlaw (acquaintance of Johnnie's) and they, fifteen, simply pull the plug out and sink the yatch and swim ashore. Pranks and stuff like that. A wild kid. A guy in New Orleans lends him his car, and Claude, fifteen, no license, nothing, wrecks it utterly on Basin Street.

What's amazing about him is his absolute physical male and

spiritual, too, beauty. Slant-eyed, green eyes, complete intelligence, language pouring out of him, Shakespeare reborn almost, golden hair with a halo around it, old queens when they saw him in Greenwich Village bars wrote odes to him starting 'O fair-haired Grecian lad.' Naturally all the girls went for him, too, and even this old dreamy hardhearted seaman and footballer, Jack, got to like him and drop tears over him.

I remember meeting a fella from Virginia gentry once told me all them New Orleans boys had tragedy written in their hearts. Even Negroes from New Orleans aint got too much luck, like Jelly Roll Morton's luck shows (invents jazz and dies broke), or poor white boys like Big Slim, but what better luck is there than Louis Armstrong's?

Anyway, the old Classical prof runs in there and wants to know all about Claude, who's trying to listen to Brahms, Franz has to run in and rescue him, by some hook or crook Claude meets Johnnie and finds that he can literally (that means really) hide out in her pad. And when I'm back with my black leather jacket from New Orleans, it makes no difference, he's been sleeping on the couch all the time anyway with Cecily. So begins our kind of apartment club.

He looks at me and says 'You're trying to write all the time but every time I see that you cant think of what to write, you look constipated.'

I give him the sidelook.

He comes in thru the roof, that is, from the roof down the fire escape, in the rainy night, with gunshots and shouts below. 'What's that?'

'Some kind of error, a fight in the bar, cops chasing, I ran over fences, you know I cant hurt anybody I'm too small . . . Now I'll sleep. Then I'll take a shower. Trouble with you Duluoz is, you're a hardhearted mean old tightfisted shitass no good Canuck who shoulda had his ass froze in the hearts of Manitoba where you and your bad blood belong, you Indian no-good bully.'

'I'm no bully.'

'Well bully for you, give me a drink.'

I saw he was trying to cow me with his language as he wasnt about to start with anything else in those days. But then I saw he was seein flaws in me I shoulda seen myself. But then I saw he was just a mischievous little prick.

So, books everywhere, he's actually attending classes at Columbia, when he hears my stories about Piccadilly in London he orders me more or less to write his composition paper for English composition, which I do, a story about some of the adventures there, and he gets an A the rat. He says 'My grandfather invented the steamer trunk and I s'pose your grandfather put potatoes in em.'

'Yep.' But he looks at me sideways because he can see what's behind all of that, going back beyond the potatoes and Canada, to, yes, Scotland and Ireland and Cornwall and Wales and Isle of Man and Brittany. Celts can spot each other. Pronounce that.

IX

Also, as he's interested in symbolistic art, Surrealism not so much but, say, Modigliani, the French Impressionists, all that darkness of my night-sea life seems to disappear and in the spring sunshine it seems that colors are being splashed over my soul. (Now *that* sounds like Swinburne!)

Anyway, one afternoon he and Johnnie are off to study nude models with George Grosz, they'd asked me to try it one afternoon, I went there and sat there as all the kids sketched and George Grosz talked, and there she was, a naked brunette looking me right in the eye and I had to leave and say to Claude at the door: 'What do you think I am?'

'What's that, a voyeur old boy?' And so they're out doing that and I've taken a shower and the door of Johnnie's apartment knocks and I open it and there's a tall thin fella in a seersucker jacket, with Franz Swinburne behind him. I say 'What?' Swinburne, already talked to me in the bar with Claude, says:

'This is the Will Hubbard they were telling you about, from out west?'

'Well.'

'He's spent a lot of time in New Orleans too, in other words, old friend of mine and Claude's. Just wants to ask you about how to ship out in the Merchant Marine.'

'Not in the service?'

'Oh no,' says Will looking around with a toothpick in his mouth, and removing it to give me the once-over, 'just 4-F, phnunk.' 'Phnunk' is where he blows out of his nose a kind of sinus condition, and also English lord expression, as his name is very old.

X

Someday, in fact, I'll write a book about Will just by himself, so ever onward the Faustían soul, só especially about Wilson Holmes Hubbard I dont have to wait till he dies to complete his story, he above all's best left marching on with that aggressive swing of his arms thru the Medinas of the world . . . well, a long story, wait.

But in this case he's come to see me about Claude, but saying it's about the Merchant Marine. 'But what was your last job?' I ask.

'Bartender in Newark.'

'Before that?'

'Exterminator in Chicago. Of bedbugs, that is.

'Just came to see ya,' he says, 'to find out about how to get papers, to ship out.' But when I had heard about 'Will Hubbard' I had pictured a stocky dark-haired person of peculiar intensity because of the reports about him, the peculiar directedness of his actions, but here he had come walking into my pad tall and bespectacled and thin in a seersucker suit as tho he's just returned from a compound in Equatorial Africa where he'd sat at dusk with a martini discussing the peculiarities . . . Tall, 6 foot 1, strange, inscrutable because ordinary-looking (scrutable), like a shy bank clerk with a partrician thinlipped cold bluelipped face, blue eyes saying nothing behind steel rims and glass, sandy hair, a little wispy, a little of the wistful German Nazi youth as his soft hair fluffles in the breeze – So unobtrusive as he sat on the hassock in the middle of Johnnie's livingroom and asking me dull questions about how to get sea papers . . . Now there's my first secret intuitive vision about Will, that he had come to see me not because I was a principal character now in the general drama of that summer but because I was a seaman and thus a seaman type to whom one asked about shipping out as a preliminary means of digging the character of said seaman type. He didn't come to me expecting a jungle of organic depths, or a jumble of souls, which b'God on every level level I was as you can see, dear wifey and dear reader, he pictured a merchant seaman who would belong in the merchant seaman category and show blue eyes beyond that and a few choice involuntary remarks, and execute a few original acts and go away into endless space a flat, planed 'merchant seaman' – And being queer, as he was, but didn't admit in those days, and never bothered me, he expected a little more on the same general level of shallowness. Thus, on that fateful afternoon in July of 1944 in New York City, as he sat on the hassock questioning me about sea papers (Franz smiling behind him), and as I, fresh from that shower, sat in the easy chair in just my pants, answering, began a relationship which, if he thought it was to remain a flat plane of an 'interesting blue-eyed dark-haired good-looking seaman who knows Claude,' wasnt destined to remain so (a point of pride with me in that I've worked harder at this legend business than they have) – Okay, joke . . . Tho, on that afternoon, he had no reason to surmise anything otherwise than shoptalk from your aunt to mine, 'Yes, you've got to go now and get your Coast Guard pass first, down near the Battery . . .'

XI

The fascination of Hubbard at first was based on the fact that he was a key member of this here new 'New Orleans School' and thus this was nothing more than this handful of rich sharp spirits from that town led by Claude, their falling star Lucifer angel boy demon genius, and Franz the champeen cynical hero, and Will as observer weighted with more irony than the lot of em, and others like Will's caustic charming buddy Kyles Elgins who with him at Harvard had 'collaborated on an ode' to 'orror which showed the *Titanic* sinking and the ship's captain (Franz) shotting a woman in a kimono to put on her said kimono and get on a life boat with the women and children and when heroic spray-ey men shout 'Madame will you take this fourteen-year-old boy on your lap?' (Claude) Captain Franz smirks 'Why of course' and meanwhile Kyles' paranoid uncle who lisps is hacking away at the gunwales with a Peruvian machete as reaching hands rise from the waters 'Ya buntha bathadts!' and a Negro orchestra is playing the *Star-Spangled Banner* on the sinking ship . . . a story they wrote together at Harvard, which, when I first saw it, gave me to realize that this here New Orleans clique was the most evil and intelligent buncha bastards and shits in America but had to admire in my admiring youth. Their style was dry, new to me, mine had been the misty-nebulous New England Idealist style tho (as I say) my saving grace in their eyes (Will's, Claude's especially) was the materialist Canuck taciturn cold skepticism all the picked-up Idealism in the world of books couldnt hide . . . 'Duluoz is a shit posing as an angel.' . . . 'Duluoz is very funny.' – Kyles I didnt get to meet till years later, doesnt matter here, but that Virginia gentryman did say (Clancy by name): 'Everybody who comes from New Orleans in that group is marked with tragedy.' Which I found to be true.

XII

The second time I saw Will he was sitting around talking with Claude and Franz in his apartment in the Village with that terrible intelligence and style of theirs, Claude chewing his beer-glass and spitting out slivers, Franz following suit with I s'pose store bought teeth, and Hubbard long and lean in his summer seersucker suit emerging from the kitchen with a plate of razor blades and lightbulbs says, 'I've something real nice in the way of delicacies my mother sent me this week, hmf hmf hmf' (when he laughs with compressed lips hugging his belly), I sit there with peasant frown getting my first glimpse of the Real Devil (the three of em together).

But I could see that Hubbard vaguely admired me.

But what was this with me with a thousand things to do?

But I bite my lips when I hear the word 'marvel' and I shudder with excitement when I hear Will say 'marvelous' because when he says it, it really's bound to be truly marvelous. 'I just saw a *marvelous* scene in a movie this afternoon,' with his face all flushed, exalted, rosy, fresh from wind or rain where he walked, his glasses a little wet or smoky from the heat of his enthused eyeballs, 'this character in this awful beat movie about sex downtown, you see him with a great horse serum injector giving himself a big bang of dope then he rushes up and grabs this blonde in his arms and lifts her up and goes rushing off into a dark field goin "Yip Yip Yipp ee!" ' But I have to ask a thousand questions to know why Will is so glad:

'A dark field?'

'Well it's one of those dreary movies, real old and full of snaps in the screen, you can hear the rolls clank and blank up in the projection booth so it's some kind of evening or dusk or somethin, a great endless horizon you see him growin smaller and smaller as he rushes off with his girl, Yip Yip Yippeeee, finally you just dont hear him anymore . . . '

'He's gone way across that field?' asks I, looking for mines and touchdowns and Galsworthy and the Book of Job . . . and I'm amazed by Will's way of saying 'Yip Yip Yip Pee' which he does with a cracky falsetto voice and never can say without bending over to hold his belly and compress his lips and go 'Hm hm hm,' the high suppressed surprised thoroughly gleeful laugh he has, or at least laughy. One afternoon probably when he'd arrived from Harvard for the summer, 1935 or so, with Kyles downtown kicked a few hours around with a sex movie in a cheap joint around Canal Street, these two great American sophisticates you might say sitting well up front (expensively dressed as always, like Loeb and Leopold) in a half-empty movie full of bums and early Thirties tea heads from the gutters of New Orleans, laughing in that way of theirs (actually Kyles' laugh, which Will had imitated since their childhood together?) and finally the great scene where the mad dope addict picks up the monstrous syringe and gives himself a big smack of H, and grabs the girl (who is some dumb moveless Zombie of the story and walks hands at her sides), he wild-haired and screaming with rain in the plip-plip of the ruined old film rushes off, her legs and hair dangling like Fay Wray in the arms of King Kong, across the mysterious dark endless Faustian horizon of Will's vision, happy like an Australian jackrabbit, his feet and heels flashing snow: Yip Yip, Yip eee, till, as Will says ,his 'Yips' get dimmer and dimmer as distance diminishes his eager all-fructified final goal-joy, for what would be greater than that, Will thinks, than to have your arms full of joy and a good shot in you and off you run into eternal gloom to flip all you want in infinity, that vision he must've had of that movie that day in that manse of his seat, legs crossed demurely, and so I picture him and Kyles sprawled then in laughter, broken up, on the floor, in tweed coats or something, unwristwatchable, 1935, laughing Haw haw haw and even repeating Yip Yip Yippeeeee after the scene has long passed but they cant forget it (a classic even greater than their *Titanic* short story). Then it is I see Will Hubbard that night after dinner at home in New Orleans with in-laws and walking under the trees and lawn lights of suburbia, going, probably, to see some clever friend, or even Claude, or Franz, 'I just saw a marvelous scene in a movie today, God, Yip Yip Yippee!'

Here I say 'And what did the guy look like?'

'Wild, bushy hair . . . '

'And he said Yip Yip Yippee as he rushed off?'

'With a girl in his arms.'

'Across the dark field?'

'Some kinda field – '

'What was this field?'

'My *Gawd* – we're getting literary yet, don't bother me with such idiotic questions, a *field*' – he says 'field' with an angry or impatient shrieking choke – 'like it's a PIELD' – calming down – 'a field . . . for God's sake you see him rushing off into the dark horizon – '

'Yip Yip Yippee,' I say, hoping Will will say it again.

'Yip Yip Yippee,' he says, just for me, and so this is Will, tho at first I really paid less attention to him than he did to me, which is a strange thing to reconsider because he always said 'Jack, you're really very funny.' But in those days this truly tender and curious soul looked on me (after that flat seaman phase) as some kind of intensity truth-guy with pride, owing to that scene one night the later week when we were all sitting on a park bench on Amsterdam Avenue, hot July night, Will, Franz, Claude, his girl Cecily, me, Johnnie, and Will says to me 'Well why don't you wear a merchant seaman uniform man like you said you wore in London for your visit there, and get a lot of soft entries into things, it's wartime isn't it, and here you go around in T-shirt and chino pints, or paints, or pants, and nobody knows you're a serviceman proud, should we say?' and I answered: ' 'Tsa finkish thing to do' which he remembered and apparently took to be a great proud statement coming straight from the saloon's mouth, as he, a timid (at the time) middleclass kid with rich parents had always yearned to get away from his family's dull 'suburban' life (in Chicago) into the real rich America of saloons and George Raft and Runyon characters, virile, sad, factual America of his dreams, tho he took my statement as an opportunity to say, in reply:

'It's a finkish world.'

Harbinger of the day when we'd become fast friends and he'd hand me the full two-volume edition of Spengler's *Decline of the West* and say 'EEE di fy your mind, my boy, with the grand actuality of Fact.' When he would become my great teacher in the night. But in those early days, and at this about our third meeting, hearing me say, ' 'Tsa finkish thing to do' (which for me was just an ordinary statement at the time based on the way seamen and my wife and I looked proudly and defiantly on the world of un-like-us 'finks,' a disgusting thing in itself granted, but that's what it was), hearing me say that, Will apparently marveled secretly, whether he remembers it now or not, and with timid and tender curiosity on top of that, his pale eyes behind the spectacles looking mildly startled. I think it was about then he rather vaguely began to admire me, either for virile independent thinking, or 'rough trade' (whatever they think), or charm, or maybe broody melancholy philosophic Celtic unexpected depth, or simple ragged shiny frankness, or hank of hair, or reluctance in the revelation of interesting despair, but he remembered it well (we discussed it years later in Africa) and it was years later that I marveled over that, wishing we would turn time back and I could amaze him again with such unconscious simplicity, as our forefathers gradually unfolded and he began to realize I was really one, one, of Briton blood, and especially, after all, one kind of a funny imbecilic saint. With that maternal care he brooded over my way of saying it, looking away, down, frowning, ' 'Tsa finkish thing to do,' in that now (to me) 'New Orleans way of Claude's,' snively, learned, pronouncing the consonants with force and the vowels with that slight 'eu' or 'eow' also you hear spoken in that curious dialect they speak in Washington D.C. (I am trying to describe completely indescribable materials) but you say 'deu' or 'deuo' and you say 'f' as tho it was being spat from your lazy lips. So Will sits by me on the bench in that irrecoverable night with mild amazement going 'hm hm hm' and 'It's a finkish world' and he's instructing me seriously, looking with blank and blink interested eyes for the first time into mine. And only because he knew little about me then, amazed, as 'familiarity breeds contempt' and bread on the waters there's a lotta fish after it.

Where is he tonight? Where am I? Where are you?

XIII

O Will Hubbard in the night! A great writer today he is, he is a shadow hovering over western literature, and no great writer ever lived without that soft and tender curiosity, verging on maternal care, about what others think and say, no great writer ever packed off from this scene on earth without amazement like the amazement he felt because I was myself.

T'all strange 'Old Bull' in his gray seersucker suit sitting around with us on a hot summernight in old lost New York of 1944, the grit in the sidewalk shining the same sad way in 'tween lights as I would see it years later when I would travel across oceans to see him just and just that same sad hopeless grit and my mouth like grit and myself trying to explain it to him: 'Will, why get excited about anything, the grit is the same everywhere?'

'The grit is the same everywhere? What on EARTH are you talkin about, Jack, really you're awfully funny, hm h mf hmf?' holding his belly to laugh. 'Whoever heard of such a thing?'

'I mean I saw the grit where we sat years ago, to me it's a symbol of your life.'

'My LIFE? My dear fellow my life is perfectly free of grit, dearie. Let us relegate this subject to the I-Dont-Wanta-Hear-About-It Department. And order another drink . . . *Really.*'

'It blows in dreary winds outside the bars where you believe and believingly bend your head with the gray light to explain something to someone . . . it blows in the endless dusts of atomic space.'

'My GAWD, I'm not going to buy you another drink if you get LITERARY!'

XIV

At this time I'm writing about he was a bartender down on Sixth Avenue (Avenue of the Americas, yet). (Okay). How my head used to marvel in those days, tug at my heartstrings, break almost, when I thought over what he meant, when he said where he worked '*There were tables with chairs where you could sit and look at the sidewalk if you wanted to.*' The utter dismalness of poor Will (I pick on him in vengeance about my own present emptiness, so dont get worried). That Harlequin hopelessness cognizing this, so that it seems as if my whole life I spend facing one way seeing endless interesting panoramas and he, Will, by God, has been placed on just such a chair, to sigh, facing the other way, where nothing happens, his long gray face hopeless. With a mince, a little uplook of his eyes playfully to a hoped-for watcher sympathetic to his plights, he sits, longlegged at the chair, looking at the empty sidewalk 'where there's nothing to look at,' by which I'd say that bloody planet he come from musta been destitute of life. ('I'm an agent from another planet,' he said.) He has in fact a destitute rocklike lifelessness, s'reason why he kept pouncing on the subject 'Blab blub you young men should go out and experience LIFE steada sittin in rooms in your blue jeans wonderin when the rain'll come again, why when I was your age . . .'

He was nine years older than me but I never noticed it.

The central vision of Will, really, is we're sitting in a yard in two chairs, later, in Morocco, and I'm reading him a letter I just wrote to a lady, wishing his opinion on whether I expressed myself politely fitly or fitly politely, one, reading: 'Discriminating readers would be interested in reading what happened so they could form in their mind an idea of Buddhism in America on the practical level.'

'How could it be any better'n at, Master?' jokes Will, quite pleased that he doesn't have to vouchsafe an opinion. So then we just sit and say nothing, I get frowning a little wondering what's with 'Master' but suddenly we're just sitting there peacefully not bothering each other at all, as usual, simply blue-eyed Will, in fact both of us listening to sounds of the afternoon or even of Friday Afternoon in the Universe, the soundless hum of inside silence which he claims comes from trees but I been out there in that treeless desert in the night and heard it . . . but we're happy. And suddenly Will says: 'Oh God, I have to go to the laundry tomorrow,' and suddenly he laughs because he realizes he just sounded like a whiny old lady sittin on the porch in Orlanda Floridy and so he says 'My Gawd, I sound like a dreary old Ka-*Ween!*'

BOOK TWELVE

I

Anyway meanwhile there's this fantastic Claude rushing across the campus followed by at least twelve eager students, among them Irwin Garden, Lombard Crepnicz, Joe Amsterdam, I think Arnie Jewel, all famous writers today, he's hurling back epigrammatical epithets at them and jumping over bushes to get away from them, and way back in the ivied corners of the quadrangle you might see poor Franz Mueller slowly taking up the rear in his long meditative strides. He might even be carrying a new book for Claude to read, see the myth of Philoctetes and Neoptolemus, which he will tell Claude reminds him so much of their own relationship, the healthy young god and the sick old warrior, and all such twaddle. I tell you it was awful, I have notes about everything that was going on, Claude kept yelling stuff about a 'New Vision' which he'd gleaned out of Rimbaud,Nietzsche, Yeats, Rilke, Alyosha Karamazov, anything. Irwin Garden was his closest student friend.

I was sitting in Johnnie's apartment one day when the door opened and in walks this spindly Jewish kid with horn-rimmed glasses and tremendous ears sticking out, seventeen years old, burning black eyes, a strangely deep mature voice, looks at me, says 'Discretion is the better part of valor.'

'Aw where's my food!' I yelled at Johnnie, because that's precisely all I had on my mind at the moment he walked in.

Turns out it took years for Irwin to get over a certain fear of the 'brooding football artist yelling for his supper in big daddy chair' or some such. I didn't like him anyway. One look at him, a few days of knowing him to avouch my private claim, and I came to the conclusion he was a lecher who wanted everybody in the world to take a bath in the same huge bathtub which would give him a chance to feel legs under the dirty water. This is precisely the image I had of him on first meeting. Johnnie also felt he was repugnant in this sense. Claude liked him, always has, and was amused, entertained, they wrote poems together, manifestoes of the 'New Vision,' rushed around with books, had bull sessions in Claude's Dalton Hall room where he hardly ever slept, took Johnnie and Cecily out to ballets and stuff downtown when I was out in Long Island visiting my folks. They tell me that Claude started a commotion in the ballet balcony, the ushers were coming with flashing lights, he led 'the gang' out thru some strange door and they found themselves in the labyrinths underneath the Metropolitan Opera House running into dressing rooms some of them occupied, out again, around, back and forth and triumphantly emerged somewhere on Seventh Avenue and got away. That on the way home, in the crowded subway all four of them laughing and gay, Claude suddenly yelled out over everybody's heads: 'WHEN THEY PUT CATTLE IN CARS THEY COPULATE!' All such Joe College stuff. Not bad style. In that same light Claude sorta looked at me as some kind of lout which was true.

Franz Mueller was jealous of Irwin, of me, of anybody Claude had anything to do with, especially of the blond college girl Cecily ('a bourgeois kitten' Claude called her) and one lilac dusk when we were all exhausted and asleep in the mad pad on the sixth floor, Will Hubbard and Franz came in quietly, saw Claude on the couch in Cecily's arms, and Mueller said: 'Doesnt he look pale, as tho he were being sucked dry by a vampire?'

One night the same two came in, but found an empty apartment, so to amuse himself that no-good pederast Mueller took my little cat, wrapped Hubbard's tie around its neck, and tried to hang it from the lamp: a little kitty. Will Hubbard immediately took it down, undamaged and just slightly hurt I guess in the neck, I don't know, I wasnt there, I would have thrown that man out of the window. It was only told to me much later on.

II

Then sometimes Mueller would catch me alone and talk to me long and earnestly over beers but always the same intention: to find out what Claude did or said behind his back, that is, behind his knowing, and who he saw, what, where, all the anguished questioning of a lover. He even patted me on the back. And he gave me detailed instructions to say this, that, to arrange meetings one way or the other. Claude was avoiding him more than ever.

Their past was unbelievable. It was exactly like Rimbaud and Verlaine. In Tulane U. Claude became depressed, blocked up all his apartment windows, put a pillow in the oven, his head on the pillow, and turned on the gas. But the amazing thing is that Mueller happened at that moment to be riding by on horseback, of all things, with a socialite girl, of all things (he was always after making women so he could get closer to Claude, this was one of Claude's casual dolls). Mueller quite accidentally got off the horse, smelled the gas at the door, broke it down and dragged the kid out in the hall.

On another occasion, after that and before Bowling Green or Andover or someplace, they actually got Coast Guard passes and seaman's papers and shipped out of Baltimore or someplace but were thrown off the ship in New York on some beef I never got clear. Wherever Claude went, Mueller followed, Claude's mother even tried to have the man arrested. At the time, Hubbard, Franz's closest friend, remonstrated again and again with him to go off someplace and find another boy more amenable, go to sea, go to South America, live in the jungle, go marry Cindy Lou in Virginia (Mueller came from aristocrats somewhere). No. It was the romantic and fatal attachment: I could understand it myself because for the first time in my life I found myself stopping in the street and thinking: 'Wonder where Claude is now? What's he doing right now?' and going off to find him. I mean, like that feeling you get during a love affair. It was a very nostalgic *Season in Hell*. There was the nostalgia of Johnnie and me in love, Claude and Cecily in love, Franz in love with Claude, Hubbard hovering like a shadow, Garden in love with Claude and Hubbard and me and Cecily and Johnnie and Franz, the war, the second front (which occurred just before this time), the poetry, the soft city evenings, the cries of Rimbaud!, 'New Vision!,' the great Götterdammerung, the love song 'You Always Hurt the One

You Love,' the smell of beers and smoke in the West End Bar, the evenings we spent on the grass by the Hudson River on Riverside Drive at 116th Street watching the rose west, watching the freighters slide by. Claude saying to me (whispering): 'Gotta get away from Mueller. Let's you and me ship out. Dont tell a soul about this. Let's try to get a ship to France. That one there's probably going to France. We'll land at the second front. We'll walk to Paris: I'll be a deaf mute and you speak country French and we'll pretend we're peasants. When we get to Paris it will probably be on the verge of being liberated. We'll find symbols saturated in the gutters of Montmartre. We'll write poetry, paint, drink red wine, wear berets. I feel like I'm in a pond that's drying out and I'm about to suffocate. I s'pose you understand. If you dont, let's just do it anyway. Franz he's desperate enough to kill me anyway.'

III

So during the days we now started to hang around the N.M.U. Hall waiting for our turn to come up for a ship. Evenings, we rejoined Hubbard at his apartment around the corner down Seventh Avenue to Greenwich Village because he was working, had his monthly trust fund check and always bought us fine dinners, in Romley Marie's, in San Remo's, in Minetta's, and inevitably Franz would always find us and join in. Claude was a great one for what André Gide called the *acte gratuite* ('the gratuitous act') the doing of an act just for the hell of it. Seeing his veal Parmesan didnt taste too hot in one of the restaurants he simply picked up the plate, said 'This is crap,' and threw it back over his shoulder with just a flick of the wrist, no expression, suavely picking up his glass of wine to sip, and nobody saw him do it except us. The waiter even rushed up apologetically to pick up the pieces. Or in a diner at dawn he'd hold up dripping egg white from his fork and say to waitress dryly 'You call this minute-and-a-half eggs?' Or, when we had a big steak in Will's room, he'd pick it up before Will could start to cut it into four sections and start ronching on it with greasy fingers and seeing that we were all amused, would start growling like a tiger, and then Franz would jump into the act and try to wrestle the steak from his fingers and they'd rip it apart with their claws. 'Hey,' I'd yell, 'my steak!'

'Ah The Louse, all you think about is food, you beefy clout!'

One time he leaped up on Jane Street to grab at overhanging branches, in the evening, and Franz sighed to Will: 'Isnt he wonderful?' Or another time vaulted over a fence and Franz tried it too, missed, 'You could hear,' as Hubbard says, 'his joints creak.' (In the effort to keep up with a young man like that, nineteen.)

It was really sad. I didn't know about the cat then, anyway, luckily.

Another evening, Claude saw a hole in the sleeve of Will's seersucker suit, stuck his finger in it, and ripped half the coat off. His bones creaking, Franz jumped in and grabbed the other sleeve and yanked it off, wrapped it around Hubbard's head, ripped up the back of the coat over his head, then they stood around making strips of it, tied them together, and made a festoon over chandeliers and bookcases all over the room. It was done in perfect good humor, Hubbard just sat there with his lips compressed, going 'thfunk' down his nose, like a bunch of Luftwaffe blades on a night off they all had all the right in the world to do anything they felt like. And of course to a 'Lowell boy' like me, destroying a coat was strange but to them . . . they all came from well-to-do families.

IV

Mueller finally got wind of what we were doing, would trail us down 14th Street and around the corner to the union hall, hiding in doorways, finally we found him in the union hall with a pleading look saying: 'Look, I knew what you were up to, so I did something about it: I arranged a lunch for the three of us with the girl upstairs who's in charge of shipping calls and such. I talked to her yesterday before you got here and this afternoon, look at this, I swiped a dozen sailing cards off her desk and here they are, Claude, put em in your pocket. Now listen: I can do this and a whole lot of other things, with my help we can all ship out the three of us in no time at all, there wont be any of this waiting around . . .'

Naturally, when Franz is out of earshot, Claude says to me: 'But the whole point of shipping out is to get away from him. *Now* what do I do?'

That night we all wind up, with the girls, and Will too, at Minetta Lane, where old Joe Gould, leaning his bearded chin on his cane, looks at Cecily and says: 'I'm a Lesbian, I love women.' So we all go to a harmless little party on MacDougal Street, eluding Franz somehow as he's going around the corner to find something, we're sitting there in that typical New York style latenight party jabber and we hear the marquee of the bar downstairs groaning and cracking, and then we see that someone is climbing it, coming into the window, boom, it's Franz Mueller.

In fact, as things got worse and Franz grew more desperate, one night (according to what he told Will) he climbed the fire escape in back of Dalton Hall and went up to Claude's third-floor window, the window was wide-open, he went in and found Claude asleep in the dark of the moon in the window. He stood there, he said, for about a half hour, just looking down at him silently, reverently, hardly breathing. Then he went out. As he was jumping the fence he was caught by the apartment hotel guard and hauled into the front foyer at gunpoint and harangued by the night clerk, the cops were called, he had to wave papers and explain, they had to call Claude and wake him up and come down and confirm that he had been drinking with Mueller in his room all night. 'My Gawd,' said Hubbard laughing with compressed lips, 's'posing you'd-a found the wrong room and hovered over a perfect stranger.'

V

In a burst of angry inspiration I went straight to the big-shot desk in the union and said I was waiting an awful long time for a ship, 'So what? Let's see your old discharges,' Suddenly he whooped when he saw the old *Dorchester* discharge: 'The *Dorchester*? You were on the *Dorchester*? Fer krissakes why dint you tell me, any ex-crewman of that *Dorchester* gets special treatment around here, I can tell you that, brother! Here! Here's your cards. Go down and give them to Blacky, you'll get a ship in a day or two. Glad times, brother.' I was amazed. Claude and I had opportunity to rejoice. We decided to got out to Long Island and see my folks.

In the bar across the street my father, in white August shirt-sleeves of beery night, looked at Claude crossways and said 'All right then, I'm going to buy a rich man's son a drink.' A shadow crossed Claude's face. He told me later he never liked that. 'If that isnt typical of the Duluozes I'll never know what is. Why did he have to bring that up just then? You clods of romantic gas land.'

'I dont like that Claude,' says me Pa to me privately that night, 'he looks like a mischievous young punk. He's going to get you in trouble. So will that little Johnnie Podlie of yours, and that Hubbard I keep hearing about. What are you doing hanging around with such a lowdown bunch as that? Cant you find good young friends anymore?' Imagine telling me that in the midst of my 'Symbolist Poet' period, with Claude and me yelling at the dark bridge waters: '*Plonger au fond du gouffre, ciel ou enfer, qu'importe?* [to plunge to the bottom of the abyss, Heaven or Hell, what matter?]' and all those other Rimbaud sayings, and Nietzschean, and here we are guaranteed to sail in no time at all and we're going to be Symbolist Isidore Ducasses and Apollinaires and Baudelaires and 'Lautréamonts' altogether in very Paris itself.

Years later I met an infantryman who was in the second front at exactly this time, who said 'When I heard you and that de Maubris guy were going to jump ship in France and walk to Paris to become poets, behind the lines, pretending to be peasants, I wanted to find you and bump your heads together.' But he forgets that we really intended to do it and almost did, and this was before the St-Lô breakthrough, too.

VI

The call did come in one afternoon. I'd written a paper for Claude (who was more intelligent but lazier than I was), he'd handed it in, in hopes of getting some kind of appeasing from the professors at Columbia, and off we went to the union hall and grabbed our call. The call was 'a Liberty bound for the second front.' We rushed off to Hoboken via the subway, a cross-town walk to North River, and the ferry. But when we got to the pier they told us she had shifted to a pier on Brooklyn at the foot of Joralemon Street (again!). So we had to wangle our way all the way back, across the river on the ferry, in heavy smoke now as there was a waterfront fire on the Jersey side (a smoke I felt was surprisingly thick, inauspicious, commenting on something that was going to go wrong), then down to Brooklyn and down to the ship. There she was.

But as we were crossing the long pier with our passes and papers all clear, and our gear on our back, singing 'Hi hee ho Davey Jones' and 'Whattaya Do with a Drunken Sailor Ear-Lie in the Mawning?' and all the seaman songs, a bunch of guys from our ship came marching up the other direction and said 'You guys going on the S.S. *Robert Hayes*? Well, dont sign on. I'm the bosun. I'm also the delegate on the ship. There's something wrong with the chief mate, he's a Fascist, we're going to see about having him replaced. Go on board, occupy your foc'sle, stow your gear, eat, but DONT sign on.'

I should have known better because when we came up the gangplank we were met in the alleyway by the port official who said: 'Allright, stash your gear, boys, and go into the captain's office to sign on for this voyage.' That sounded more like it. But Claude and I wondered what to do really. We wondered if we'd be thrown off the ship by the union if we did sign. We hung around the foc'sle discussing it. We put away our clothes and went down to the stores below, found a huge can of ice-cold milk (dairy can five gallons) and drank most of it, chawing on cold roast beef meanwhile. We walked around the ship trying to figure out the complicated lines and ropes and winches. 'We'll learn!'

On the poop deck we looked toward the towers of Manhattan, right across the river, and Claude said, 'Well, by God, at last I'll be free of F.M.'

But just then a great big redheaded mate who looked exactly like Franz Mueller without a beard came storming at us and said 'Are you the two boys who just walked on board?'

'Yeh.'

'Well werent you told to go sign up in the captain's mess?'

'Yeh . . . but the bosun told us to wait.'

'Oh did he now?'

'Yeh, he said there was some kind of beef . . . '

'Listen wise guy, beef is right, I saw you two bums go down in the stores and eat beef and drink milk, that's your beef. Leave some money on this ship to pay for that beef, pick up your gear, and get off. You're fired along with the bosun and all the rest of you no-good bastards. We're going to get a crew on this ship if it's the last thing I do you cocksucking no-good little pearly-assed punks.'

'But we didnt know.'

'Never mind the we didnt know, you knew well enough you sign on a ship or you dont, now get in that foc'sle, get that gear, and beat it and beat it good!' He was such a big guy I was afraid to get into explanations, he just didnt want explanations, also he scared me, as for Claude he was as pale as a sheet.

Here we went, five minutes later, straggling back down the long cool pier with our gear on our backs, headed for the hot sun of the hot murderous streets of New York at four o'clock in the afternoon.

So sunny hot, in fact, we had to stop for Cokes with our last few dimes at a little store. Claude looked at me. I looked down. I should have known better. On the other hand, what was that silly bosun up to? Trying to get his own friends on the ship? And it was bound for the second front, too . . . war bonus pay and no more danger from German artillery, either. I'll never know.

VII

I'm neglecting Johnnie of course, who in those days looked about what Mamie Van Doren looks like today, same build, height, with the same almost buck-toothed grin, that eagering grin and laugh and eagerness entire that makes the eyes slit but at same time makes the cheeks fuller and endows the lady with the promise that she will look good all her life: no lines of drawnness.

As Claude and I return from that long foolish day, throw our gear on the floor, the apartment is all darkened, sun going down, Union Theological Seminary bell tolling, nobody in there but Cecily sleeping on the sofa in a litter of books, bottles, empties, butts, manuscripts. Without turning on the light Claude immediately lies down beside her on the couch and holds her tight. I go into Johnnie's (and my) bedroom and lie down and take a nap. Grinning Johnnie comes in about an hour later with some food she bought after borrowing a few bucks from a funeral director she knows and we have a gay supper in our bare feet. 'Ha ha ha,' chides Johnnie, 'so you two bastards aint goin to France after all! I shouldna wasted my good film on those pictures I took of you yesterday afternoon thinkin I'd never see either one of you again.'

These pictures, in the sunlight of the plaza of fieldstones in front of Low Memorial Library, Columbia University, show Claude and I leaning casually, one leg up on fountainside, smoking, frowning, tough guy seadogs. Another one is of Claude alone with arms hanging at sides, with butt in hand, looking like a child of the rainbow, as Irwin later called him in a poem.

Some rainbow.

Claude and I later go down to the West End Bar to drink a few beers and discuss our next attempt at the union hall. He gets into a big metaphysical argument with Roy Plantagenet or somebody and I go home to sleep some more, or read, or take a shower. As

I'm passing the St Paul's Chapel on the campus, and going down the old wood steps they had there, here comes Mueller bounding eagerly, bearded, in the gloom, up my way, sees me, says: 'Where's Claude?'

'In the West End.'

'Thanks. I'll see ya later!' And I watch him rush off to his death.

VIII

Because at dawn I'm woke up from my sleep at the side of Johnnie, it's been so hot we had to open the Claude sofa and spread it afar with wide sheets, in the breeze crossway of windows, and there's Claude standing over me with his blond hair in his eyes, shaking me by the arm. But I'm not really asleep either. He says 'Well I disposed of the old man last night.' And I know exactly what he means. Not that I was Ivan Karamazov to his Smerdyakov but I knew. But I said:

'Why'd you go and do that?'

'No time for that now, I've still got the knife and his glasses covered with blood. Wanta come with me see what we can do to dump em?'

'What in the hell didja go and do that for?' I repeated, sighing, as tho someone'd woke me up with the news of a new leak in the cellar or in the kitchen sink there's another cat turd, but I raise my weary bones like a seaman has to do another watch and I go shower, dress in chinos and T-shirt, and come back to see him standing in the window looking out on the alley bemused. 'What'd you really do?'

'I stabbed him in the heart twelve times with my boy scout knife.'

'What for?'

'He jumped me. He said I love you and all that stuff, and couldnt live without me, and was going to kill me, kill both of us.'

'Last I saw, you were with Plantagenet.'

'Yeh, but he came in, we drank, went down to the Hudson River grass, had a bottle . . . I stripped off his white shirt, tore it into strips, tied rocks with the strips and tied the strips to his arms and legs, took all my clothes off and pushed him in. He wouldnt sink, that's why I had to take my clothes off, after, I had to wade in to my chin level and give him a push. Then he floated off somewhere. Upside down. Then my clothes was there on the grass, dry, it's hot as you know. I put it on, hailed a cab on Riverside Drive and went to ask Hubbard what to do.'

'In the Village?'

'He answered the door in his bathrobe and I handed him a bloody pack of Luckies and said "Have the last cigarette." Like you he seemed to sense what happened, you might say. He put on his best Claude Rains manner and paced up and down. Flushed the Luckies down the toilet. Told me to plead self-defense which is what it was, for god's sake, Jack, I'm going to get the hot seat anyway.'

'No you aint.'

'I've got this here knife, these eyeglasses of poor old Franz ... all he kept sayin was "So this is how Franz Mueller ends." ' He turned away like a seamen turning away to cry but he didnt cry, he couldnt cry, I guess he'd cried enough already. 'Then Hubbard told me to give myself up, call my grandmother and get a good New Orleans lawyer and give myself up. But I just wanted to see you, old boy, have a final drink with you.'

'Okay,' I says, 'I've just picked up three bucks from Johnnie last night, how much you got? We'll go out and get drunk.'

'Hubbard gave me a fiver. Let's go down to Harlem. On the way I can dump the glasses and the knife in the weeds down there in Morningside Park.' In fact we were running down the six flights of stairs as we were saying this and suddenly I thought of poor Johnnie sleeping there, not knowing a thing, so when we hit the street I told Claude to wait a second and I rushed back up the stairs double time, two, three steps at a time, in all that heat, puffing, just to go in and plant a little un-waking kiss on her (that she remembered, she said later) then ran down again to Claude and we took off down 118th and down the stone steps of Morningside Park. All of the rooftops of Harlem and of the Bronx further you could see spewing up heat and smoke of August of 1944. A disgusting heat already in the early morning.

In the bushes down near the bottom I said 'I'll pretend I'm taking a leak here, look around real anxious, to draw attention to anybody watching, and you just bury the glasses and the knife.' By God I had the right instinct, in a previous lifetime it must have been where I learned this, I certainly didnt learn it in this one, but anyway he did just that, kicked some clods, dropped the glasses, kicked clods back over them (rimless, sad) and some leafy twigs and we walked on, hands-a-pockets, wearing just T-shirts and alone the two of us toward the bars of Harlem.

In front of a bar on 125th Street I said 'There, look, a good subway grate, that's where money keeps falling down and little kids put bubblegum on the end of long sticks and gum it up. Drop the knife down in there and let's go in this cool zebra-striped lounge and have a cold beer.' Which he did, but instead of hiding now, in full view of everybody, he dramatically knelt at the grate and let the knife drop from his stiff fingers very dramatically, as tho this was one thing he really didnt want to hide, but it fell, hit the grate, stuck there, he kicked it, and it fell down 6 feet to the gum wrappers and junk below. Nobody who saw him cared anyway. The knife, the boy scout knife I s'pose he had when he was fourteen and joined the boy scouts to learn woodcraft but only ran into the Marquis de Sade scoutmaster, lay there now probably among a stash of dropped heroin, marijuana, other knives, cundroms, what-all. We went into the air-conditioned bar and sat at cool swivel stools and ordered cold beers.

'I'll get the hot seat for sure. I'll burn in Sing Sing. Sing you sinners, boy.'

'Ah come on, Will's right, it's just a question of defending your whole goddamn life from – '

' – 'member that movie we saw last week with Cecily and Johnnie, *Les Grandes Illusions*, Jean Gabin is the peasant soldier, Claude Lebris de la Merde or whatever his name was who wears white gloves, they escape from the German prison camp together? You're Gabin, you're the peasant, and me, my white gloves are starting to chafe.'

'Get off that, my ancestors were Breton barons.'

'You're fulla you know what, I wouldn't look it up even if it was true because I do know they musta been peasantish barons.' But he said it all so kindly, in soft voice, and it didn't matter. 'What we gotta do today is get drunk, borrow some money even, then I'll give myself up in the evening. I'll go home to Mater's sister, as prophesied. I'll get the chair for sure, I'll burn. He died in my arms. So that's the story of Franz Mueller, he kept saying, so that's how it ends, so that's what happened to me. "Happened" mind you, like it already happened before. I shoulda stayed in England where I was born. I stabbed him in the heart, that section here, twelve times. I pushed him in the river with all those rocks. He went off floating with his feet upside down. His head's down below. All those ships goin by. We missed that damned ship in Brooklyn. I knew something would go wrong when we missed that damned ship. That damned first mate with the red hair looked like Mueller.'

'Let's take a subway downtown go see a movie or something.'

'No, let's take a cab go see my psychiatrist. I'll borrow a five from him.' And we went out in the street, hailed a cab immediately hove in sight, rode down to Park Avenue and went into a fancy foyer, up in an elevator, and I waited outside while he went in and confessed to his psychiatrist. He came out with a five-dollar bill and said 'Let's go, he washes his hands. Let's go fast, around the corner and down to Lex. He probably doesnt believe me.'

We kept walking and came to Third Avenue where we saw the movie *Four Feathers* announced on a marquee. 'Let's go in there.' We come in there just about in time for the beginning of J. Arthur Rank's production of said *Four Feathers* in which there is a fellow called Hubbard in the story. We both wince to hear the name in the dialogue. The picture is Technicolor. Suddenly thousands of Fuzzy Wuzzies and English soldiers are hacking and massacring on all sides in the Battle of the Nile near Khartoum.

'They can murder em by the thousands,' says Claude in the dark show.

IX

We come out of there and idle down Fifth Avenue to the Museum of Modern Art where Claude comes to a meditative stop before a portrait by Amedeo Modigliani, for some reason his favorite modern painter. A queer is standing in the back watching Claude intently, drifting around, coming around again to get another look at him. Claude either does or doesnt notice but I do. We stop in front of Tchelitchew's famous painting 'Cache Cache' and delight in all the little touches, of little wombs, little fetuses (feti?), sperm coming out of blossoms, that marvelous painting that was damaged in a fire decades later, or decade and a half. We then go down thru Times Square and down to the N.M.U. Hall just for nostalgia's sake, I guess. Claude says 'That Sabbas of yours used to moon around the streets of New York and Lowell with you, with all his poems, about "Hello Out There" and "We'll Go No More A-Roaming," wish I'd have met him.'

X

We eat hotdogs, have to eat, walk around, come back up Third Avenue, inching back toward his aunt's house at 57th Street thereby, stop in a bar and two sailors accost us asking to know where they can find girls for hire. I tell them the Letters-to-Your-Son Hotel. (At the time, that was right.) Then Claude says 'See this vest I'm wearing, it was Franz's, it's also covered with blood. What I do with it?'

'When we leave the bar just drop it in the gutter, I guess.'

'These white gloves are chafing. You want them, peasant?'

'Okay, hand em over.' He goes through the routine of imaginarily handing me them white gloves, 'in a gesture' as Genet would say, but with me it's just dumb show and he dont know what to do. Allow me grammatical lapses as well laid on clearly in every bar from here to St Petersburg.

XI

So in the Third Avenue late afternoon he just drops the vest (sorta leather) in the gutter, nobody cares, and says: 'Now I go up two blocks alone, turn right to Fifty-Seventh Street, tell my aunt, she calls lawyers on Wall Street, as we've got connections you know, and I dont ever see you anymore.'

'Yes you will.'

'In any case, I'm off now. It's been a grand day, old boy.' And head down he plunges on up the street, fists in pockets, and does that right turn, and just then a big truck saying RUBY SOUTH CAROLINA rumbles and thunders by and I think of hopping it yelling 'Ha haaaa' and getting out of town to go see my South again. But first I gotta go see Johnnie.

But of course the New York police are faster than that. I go see Johnnie, dont tell her anything, but in the evening the door knocks and in saunters real casual-like two plainclothesmen who begin to look in drawers and turn books over. Johnnie yells 'What the hell is this?'

'Claude has confessed he killed Franz last night on the river.'

'Killed Franz? How? Why didnt you tell me? Is that why you kissed me when you left with him this morning? Tell these guys I think Mueller deserved it!'

'Easy young lady. Anything around here?' asks the cop, looking at me with frank blue eyes.

'Just a simple case of self-defense. Nothin to hide.'

'You're coming with us, you know that dont you?'

'For what?'

'Material witness. Dont you know that when someone confesses a homicide to you, you're supposed to tell the police right off? And where is the murder weapon?'

'We dropped it in a grate in Harlem.'

'Well there you are, you're an accessory after the fact. We'll take you down to the local precinct, but wait a coupla fifteen minutes or so, there's some photographers down there waiting to take your picture.'

'Picture? Why?'

'They took Claude's picture already, boy. I'm tellin you, just sit easy. As long . . . hey, Charley, okay, see you down at the precinct.' Charley leaves and after a half hour of sitting we go off, in his car, to the precinct down around 98th Street and I'm ushered into a cell with a board for a bed, no windows, who cares, and I curl up and try to sleep. But there's noise all night. Jailer comes to my bars at midnight and says:

'You're lucky, kid, there was a big bunch of photographers from the New York papers waitin for you here for a half hour.'

XII

So in the morning I like my arresting officer, who thought of that half hour, and he comes back, quiet, burps saying he had a heavy breakfast, says 'Come on,' has blue eyes, is Jewish plainclothesman, and we go downtown to the D.A.'s office for all the paper work and interrogation.

He drives placidly down West Side Highway, slowly and saying, 'Nice day,' for some reason he realizes I am not a dangerous prisoner.

I am ushered into the District Attorney's office, it's Jacob Grumet at the time, little mustache, Jewish too, pacing swiftly up and down, papers flying, and he says to me 'First off, kid, there's a letter we received this morning from the Y.M.C.A. on Thirty-Fourth Street. Read it. Here. Sit down.' I read this letter, in pencil, saying:

'*I told you Claude was bad and that he would kill. When we met in the El Caucho that night and I told you, hah! you wouldnt believe. He is a rat. I've always told you so, ever since I met you in 1934.*' And so on. I look up at Grumet and say:

'This is a fraud.'

'Okay,' filing it. 'Every homicide case of this kind some letters like this show up. Why particularly is this letter a fraud?'

'Because,' laughing, I, 'in 1934 I was twelve years old and I never heard of the El Gaucho and I dont know a soul in the Thirty-fourth Street Y.M.C.A.'

'God bless your soul,' says the D.A., 'and now, kiddo, here's Detective Sergeant O'Toole who's going to take you in the outer office and ask you a further question.'

Me and O'Toole go in the other room, he says: 'Sitdown, smoke?,' cigarette, I light, look out the window at the pigeons and the heat and suddenly O'Toole (a big Irishman with a gat on his chest under the coat): 'What would you do if a queer made a grab at your cock?'

'Why I'd k-norck him,' I answered straightaway looking right at him because suddenly that's what I thought he was going to do. (Note: 'K-norck' is Times Square expression of 'knock,' sometimes known, then, as 'Kneeazorck.') But anyway O'Toole immediately takes me back to the D.A.'s office and D.A. says 'Well?' and O'Toole yawns and says 'O he's okay, he's a swordsman.'

Well, that was no Cornish lie.

Then the D.A. said to me 'You're very close to having become an accessory after the fact of this homicide because of your assistance, nay, advice, to the accused, in burying and concealing the weapon and evidence, but we understand that most people dont know the law, that is, a material witness is a witness after the fact who's been apprized of the fact by the accused but doesnt bring it to the attention of the law. Or before the fact. You went out and got drunk with the accused, you helped him bury and dump the evidence, we understand that not only you dont, or didnt, know this aspect of the law, but most guys would act the same way in the same circumstances with, as you might say, their buddies, or friends, who are not habitual criminals. But you're not out of hot water yet. Either as accessory after the fact, or as a guest in the Bronx Jail, which we call the Bronx Opera House, where pigeons sing arias, and you're never going to be out of hot water if we find this kid guilty of murder instead of manslaughter. Now, the *Daily News* is calling this an "honor slaying," which means the kid was defending his honor from a known homosexual, who was, also, by the way, much bigger. We've got the record here of how the guy followed him around the country from one school to another getting him in trouble and getting him expelled. The case hinges on whether Claude de Maubris is a homosexual. We're trying to establish whether he is, you are, or whatever. O'Toole thinks you're not a homo. Are you?'

'I told O'Toole I wasnt.'

'Is Claude?'

'No, not in the least. If he was, he'd have tried to make me.'

'Now we have this other material witness, Hubbard, whose father just flew in from out west with five grand in cash and bailed him out. Is he a homo?'

'Not that I know of.'

'Allright . . . I believe you. You might be lucky and then again you may not. Your wife is down the hall if you want to go see her.'

'She's not married to me.'

'That's what she told us, among other things. She's pregnant aint she?' (grinning).

'Of course not.'

'Well, go down and see her and wait there. I've got to talk to de Maubris now.'

I go down into the hall with O'Toole, they bring Johnnie, we talk and cry in an office, and like in Jimmy Cagney movies when time's up they tell us it's time, she cries, hugs me, holds me, she wants to be dragged away like in the movies? I see Claude being led down the hall by two guards. They bring me a *Daily News* showing pictures of Claude on the river grass pointing to where he dumped Franz. Headlines say HONOR SLAYING and call him a SCION OF A EUROPEAN FAMILY. I mean it, headlines in the New York *Daily News*, I must say they musta been starved for news in those days, I guess they were sick of Patton's tanks busting on the German front and wanted a little spicy scandal.

XIII

They bring me the early evening edition of the New York *Journal American* and it shows a photo of handsome blond Claude being led by cops into a Tombs entryway (the Tombs Jail down on Chambers Street) and he's holding two slim volumes in his hands, God knows where he picked them up, I guess at his aunt's house for something to read during the proceedings. The books are described by the *Journal American* as *A Vision* by William Butler Keats (that's right, KEATS) and *A Season in Hell* by Jean-Arthur Rimbaud.

Then, lo, on the bench in the 'waiting' room beside Johnnie, Cecily and all the other questionees, is Irwin Garden all eager with a buncha books and leaning forward from the edge of his bench ready to be interrogated. He wants to explain the 'New Vision' to the D.A. and to all the newspapers of New York. He's only seventeen and only a minor, in fact completely useless witness, but he wants to be in on it all the way, not like Snitkin really but more like the old litterateur in *The Possessed.* It's his first big chance to get in the newspapers, he who, a year ago at sixteen had vowed on the Hoboken ferry: 'I shall devote my life to the liberation of the working class,' tho the only honest lick of work he ever done in his life was when he was a bus boy in a California cafeteria and shoved his mop cloth right in my kisser when I said something un-nicetized about his slaving position, calling him a Puerto Rican nonentity bus boy in a nowhere void. But bless Irwin, Claude, Johnnie, even Franz, the D.A., O'Toole, the whole lot, it was all done and done as a fact.

XIV

It started to pour cats and dogs and Claude and I, together again now, with cops, go briefly in some alleyways and paddywagons, to a judge's bench not far from Chambers Street and are 'arraigned' or whatever they call it but in the drenching roar of that rain, which dins throughout the courtroom like invasions and attacks from outside, Claude takes advantage to say to me out of the corner of his mouth: 'Heterosexuality all the way down the line.'

'I know, you jape.' Because, after all, what else, and 'you jape' I only just added now, in those days I just said 'I know.' Then after another night in the 98th Street Precinct I'm brought before another judge, star chamber or something, with lots of people there, and as always the judge winks at me, every time I face a judge he winks at me, and the judge sings (and it's still raining out):

'Well as the old Swedish sailmaker said to the old Norwegian sailor, a sailor is safer in a storm at sea than he is on land. Hor hor hor.' And he signed things, and banged gavels, but to my surprise it said in the paper next day that I was whistling a tune while all this was going on, which I dont doubt, because when I was young and I heard a tune in my head I just simply whistled it, and knowing the hit song of that summer I'm sure I must have been whistling 'You Always Hurt the One You Love.' A big bunch of people rushed up to me after, a certain to-do was done with on the bench, I turned, I thought it was a mob of eager law students, so that to every question they asked me I gave a precise answer: my full name, birthplace, hometown, present address, etc., and only afterward my kind plainclothesman sighed in the car as he drove me up to Bronx Jail saying:

'My God, man, those were newspaper people, didnt you know that?'

'I thought they were lawyers taking notes.'

'You . . . now your father's going to see your name in the paper, and your mother too.'

'What'd the judge mean by land and sea, that was some joke?'

'He's a card, Judge Moonihan.'

We drove up to the Bronx Opera House. 'Now lissen Jack, this is the jail where all material witnesses to homicides are kept, you're not under arrest, understand this, you're simply what we call detained. You're going to be paid three bucks a day while you stay here. The reason why we keep material witnesses to homicides in here, that is to say, people who know about certain killings, is so that when the trial comes up, he, you, the material witness, wont be hidin out in Detroit or someplace, or Montevideo, and, but, you're going in here on the same floor with all the material witnesses of the killings of New York which includes Murder Incorporated boys so take it easy and dont let them scare you. Just keep your nose clean, read those boys in silence, study those books we picked up for you, that there cakes and ales is it? by Somerset Mann, and sleep most of the time, you can play handball on the roof, most of these guys are Italians, they come from the old syndicate and Brooklyn Murder Incorporated, they're all serving over one hundred ninety-nine years and what they got to do is get a confession out of guys like you that can lop fifty years off their convictions. But since you've got nothing to confess, just take it easy. Tomorrow I'll be over and see you for probably the last time: I gotta drive you to the Bellevue Morgue to identify the body of Franz Mueller, which they just found in the river.'

XV

I'm ushered in, evening, the Mafia boys are playing cards before each individual cell on the open cell block which is slammed shut at ten, they wanta know if I play cards: 'I cant, I dont know how,' I say, 'my father can.'

They give me the once-over. 'What's this wit the fadder?'

XVI

The gates of each individual cell are slanged shut at ten and we all go to sleep, and O boy, a cold wave has suddenly hit New York from the northwest and I actually have to wrap in my flimsy blanket, even have to get up and put on all my clothes, reach down for a bite of my chocolate candy bars and see by the dim hall light that a mouse has already taken a few nibbles out of it. But I've got my little individual toilet bowl, little individual sink, and in the morning there's breakfast, which tho it's only dry old French toast at least there's syrup to go on them, a little coffee, and okay. My wonderful Jewish plainclothesman comes and drives me down to Bellevue Morgue through all kinds of interesting clanging doors and we come there, are told to wait till the coroner's done, have to go down and see District Attorney again and spend a dull afternoon smoking cigarettes on benches in the anteroom. (He tells me I can get out on bail bond, by the way.)

But the D.A. comes out in late afternoon and does indeed say 'Well, you're all right kid. We've checked out everything and you'll be okay. You're not going to be an accessory after the fact. And if Claude cops out on a manslaughter plea there'll be no trial and you'll be free and paid for your time in the opera house. Now if you want to call your father . . . '

I got the phone book and called Pa at his printing plant on 14th Street, where he was a linotypist working out of the New York City union, got him on the phone and said: 'All I need is a hundred dollars bond, for this five-thousand-dollar bail, and can go home. Everything's okay.'

'Well everything's not okay with me. No Duluoz ever got involved in a murder. I told you that little mischievous devil would get you in trouble. I'm not going to lend you no hundred dollars and you can go to hell and I've got work to do, good BYE.' Bang, the phone.

D.A. Grumet comes out again, says 'How's the girl Johnnie?'

Every time I'm involved the police of New York seem to take more interest in my girlfriend.

Me and the plainclothesman drive down to Bellevue Morgue in the gathering darkness and rain. We park, walk out, stop at the desk, papers are shuffled, and out comes a one-eyed Lesbian woman in a big bleak apron who says 'Okay, ready for the elevator?'

ELE-vator? DEPRECIA-tor I'd say, we go down with her, into a sinking smell of human refuse, you know what I mean, the smell of shit, pure shit, down, down, into the basement of Bellevue Morgue, her one eye glaring at me, as John Holmes would say, banefully. Gad I still hate that woman. She was like that character who charades you across the Styx into the Hell Regions of Greek Mythology. She looked the part and moreover was a woman, fat, sinister, the very Wraparound for the Devil's Counterpart in a Counterpane in Counter-Town's Beelzabur Fair and worse: if she ever danced ring-around-the-rosy with a Maypole in some old Celtic or Austrian celebration, I'd as lief bet that this here Maypole warn't gonna last more than into May Two.

Yessir, we were disposed and displeased into the bottom basements of Bellevue by her, and walked across a lot of file cabinets that you might think were handled by blue-eyed executive girls with Belgian builds, but no, it's this big Irishman with a sleeveless undershirt, munching on a sidewalk or a sandwich or something, waltzes up from the rainy cellar doorway of the morgue where I see an ambulance opened at the back and some guys easing out a box with a body in it, and says: 'What is it?'

'We've got to identify one sixty-nine,' says my cop.

'Right this way,' says he munching on his sandwich, comes to a Number 169, and whips it open like I whip open my files in which all the old records are kept in mothballs only in this case the old record is the actual body of poor Franz Mueller after he floated in the Hudson River some fifty hours, all bloated and blue but with his red beard still there and his familiar sports shirt along his side and his sandals too.

I swear he looks like a bearded old patriarch, there lying on his back with beard jutted up, whose unimaginable spiritual torment had turned him physically blue.

And his dong's still preserved.

XVII

'That's him, the red beard, the sandals, the shirt, the face aint there,' I said and turned away but the attendant kept munching on his sandwich and as I say yelled at me grinning (with cheese sandwich stuck in his teeth): 'Wassamatter boy, aint you ever seen a weenie before?'

Today I dont think it would bother me as much. Today I

could even be a coroner maybe. Looking at all those different file cabinets, if you ever go down into the Bellevue Morgue of New York, go ahead, write a poem about endless death in the big city train.

I'm driven back to Bronx Jail and in I go and we're all asleep as the rain drums on Yankee Stadium right outside the window.

When they televise a game from Yankee Stadium and you're looking from behind the home plate at the flags whipping over the right field stands, look further at that boxy structure there, white, it's the Bronx Opera House where people sing. As a matter of fact we could even watch ballgames from up there tho we couldnt tell if it was Mickey Mantle or Ty Cobb at bat, with all those 199 years behind us, maybe it was mustachio'd Abernathy McCombrie Fitch Doubleday himself at bat with a gourd he shoulda floated away in down the Ma River.

Tao Yuan-ming was a great Chinese poet a hundred times greater than Mao Tse-tung. Tao Yuan-ming said:

The bitter-cold year comes to an end.
In my cotton gown I look for the sun in the porch.
The southern orchard is bare, without leaves.
The rotting branches are heaped in the north garden.
I empty my cup and drink to the dregs.
And when I look in the kitchen, no smoke rises from the hearths!
Books and poems lie scattered beside my chair,
Yet the light is dying, and I shall have no time to read.
My life here is not like the agony in Ch'en, where Confucius nearly starved to death,
But sometimes I suffer from bitter reproaches.

Then let me remember, to calm my distress,
That the sages of old suffered from the same melancholy.

– TAO YUAN-MING, A.D. 372-427

XVIII

In the morning the main switch opens all the gates of the individual cells and guys can wander out and walk around, go down to the end where the card game is, pass idly by, say, the Chinamen's cell where the two Chinese brothers spend all the time with silk stockings in their hair ironing clothes for the family in Chinatown: both of them convicted murderers, but only one of them guilty, neither one will tell who did it, orders from the Father. (Girl, Coca-Cola bottle.) The card game is going on all the time. There's even a Negro trusty who gives shaves and haircuts, I mean by 'trusty,' I guess, that he's allowed to handle a razor blade tho there are no precautions against suicide.

But let me explain by cats: into my cell, as I'm lying there reading Somerset Maugham's *Cakes and Ale* and Aldous Huxley's *Brave New World*, waltzes Vincent the Falcon Malatesta arm in arm with Joey Angeli. I mean, arms over each other's shoulders, smiling Italian smiles, dark eyes, scars, eyepatches, shot-out ribs, bathrobes, kicks and dont ask me the rest as tho I knew. They say, 'Do you realize who we are?'

I say 'No.'

They say 'We were both hired assassins.'

'Now look,' says Falcon, 'I was hired to shoot Joey Angeli here, my buddy, who at de time was The Mouthpiece's bodyguard, remember, World War Two, about 1942, so I come out and we pick him up and hold him in the back of the car, take him out to New Jersey, throw him out of the car and pump shells into him about fifteen, and we drive away. I get paid, the job is done. But Joey here, he aint dead. He crawls on his belly to the nearest farmhouse, gets a phone (at gunpoint he dont even have to ask), calls the hospital, boom, in six months they've healed him up and he's almost as good as ever. Now he gets the order to hit ME, you see. So there I am innocently playing poker chips in a pile in Mott Street Italian section down near Chinatown near the Scungili Restaurant, and lo and behold, I look up and there's Joey the Angel in the door. Boom, he shoots me in this eye.' He points at the black patch over his eye. 'So I'm taken to the hospital and turns out the bullet went in and came out the other way without damaging the inner vittles of my brain.'

'I knew a guy the same thing happened in the Navy.'

'That's right, it happens sometimes, but we were paid to do these things, we got nothing personal against each other. We're just professionals. So here we are now standing up to one ninety-nine and two ninety-nine and a million years and we're the best friends you ever saw. We're like soldiers, you get it?'

'That's amazing.'

'And what's even more amazing is to find a nice kid like you in a joint like this. What's with this Claude kid we been readin about in the *Daily News*? Is he a pansy? Did he knock off his pansy friend?'

'No, Claude aint no queer, he's straight. The guy he knocked off was a pansy.'

'How do you know?'

'Well he never tried to make me.'

'Who would try to make an ugly prick like you? Hor hor hor.'

'Well also, he's a regular kid, you know what I mean? Va va voom,' I held up my hand, 'a regular.'

'So what's with the Italian va va voom regular? You're not Italian? What kinda name is your name there?'

'Breton French . . . ancient Irish actually.'

'Well how can you be French and Great Britain and ancient Irish at the same time?'

'In Roma they call it Cornovi.'

'What's Cornovi?'

'It's English, British.'

'So now he's English, British, hear that Joey?' And they start to wrestle playfully, pushing and mauling each other in my cell, then they get quiet and say 'Well we see you like to be alone by yourself, says you cant play cards, wanta read books, we just wanted to know what you were like, kid. But remember, no matter what happens, you look at us two guys right now and remember that we were hired to kill each other, we tried, we missed, and here we are together for life arm in arm two buddies for life, like two soldiers, what do you think of that?'

'That's great.'

'Great, he says,' they say sighing, leaving.

Then in comes Yogi the Hijacker. Yogi is Jewish. has big muscles, says 'Look at them muscles. In my cell, you come by my cell around the corner this afternoon. I have manuals on yoga lessons, breathing exercises, diaphragm control, Vedanta, all that stuff. In New Jersey I used to hijack trucks. Then I got mixed up in the vendetta, you know. Meyer Lansky and Maranzara and Kid Reles and the rest. Everybody here's mixed up with Murder Incorporated. They're all a bunch of bums. Kid, dont trust any of them. You can trust me, that's one thing sure. All I want to know from you is this: what that kid Claude the Maybreeze was, was he a shnook went for men's pants?'

'No, not in the least. What the hell you expect him to find there?'

'Find something might interest him.'

'Might interest somebody I can think of, but not him.'

Then in the evening the Falcon with the black patch comes in alone and says 'I came in here with Joey but was just kiddin around you know, like Tami Mauriello and I used to do roadwork with Mouthpiece when Tami was gettin in shape for a fight, I know everybody, and I wouldnt want Joey to hear what you got to say, but is that kid Claude a dilly dilly daisy? You know what I mean, a guy who waits around subway toilets for characters to come in? A guy who writes on walls? You know, like in the W.P.A. art theater place? A queer? A homo?'

'No I told you, Vincent, he's just a regular kid who's good-looking who got set upon by a homo. It's been happening even to me all my life. You remember when you were young . . . '

'Hey hey, I couldnt even play handball,' he says, holding out his hands . . . 'Soon's I put on my bathingsuit all those creeps from Sheepshead Bay was watching. But dont trust anybody else in this joint, I'm Vincent Malatesta and I may be an assassin on pay but I'm honest, my father was an honest cabinetmaker, best in Alcamo and in Brooklyn too, come to me and tell me anything's on your mind anytime. And dont be afraid of me because of my black patch and my reputation.'

I wasnt.

At least not in there.

A few months later he was shipped out to an unknown hideout forever.

XIX

If it was Sicily, did they get him? Then Joey Angeli comes in alone and says 'Dont trust Falcon, tho he's a nice guy. The only guy in here you can trust is me, Joey Angeli. All I wanta know is, is that kid Claude a queer? Did he ever feel up your leg with his knee?' he asked lasciviously.

'No, and if he did try to feel up my leg with his knee, I wouldnt talk to him anymore.'

'That's funny, now why not?'

'Because I think it would add up to an insult to my person as a male person.'

'Well that's well put. You know, I was intelligent. I shouldna sold out to the assassination business, The Mouthpiece liked me and told me I could go a long way. How you like my silk dressinggown?'

Then a note comes in for me that I can call for bail bond money. I ask for my Johnnie's number and call her up in front and say: 'Lissen, my father is mad as hell, wont lend me a hundred for the bond, the hell with him. Johnnie, you borrow that money from your aunt, I'll get out of here, we'll get married, right now, we'll go to Detroit and I'll get a job in a war plant and pay her off her hundred dollars (or your father might lend it) but in any case let's get married' – my father having abandoned me the first thing I thought of was getting married – 'and then I'll get a ship and ship out to Italy or France or someplace and send you my allowance.'

'Okay Jackie.'

But meanwhile, back in my cell trying to read, here comes the rest of them, the whole bunch (except the Chinese, who were Tong), everyone of them saying they were the only honest individual in the cellblock and to tell them the Gospel truth alone would save me.

But the Gospel truth was simply that Claude was a nineteen-year-old boy who had been subject to an attempt at degrading by an older man who was a pederast, and that he had dispatched him off to an older lover called the river, as a matter of record, to put it bluntly and truthfully, and that was that.

That was why he was really a 'child of the rainbow,' even at fourteen he could see through that guff, and the particular way it was laid down in this case, which was amounting to pursuit almost to the point of strong-arm threat, or extortion.

A man has a right to his own sexual life.

Demeaned by exhibitionism, ragged, hagged, witched-at, not left in peace of own soul, right in the face of mankind's pleasaunces he just dumped the malicious child-mongerer in the bloody drink and brook me that. Brool me that. (And duel me not that.)

XX

Shades of the prison-house. It's Saturday evening in August, in New York, a late sunset goldenly appears in a gap in the firmament between great dark cloudbanks so that the early lights of the city in the streets and on the watchers in the wallsides of high buildings suddenly shine quite feebly in the big light that was like the glow of a golden rose in all the world: and people look up and around with strange mulling thoughts. All day it has been gray, and really depressing, in the morning it's even rained some, but now's the dull clouds empurpled and made to flame at borders in evening and the one great hit and visitation of the Heavens throbs just widespread in the atmosphere like a great big golden old blue balloon and alike a harbinger, you might say, of mysterious new kindsa glory for everybody even over the soft tremblings of Times Square, and of 14th Street, and of Borough Hall in Brooklyn, even over the darkling waters by the piers where planks float, even where the Narrows soften by Staten Island and her silly wretched statue to the rose night true sea, even over the buzzing hums and great rumorous neons of rooftop Harlem and the Upper Italian East Side, and even over the millions of packed places where in my New York life I'd seen so many people who were preparing for the soft air and whatever celebrations and occasions that must, and do, arise in piddling earth in the vast night's camp.

And so, gentle lug heads, how sad, how true, how necessary that a whole day might have to be like a sodden rag, lumpish, distress-ful, like the last day of the world (which it oughta be sometime) when all the 'windows be darkened and the daughters of music brought low,' and men can go about with a kind of jaundiced toolbag sorrow and black hats and coats to a card game like Cezanne's which is more sorrowful than sources of disenchanted soul itself. Workmen who sweated all day did sweat without joy, and hated dumb labor, and thought of home without consolation, except for pizza and the *Daily News* and the Yankee game. Indoor workers gaped with itchy pants and embarrassment at windows. Housewives and storekeepers Vergilized a gray empty doom and led their whoresons on. Children marveled like lepers at the amazing sadness of day, turning little faces downward, tho, not at ships, nor trains, nor great trucks from South Carolina arriving over bridges and all the smoky fanfares, movies, museums, bright toys, but to awful fogs in which, yet, the central joyous source of the universe there still hung on, clear as a bell ever, the pearl of Heaven flaming on high. So that even in jail, men look up from whatever they're thinking with the same struck mull thought, say 'Yah, red out there, ugh,' or they say, 'What's that, no rain?' or say nothing and watch awhile before returning to the feverish waiting mat.

On the fourth floor of the Bronx Jail, I, a young man, standeth silent outside the cell in the barred hall of the tier, I look across another hall thru the bars of a window that opens on that immense silly blushing New York with its awestruck, yet sad, pot-of-man look. And down the hall, there's the card game. There's the evening guard sitting among the men in shirtsleeves with his cap thrown back. Maybe he's got a quarter. Last few hours before lights out. Harsh white light burns over the muttering concentrations. Every now and then some guy looks up from the ring of heads and says 'What, no rain?' A gaunt man with a black patch over one eye, that being, of course, Little Red Riding Hood, says 'Stick to your guns, Rocco, by the time you get out there you'll be the last rose of summer.'

'In the spring a young man's fancy? Give me three.'

'In a year, Eddie, you can kiss the boys goodbye and go home.'

'Never mind, that's allright, dont think about *abiyt nem dibt wirrt hyst ren nberm t isegyts, yuck.*'

'What's he talkin, Ay Rabic?'

'I'll remember it,' says Red looking away.

Anyway, see? No time for poetry. And anyway, see? No time for poetry.

XXI

So the next day I have them call the D.A., Grumet, to tell him I want to be let out for a few hours to marry Johnnie. I can see the D.A. rubbing his hands together thinking gleefully 'I KNEW she was pregnant.' He gives the go-ahead. A big Irish dick from Ozone Park, clothes plain, comes for me and says 'Come on.' We go out together. He's carrying a thick gat under his coat. It's cool now August, but the subway's still hot and so we ride downtown together hanging onto straps and reading the *Daily News* and the *Daily Mirror* respectively. He knows I aint going to make a run for anything but because there's nothing on me in the Bronx Opera House maybe he thinks I'm a nut, what I mean is, anyway, he's got his eye on me. We get downtown and meet Johnnie and Cecily. Cecily is going to be the best woman and Detective Shea the best man.

When he gloms Cecily his lips ooze out 'OO' and we go down to City Hall and get the license. In two minutes flat a justice of the peace is marrying us. Shea is standing proudly in the back with beauteous Cecily at his side and me and Johnny are married.

Then we repair to a bar for an afternoon of pleasant drink and talk. Evening comes. One more for the road. Shea is about forty-seven years old and about to retire. He's never been a best man at an impromptu wedding with a bourgeois doll like Cecily, actually that's mean, a beautiful doll like Cecily, only twenty, and he's flushed and good times, in fact he buys all the drinks, but anyway I'm married to Johnnie and I give her a big kiss as Shea and I have to return to Bronx Jail to put me back in my cell. She's going to wire home for that one hundred and I'll be sprung in a few days. The wife of my youth I married anyway.

When I'm being escorted down the evening hall to my cel that night around nine all the prisoners are going 'Ye, ye, ye, that's some wedding night for that boy, ha ha ha.'

In the middle of the night everybody is silent, snoring, or thinking quiet thoughts one way or the other, and the only thing I hear is the Chinese brothers going quietly in the dark '*Hungk-ya mung-yo too mah to.*' I think of all the rice in their father's shop. I think of all the ink in my father's fingernails. I think of all the absurdity of going on when there's no place to go. Then I think:

'Absurdity? Of course there's someplace to go! Go mind your own business.'

BOOK THIRTEEN

I

Talk about 'widening your consciousness' and all that crap they talk about nowadays, if I'da widened my consciousness enough to narrow down the piecework numbered on the counters of the piecework ballbearing laborers in Federal Mogul Factory in Detroit that September, where I went to earn and save that one hundred dollars I owed my new wife's aunt, they'da widened my arse and narrowed my head with a monkey wrench and not a left-handed one at that.

It was the best job I ever had. From midnight till eight in the morning, it was gotten for me through the influence of Johnnie's well-known society father, via friends thereof, and I dont know what the ballbearing boys thought of me but they saw that after twelve, when I checked their opening count on the counter, I had nothing to do till eight but occupied myself the entire noisy night sitting at the foreman's desk I guess it was, on a high dunce stool, reading and taking down notes endlessly. What I was doing. I was studying very carefully a list of books dealing with American literary criticism so I'd be ready for the wars up ahead other than those we were making ballbearings for.

Ballbearings, of all things, my boyhood joy because they could always outroll the marbles and win the horse races . . .

Because D.A. Grumet let me out of Bronx Jail not long after Johnnie and I were married, on that one-hundred-dollar bail bond for the five-thousand-dollar bail, and we went west to live with her aunt, in Grosse Pointe Michigan. First my Pa and Ma came to see me, tho, in the jail, sat at the long table and talked to me in front of a guard just like in the John Garfield movies. They were surprised I had decided to marry Johnnie, they understood I did it because I had no friends, had to get out, try something new, they looked on me as an errant but innocent son victimized by decadent friendships in the evil city, which was true, in a way, but anyway, everything was forgiven.

In Johnnie's aunt's house in Grosse Pointe, everything was fine, we had wonderful dinners every evening at seven on laced tablecloth with regular china dishes and casseroles of silver and chandelier above, albeit cooked by Johnnie and served by her aunt, no maids, but a beautiful quiet home and a beautiful quiet woman her aunt. Of course she had nothing for me over roast beef and brown potatoes but words that would make me feel slightly guilty but when I sat with her in the parlor after dinner and continued my reading and note-taking she began to realize I might be serious about the 'writing game.'

'Well,' she'd say, 'I've heard of some people who made a living out of writing books, Pearl Buck, they told me today at the club, and Harriet van Arness of Pinckney Michigan made quite a renown for herself.' Pinckney Michigan was where they had a farm, occupied by relatives, right near Henry Ford's farm, near Ann Arbor or a few miles, a lovely farm we visited for Sunday dinner and across the fields of which, in the lovely northern October of Michigan, Johnnie and I roamed, to go lie down in yellow weeds by creeks exuding cold of coming winter, wishing someday we could own a farm and lie around in corduroy slacks and wool sweaters and smoke fragrant pipes and raise healthy little butter eaters, creamery butter from the cows, that is. But Johnnie was unable to have children because of a dangerous anemic condition, and as for me, it turned I found out a few years later I was like my uncles Vincent and John Duluoz, and my aunt Anne Marie, well nigh sterile. That Duluoz family being so very old . . .

I guess it's not unusual that by the time my father and I came around at the bottom of that pot of Duluozes, the only good thing we could figure had ever happened to us was that we could fall asleep at night and dream, and the only bad thing, wake up to this gnashing world. At least the early Duluozes had fields of green in Cornwall and Brittany, horses and mutton chops, barks and rigging and salt spray, shields and lances and saddles, and trees to look at. Whoever they were, them Duluozes (Kerouac'hs), their name meant 'Language of the House' and you know that's an old name, and that's Celtic, and that any family that old cant go on much longer. 'Bad blood' as Claude used to say of me. But anyway the 'wife of my youth' and I could never have children.

Palmer was probably an old family too, she was the granddaughter of a Scottish furniture tycoon whose fortune had been squandered by her Pop but all in good fun. Think of all the literary and political asses who get prizes for being abstract telling you that life and its 'values' are wonderful, in great chosen terms deliberately stuffed with cover-up platitudes, who dont know what it is to come from an old family which is too old to lie anymore.

I worked for the whole month of September into October till I had paid back Mrs. Palmer in twenty-dollar-a-week installments, cleared my debt, then got old Mr Palmer now to arrange me a free truck ride to New York City so I could ship out again. It was October 1944, ships were now headed for other interesting shores like Italy, Sicily, Casablanca, I think even Greece.

II

So I kissed Johnnie goodbye, to Mrs Palmer's approval, and got on that truck in the evening. In the morning we were in the smoky Pennsylvania hills in their autumn haze and apple smell. At night I was back on the New York waterfront talking to some guys near the hall, in the morning I signed on as an acting able-bodied seaman on the S.S. *Robert Treat Paine*, AGWI Lines again, as the *Dorchester* had been. They were so short of seamen now they were making ordinary seamen like myself into acting able-bodied seamen. I didnt even still know how to figure the lines and bits and gadgets of the deck. The bosun of the ship spotted that right away and said 'Who the hell do you think you are signing on this ship as an A.B. when you dont even know what to do to swing a lifeboat out?'

'Ask the union, at least I can make coffee and stand bow watch and hold the wheel at sea.'

'Lissen punk, you're going to learn one hell of a lot on this trip.' But in front of the rest of the guys he didnt call me 'Punk,' he called me 'Handsome,' which was worse and much more sinister. But we were docked on the North River loading up so I got out at 5 P.M. to go up to the Columbia campus and look up Irwin and Cecily and the others.

The Claude-Mueller murder story was still the talk of the campus and the bar. A little story by Joe Amsterdam in the *Columbia Spectator* about the murder was illustrated in ink, showing Russian hovel steps leading up to glooms, making it look romantic and *fin de siècle.* He was also congratulating me for giving up 'rock-ribbing football to turn to Wolfean novels.' I'd already lost the long novel I had been writing for Claude's and Irwin's pleasure, in pencil, printed, in a taxicab: never heard from it again. I was wearing my London outfit of black leather jacket and chinos and phony goldbraid hat. The big sad salesman took my picture in the Columbia bookshop. I've never seen it again but it was a picture of despair in bone and flesh, I'll tell you.

But beauteous blond Cecily started to turn on the come-on, which is enough for me, and I did the rattiest thing of all my life, I'd say, by reciprocating in kind and trying to make her. But she was just 'teasing.' Still I necked with her all night. I think if Claude had known about this in his cell at reform school, where he'd gone after copping a manslaughter plea, he would have wept. She was after all the symbol of his ninteen-year-old year. Anyway he never learned of it till after he came out two years later. That woman was a menace anyway.

Because sitting in the West End Bar with me and poor little Irwin and Dover Judd a garrulous poet-student from Georgia, she even started to flirt with two Naval officers, who got sore because we were 'all queer' and here this great blond beauty was going to waste. They even addressed me directly, threatened to bat Irwin and Dover on the head and were acting like they had Cecily made to go out to the Ritz. I went to the men's room, like that time in Hartford, practiced a couple of punches on the wall, and came out and yelled 'Allright, let's go outside.'

Outside, the first Naval lieutenant held up his fists à la John L. Sullivan which suddenly made me laugh. His buddy right behind him. I waded into him with a series of little slaps right and left that were swift and hard and knocked him on his back on the sidewalk. Some Navy man I was. Then the other was flying at me through the air and I just instinctively held up my elbow with the fist cocked at my own face. He hit the hard bone point and slid 6 feet on the sidewalk on his face. They both got up bloody and sore as hell. Now they combined to wrassle me down to the sidewalk where they grabbed my long black hair and began to try to bang my head on the pavement with that grip. I held my neck tense so the hair just ripped out, ouch. Then little Irwin Garden waded in trying to help. I began to like him. They just pushed him away. Finally Johnny the Bartender, my big buddy, came out and, with a bunch of others, and his brother, said 'Okay that's enough, two on one wont do. Fight's over.'

So I went to my new room in Dalton Hall with Irwin and Cecily and wept on her belly all night. I felt it was horrible, the feel of flesh smacking on sidewalks, the terror of it. I should've thrown her right out of the room for starting the whole thing anyway. Also I kept picturing those two Naval officers suddenly rushing in the door to finish the job. But nope, the next day I went back to the West End for a beer, about ten in the morning, and there they were, all bandaged up, drinking quiet beers and not even looking up at me: probably got hell from the captain of their ship. They had bandages because they had corpsmen, I had nothing but the mindless seaman's waterfront and went down there that afternoon to get more hell from the bosun about how stupid I was on deck. As if he'd notice the blood in my hair.

But the mysterious beautiful thing of going to sea occurred that night: just a few hours after all that junk of bars, fighting, streets, subways, boom, there I am standing by whipping shrouds and snapping lines in the Atlantic Ocean in the night off New Jersey, we're sailing south to Norfolk to load on for Italy, everything is washed away by the clean sea, I can remember the judge's remark about the sailor in the storm is safer than the sailor on land. The stars are big, they rock side to side like Galileo drunk and Kepler stoned and Copernicus thinking, like Vasco da Gama in his bunk in thought, the wind, the cleanness, the dark, the quiet blue light in the bridge where hand holds wheel and course is set. The sleeping seamen below.

III

Strangely, when we arrive in Norfolk I'm put on the wheel for the first time in my life. As we approach the mine nets of the harbor I have to turn a few times to stay on course, as indicated on the Kelvin compass, but this isnt like turning softly right with the wheel of a Ford or a Pontiac, the whole huge serpentine length of iron ship behind you doesnt turn to the wheel till about ten seconds later, and when it does you realize you've got to ease it because it's going to keep on turning and go into a slow spin, so you angle the wheel left (port) again, it's one vast hell of a way to drive. Not only that but a bumboat rushes up, they throw down the Jacob's (rope) ladder, up comes the harbor pilot, strides into the bridgehouse, doesnt even look at me and says 'Keep her to course one ninety-nine, steady as you go.' He says 'We're going through those mine nets there, that opening, which is directly on course two hundred one. Keep her steady. Just listen to me.' He, the captain, myself and the first mate are all standing there looking straight ahead but why they let me handle the wheel I'll never know. I guess because it's easy anyway. It's broad sunny noon. We slide right through the nets and there's plenty of room. Now for the business of coming into dock they bring up the regular A.B. on my watch. I guess they were trying to train me. Dont ask me what was going on here, there or anywhere, I really dont know, all I wanted to do was go back to sleep or go cry on Cecily's slippy belly.

When we docked me and the (other) ordinaries put out rat guards to the cheers of several girls in cotton dresses on the pier, my God them Norfolk gals used to go right out to meet the seamen even before the rat guards were out.

'Where you goin?'

'Dont know.'

'Take us along.'

The captain: 'Get those girls off the pier!'

But now again the bosun starts to call me 'Handsome' and even 'Pretty Boy' as we're winching up the lines and I turn to him and say: 'What the heck's the matter?'

'You know what, Pretty Boy, Baby Face, you aint no able-bodied seaman. By the time I'm done with you . . . ' I sensed he wanted a fight. The other guys didnt care. I began to see that there was something homosexual about his prod and dare. I wasn't about to sail all the way to Naples with a 230-pound homo bosun.

IV

I really pondered the problem in my bunk that sundown. The boys went ashore to dig Norfolk, nothing there but thousands of sailors and cars and movie shows and whores who charged too much. The bosun had on his side the carpenter who also gave me the evil eye. Nothing I'd done on the ship except showing a lack of knowledge of some of the deck work. But that may have been enough. There would be a fight. Even after the next day, a whole day I spent on the smokestack with another deckhand fixing the filter with wires, and down below fixing other stuff, he wasnt satisfied and kept calling me 'Sweetie Face' and making the other guys laugh, some of them, but some of them looking away.

Shall I tell you where I met that guy years later? Fifteen years later as I was reading poetry in a MacDougal Street coffee-house for free, he was there tape-recording the whole thing and I recognized him immediately but in the gaiety of poetry just put my fist under his chin and said 'You, I remember you, bosun, what are you doing taking all this down?' As I saw his crewcut and tweed jacket I realized now, fifteen years later, 1959, that he was some kind of investigator for the government. He must have remembered my name over the fifteen years and figured I was a Communist, maybe the Navy told him about my interview with Naval Intelligence at Newport R.I. I've always had the feeling the F.B.I. is watching me, or the like, because of my bum record in the Navy tho I'm still proud of having had the highest I.Q. in the history of Newport Naval Base.

But anyway, to compound all the horror, I had to get away from that horrible bosun. So I put all my clothes on, put my chinos and black jacket over that, folded the empty duffel bag into my belt under, and walked off the ship that night the fattest able-bodied seaman you ever saw. The guard on watch was from the dock and didnt know me personally, how I was built, and just watched me walk off showing my papers to the pier people below. I looked like Mister Five-by-Five. A fat happy seaman going ashore to look at girls' legs. But it was only I.

I walked across the endless piers, got to the highway, where Naval lieutenants I could see inside of swank restaurants dining with blondes, and got into the toilet of a Texaco filling station. There I undid all my clothes, packed in back in the duffel bag, and emerged light as a feather in the cool southern autumnal evening. With the duffel bag I hailed a bus confidently, but who do you think was sitting in the front seat of the bus leering at me: the bosun and the carpenter! 'Where you going with your duffel bag? How'd you get that off the ship?'

'It's not mine, I picked it up at a gas station for my friend from Mass., he's downtown waiting for it.'

'Yeh?'

'Yeh.'

'Dont forget, we sail tomorrow night at five P.M. Have a good time, kid,' as I moved to the back of the bus among the standing sailors.

So, at midnight, after having stashed my bag in the bus station lockers, and even seeing a movie, and by God even digging Norfolk just because I was there, and in fact even running into an old boyhood Navy chum from Lowell (Charley Bloodworth who was also in love with Maggie Cassidy during the 1939 track season), I was on the bus and riding back up across the southern dark toward New York. A ship jumper, to add to the rest.

V

And in New York, I went straight to the Columbia campus, occupied a room on the sixth floor of Dalton Hall, called Cecily, held her in my arms (still a tease, she), yelled at her, then when she left settled out my new notebooks and embarked on a career as literary artist.

I lighted a candle, cut a little into my finger, dripped blood, and wrote 'The Blood of the Poet' on a little calling card, with ink, then the big word 'BLOOD' over it, and hung that up on the wall as reminder of my new calling. 'Blood' writ in blood.

From Irwin I got all of the books I wanted, Rimbaud, Yeats, Huxley, Nietzsche, Maldoror, and I wrote all kinds of inanities that are really silly when you think of me, like, 'Creative pregnancy justifies anything I do short of criminality. Why should I live a moral life and inconvenience pre-disinterested emotions towards it?' And the answer came in red ink: 'If you dont, your creation will not be sound. Sound creation is moral in temper. Goethe proved that.' I reopened the wound and tourniqueted more blood out of it to make a cross of blood and a 'J.D.' and a dash over the inked words of Nietzsche and Rimbaud:

'NIETZSCHE: Art is the highest task and the proper metaphysical activity of this life.'

'RIMBAUD: *Quand irons-nous, par delà les grèves et les monts, saluer la naissance du travail nouveau, la sagesse nouvelle, la fuite des tyrans, et des démons, la fin de la superstition, adorer . . . les premiers! . . . Noël sur la terre?*' Translated it goes: 'When shall we go, over there by the shores and mountains, to salute the birth of new work, the new wisdom, the flight of tyrants, and of demons, the end of superstition, to adore . . . the first ones! . . . Christmas on Earth?'

And this I pinned up on my wall.

I was completely alone, my wife and my family thought I was at sea, nobody knew I was there except Irwin, I was going to embark on an even deeper solitary room writing than I had done in Hartford Conn. with the little short stories. Now it was all

Symbolism, all kinds of silly junk, the repertory of modern ideas, 'neo-dogmatism à la Claudel,' 'the neo-Aeschylus, the realization of the need for correlation of introspective visionaryism and romanticist eclecticism.'

Now I only mention these few quotes to show the reader what I was reading and How (and How!) I was absorbing it and how serious I was. In fact I had endless things lined up some of which might just about cover the tone of the period I was undergoing:

They went:

'(1) The Huxleyan (?) idea of ceaseless growth (also Goethean). *Élan vital.* The course in conversation (polemicism), reading, writing, and *experiencing* must never cease. *Becoming.*

'(2) Sexual neo-Platonism and the sexual understanding of a *grande dame* of the eighteenth century as a modern trend.

'(3) Political liberalism in the critical throes of adolescence (post-Marxian, pre-Socialistic). Bloody modern Europe. Materialism has picked up a bludgeon.

'(4) The conflict between modern bourgeois culture and artistic culture in Thomas Mann, in Rolland, in Wolfe, in Yeats, Joyce.

'(5) The new aspect, or the new vision – in Rimbaud, in Lautréamont (Maldoror), or as in Claudel.

'(6) Nietzscheanism – "Nothing is true, everything is allowed." Superman. Neo-mysticism as exemplified in Zarathustra. An ethical revolution.

'(7) The decline of the Western church – Hardy's crass casuality in the same instant made subject to the fortitude of Jude.

'(8) Freud's mechanistics in practically the same instant made subject to emotions (as in Koestler) or to a new morality (as in Heard's vague sense).

'(9) From the humanism of H. G. Wells, from the naturalism of Shaw and Hauptmann and Lewisohn, immediately to the neo-Aeschylus Stephen Dedalus (*Bous Stephanoumenos*) and to universal Earwicker himself.

'(10) Spengler and Pareto – a resultant return, as in Louÿs or Rimbaud, to the East. (Malraux.) Why do the French return to the South? (Those Marseilles decadents in the mahogany tropics of Alfredo Segró.) Anglo-Catholicism and classicism of Eliot. "Fine sentiment," comments the Kensington Garden intellectual in Royal Albert Hall.

'(11) Music . . . toward conflict and discordance. The prophecy in end of third movement of Beethoven's Ninth. Shostakovich, Stravinsky, Schoenberg. Freud's ego-concept has risen to the surface and is now *heard* conflicting. *Seen* in painting as in the Impressionists, in Picasso, in Dali, *et al.*

'(12) Santayana's grandee mysticism . . . De Boeldieu and his white gloves in *Les Grandes Illusions*. High-consciousness.

'(13) Francis Thompson's lesson of the impalpability of human life. Melville: "I seek that inscrutable thing!" Also Wolfe, Thompson, like the latter is haunted by the *truth of loneliness* until he is forced to accept it (!).

'(14) Gideanism . . . *acte gratuite* as abandonment of reason and return to impulse. But now our impulses exist in a society civilized by Christianity. Gideanism is richness in contradiction's Proteanism, immorality . . . is, in essence, the Dionysian overflow of the artistic morality.' Etc.

VI

Artistic morality, that was the point, because then I devised the idea of burning most of what I wrote so that my art would not appear (to myself as well as to others) to be done for ulterior, or practical motives, but just as a function, a daily duty, a daily scatalogical 'heap' for the sake of purgation. So I'd burn what I wrote, with the candle flame, and watch the paper curl up and squirm, and smile madly. The way writers are born, I guess. A holy idea, I called it 'self ultimacy,' or, S.U.

Also, to show you, the intellectualism that Claude and Irwin had now influenced over me. But the word 'intellectualism' just made Hubbard snuff down his nose when he showed up early that December after much candle-writing and bleeding on my part, 'My God, Jack, stop this nonsense and let's go out and have a drink.'

'I've been eating potato soup out of the same bowl with Irwin in the West End.'

'What about your shipping out and stuff?'

'I jumped the ship in Norfolk thinking I was coming back here for a big love affair with Cecily but she doesn't care.'

'Oh you're a card. Let's go have dinner, then go see Jean Cocteau's movie *The Blood of the Poet* if that's in your line these days, then we'll repair to my apartment on Riverside Drive, me boy, and have a bang of morphine. That oughta give you some new visions.'

This may make him sound sinister but he wasnt sinister at all, morphine came my way from other directions and I turned it down anyhow. Why, old Will in that time, he just awaited the next monstrous production from the pen of his young friend, me, and when I brought them in he pursed his lips in an attitude of amused inquiry and read. Having read what I offered up, he nodded his head and returned the production to the hands of the maker. Me, I sat there, perched on a stool somewhat near this man's feet, either in my room or in his apartment on Riverside Drive, in a conscious attitude of adoring expectation, and, finding my work returned to me with no more comment than a nod of the head, said, almost blushingly 'You've read it, what you think?'

The man Hubbard nodded his head, like a Buddha, having come to ghastly life from out of Nirvana what else was he s'posed to do? He joined his fingertips resignedly. Peering over the arch of his hands he answered 'Good, good.'

'But what do you specifically think of it?'

'Why . . . ' pursing his lips and looking away toward a sympathetic and equally amused wall, 'why, I dont specifically *think* of it. I just rather like it, is all.' (Only a few years before he'd been with Isherwood and Auden in Berlin, had known Freud in Vienna, and visited the Pierre Louÿs locales in North Africa.)

I returned the work to my inner pocket, again blushed, said 'Well at any rate, it was fun writing it.'

'I daresay,' he'd murmur. 'And now tell me, how is your family?'

But, you see, late that night he'd, alone, with fingers counterpoised under the glare of the lamp, with legs crossed and eyes heavy lidded in patience and waiting, remember again that tomorrow the young man would return with the records of his imagination . . . and ill-advised and importunate tho he might consider them . . . he, yes, waited for more. Elsewhere there was only established fact and ruinous retreat.

VII

So just about the whole next year I spent hungering to go see him, to be handed books by him, Spengler, even Shakespeare, Pope, a whole year of drug-taking and talking with him and meeting characters of the underworld he'd started to study as an *acte gratuite* of some kind.

Because around Christmas of 1944 Johnnie came back to me from Detroit, we lived and loved briefly in Dalton Hall, then moved in with her old girlfriend June up on 117th Street now and then persuaded Hubbard to move in too, in the empty room, and he later married June (Johnnie and I knew they would like each other).

But it was a year of low, evil decadence. Not only the drugs, the morphine, the marijuana, the horrible Benzedrine we used to take in those days by breaking open Benzedrine inhalers and removing the soaked paper and rolling it into poisonous little balls that made you sweat and suffer (lost thirty pounds in three days the first time I tried in on an overdose), but the characters we got to know, Times Square actual thieves who'd come in and stash stolen gumball machines from the subway, finally stashing guns, borrowing Will's own gun, or his blackjack, and worst of all, on June's huge doublebed with the Oriental drapecover on it we had ample room for sometimes six of us to sprawl with coffee cups and ashtrays and discuss the decadence of the 'bourgeoisie' for days on end.

I'd come home to Ozone Park from these endless debauches looking like a pale skin-and-bones of my former self and my father would say 'O that Hubbard and that Irwin Garden are going to destroy you someday.' To add to everything my father had begun to develop Banti's disease, his belly would swell up every two or three weeks and have to be drained. He soon couldnt work anymore and was about to come home and die. Cancer.

I ran with horror from home to 'them' and then from 'them' to home but both equally dark and inhospitable places of guilt, sin, sorrow, lamentation, despair. It wasnt so much the darkness of the night that bothered me but the horrible lights men had invented to illuminate their darkness with . . . I mean the very streetlamp down at the end of the street . . .

It was a year when I completely gave up trying to keep my body in condition and a photo of myself on the beach at the time shows soft and flabby body. My hair had begun to recede from the sides. I wandered in Benzedrine depression hallucinations. A 6-foot redhead applied pancake makeup to my face and we went in the subway like that: she was the one who gave me the overdose: she was a gun moll. We met furtive awful characters at certain subway stops, some of them were subway 'lush workers' (rolling subway drunks), we hung out in the evil bar on 8th Avenue around the corner from 42nd Street. I myself took no part in any crime but I knew personally of many indeed. For Hubbard it was a jaded study of how awful poeple can be, but in his vacuity, how 'alert' they could also be in a 'dead' society, for me it was a romantic self-torture like the blood business in my Self Ultimacy writing garret the fall before. For Irwin, now a shipyard worker, and occasional merchant seaman coastwise to Texas, *et al.*, a new kind of material for his new Hart Crane poetry kick.

One of our 'friends' who came in to stash a gun one day turned out, after he hanged himself in the Tombs some months later, to have been the 'Mad Killer of Times Square,' tho I didnt know about that: he'd walk right into a liquor store and shoot the proprietor dead: it was afterward confessed to me by another thief who couldnt hold the secret he said because he hurted from holding it.

VIII

My poor father had to see me, while dying of cancer, come down to all of this from that beginning on the sandlot football field of Dracut Tigers Lowell when the ambition was to make good in football and school, go to college, and become a 'success.' It was part of the war, really, and of the cold war to come. I can never forget how June's present husband, Harry Evans, suddenly came clomping down the hall of her apartment in his Army boots, fresh from the German front, around September 1945, and was appalled to see us, six fullgrown people, all high on Benny sprawled and sitting and cat-legged on that vast double-doublebed of 'skepticism' and 'decadence,' discussing the nothingness of values, pale-faced, weak bodies, Gad the poor guy said: 'This is what I fought for?' His wife told him to come down from his 'character heights' or some such. He divorced her awhile later. Of course we know the same thing was going on in Paris and Berlin of the same month and year, now that we've read Günther Grass and Uwe Johnson and Sartre and even, of course, Auden and his *Age of Anxiety*.

But this didnt jibe with my dying father's continuing notion that people 'should make the best of it, look hopefully to tomorrow, work, do well, make an effort, shake a leg,' all the old 1930's expressions that were so stirring, like cranberry sauce, when we thought Prosperity was right around the corner and it sure was.

I myself, as you can see from this whole insane tirade of prose called a book, had been thru so much junk anyway you can hardly blame me for joining in with the despairists of my time.

Still, there were guys coming home from the war and getting married and going to school on the G.I. Bill who had no taste for such negativism and who would have punched me on the nose if they knew about how low I'd fallen from the time, maybe, when they had a beer with me in 1940. But I had goofed throughout entire wartime and this is my confession.

(At this time also, I let Johnnie my wife handle the annulment papers in Detroit, I was of no more use to her as a husband, I sent her home.)

IX

I took so much Benzedrine that year out of those cracked tubes, I finally made myself real sick, developed thrombophlebitis, and by December had to go to the Queens General Hospital (on the V.A.) to lie there with my legs up on pillows swathed in hot compresses. There was talk at first of surgery, even. And even there I'd look out the window at the darkness of the Queens night and feel a nauseating gulp to see those poor streetlamps stretching out into the murmurous city like a string of woes.

Yet a little bunch of kids, twelve and thirteen, who were patients there, actually came to the foot of my bed and serenaded me with guitars one evening.

And my nurse, big fat gal, loved me.

They could see in my eyes what had been there in 1939, 38, nay 22.

In fact I began to bethink myself in that hospital. I began to understand that the city intellectuals of the world were divorced from the folkbody blood of the land and were just rootless fools, tho permissible fools, who really didn't know how to go on living. I began to get a new vision of my own of a truer darkness which just overshadowed all this overlaid mental garbage of 'existentialism' and 'hipsterism' and 'bourgeois decadence' and whatever names you want to give it.

In the purity of my hospital bed, weeks on end, I, staring at the dim ceiling while the poor men snored, saw that life is a brute creation, beautiful and cruel, that when you see a springtime bud covered with rain dew, how can you believe its beautiful when you know the moisture is just there to encourage the bud to flower out just so's it can fall off sere dead dry in the fall? All the contemporary LSD acid heads (of 1967) see the cruel beauty of the brute creation just by closing their eyes: I've seen it too since:

a maniacal Mandala circle all mosaic and dense with millions of cruel things and beautiful scenes goin on, like say, swiftly on one side I saw one night a choirmaster of some sort in 'Heaven' slowly going 'Ooo' with his mouth in awe at the beauty of what they were singing, but right next to him is a pig being fed to an alligator by cruel attendants on a pier and people walking by unconcerned. Just an example. Or that horrible Mother Kali of ancient India and its wisdom aeons with all her arms bejeweled, legs and belly too, gyrating insanely to eat back thru the only part of her that's not jeweled, her yoni, or yin, everything she's given birth to. Ha ha ha ha she's laughing as she dances on the dead she gave birth to. Mother Nature giving you birth and eating you back.

And I say wars and social catastrophes arise from the cruel nature of bestial creation, and not from 'society,' which after all has good intentions or it wouldn't be called 'society' would it?

It is, face it, a mean heartless creation emanated by a God of Wrath, Jehovah, Yaweh, No-Name, who will pat you kindly on the head and say 'Now you're being good' when you pray, but when you're begging for mercy anyway say like a soldier hung by one leg from a tree trunk in today's Vietnam, when Yaweh's really got you out in back of the barn even in ordinary torture of fatal illness like my Pa's then, he wont listen, he will whack away at your lil behind with the long stick of what they called 'Original Sin' in the Theological Christian dogmatic sects but what I call 'Original Sacrifice.'

That's not even worse, for God's sake, than watching your own human father Pop die in real life, when you really realize 'Father, Father, why hast thou forsaken me?' for real, the man who gave you hopeful birth is copping out right before your eyes and leaves you flat with the whole problem and burden (your self) of his own foolishness in ever believing that 'life' was worth anything but what it smells like down in the Bellevue Morgue when I had to identify Franz's body. Your human father sits there in death before you almost satisfied. That's what's so sad and horrible about the 'God is Dead' movement in contemporary religion, it's the most tearful and forlorn philosophical ideal of all time.

X

Because we do know that the brutish, the mean-hearted, the Mad Dog creation has a side of compassionate mercy in it, as witness the mother cat (Mother Nature) how she washes and soothes her little kittens in the basket (almost said 'casket') and gives of her own milk of kindness without stint: we have seen the brutal creation send us the Son of Man who, to prove that we should follow His example of mercy, brotherly love, charity, patience, gave Himself up without a murmur to be sacrificed. Otherwise we would have taken His example lightly. Seeing that He really meant it right down to the cross, we are impressed. Impressed so much that it comes to the point of being by way of a kind of redemption, a plucking from the sea, a saving hooray. But we cant be redeemed 'unless we believe,' it says, or follow His example. And who can do that? Not even Count Leo Tolstoy who still had to live in a 'humble hut' but on his own lands even tho he'd signed over his 'own lands' of course to his own family, and had the gall then, from that solid earthly vantage point of vaunt, to write *The Kingdom of God Is Within You.* If I, myself, for instance, were to try to follow Jesus' example I'd have first to give up my kind of drinking, which prevents me from thinking too much (like I'm doing now in awful pain this morning), and so I'd go insane and go on public debt and be a pain to everybody in the blessed 'community' or 'society.' And I'd be furthermore bored to death by the knowledge that there's a hole even in Jesus's bag: and that hole is, where He says to the rich young man 'Sell everything you have and give it to the poor, and follow me,' okay, where do we go now, wander and beg our food off poor hardworking householders? and not even rich at that like that rich young man's mother? but poor and harried like Martha? Martha had not 'chosen the better part' when she cooked and slaved and cleaned house all day while her younger sister Mary sat in the doorway like a modern beatnik with 'square' parents talking to Jesus about 'religion' and 'redemption' and 'salvation' and all that guck. Were Jesus and young Mary McGee waiting for supper to be ready? While talking about redemption? How can you be redeemed when you have to pass food in and out of your body's bag day in day out, how can you be 'saved' in a situation so sottish and flesh-hagged as that? (This was also the hole in Buddha's bag: he more or less said 'It's well for Bodhisattva sages and

Buddhas to beg for their food so as to teach the *ordinary* people of the world the humility of charity,' ugh I say.) No, the spring-time bud I talked about with rain dew on its new green, it's the laugh of a maniac. Birth is the direct cause of all pain and death, and a Buddha dying of dysentery at the age of eighty-three had only to say, finally, 'Be ye lamps unto thyselves' – last words – 'work out thy salvation with diligence,' heck of a thing to have to say as he lay there in an awful pool of dysentery. Spring is the laugh of a maniac, I say.

XI

Yet I saw the cross just then when I closed my eyes after writing all this. I cant escape its mysterious penetration into all this brutality. I just simply SEE it all the time, even the Greek cross sometimes. I hope it will all turn out true. Madmen and suicidists see this. Also dying people and people in unbearable anguish. What SIN is there, but the sin of birth? Why doesnt Billy Graham admit it? How can a sacrificial Lamb of birth itself be considered a sinner? Who put it there, who lit the fires, who's the longnosed rat who wants to waft Lamb smoke to Heaven so he can stash away a temple for himself? And what use the materialists who are even worse because of their clunkhead ignorance of their own broken hearts?

Like, silly behaviorists of the sociology and computer sciences today are more interested, mind you, in measuring the reactions to the pain of life, and in pinpointing the cause of pain on their own fellow humans, *i.e.*, society, than in pinning it down once and for all on what it comes from: birth. Even metaphysical gurus and philosopher prophets on the lecture circuit are absolutely certain that all the trouble can be attributed to such and such a government, a secretary of state, a defense minister (think of a 'philosopher,' mind you, like Bertrand Russell), trying to lay the blame on such born victims of birth as that, than on the very metaphysical causes they're supposed to propose to argue, that is, what comes before and after the physical, *i.e.*, being born so that there can be dying.

Who's going to come out and say that the mind of nature is intrinsically insane and vicious forever?

XII

What to do meanwhile? Wait? S'posing you're a soldier who gets the diarrhetic runs just as the enemy is attacking and you're supposed to crawl up already smelling of death in your pants to take a look at somebody else's poor pants, do you blame that on society? Do you blame it on society that a seventy-year-old woman lies in bed paralyzed as if a great stone was on her chest even after ten months of hopeful waiting and perfect care from her children? Blame it on society that a New Bedford fisherman is caught in ice-cold water in raging seas afloat in his life belt in the night, crying to God, to Stella Maris, forgot to bring his razor blade in his watchpocket (as I'd done throughout the sea war) so he could at least let the blood out of his wrists and faint before choking, before choking like my German boy, alone, forsaken by his father in both ways, weeping for mother mercy that aint there in your brute creation sea?

No, blame it on poor hunks Springtime Bud with the rain dew on it. Blame it on the 'sticky little leaves' that Claude said was the first thought that made him cry in the reformatory.

XIII

So, partially well, I went home and, in the general vanity of Duluoz, I decided to become a writer, write a huge novel explaining everything to everybody, try to keep my father alive and happy, while Ma worked in the shoe factory, the year 1946 now, and make a 'go' at it.

But slowly he withered before my eyes. Every two weeks his belly became a big bag of water and the poor Jewish doctor had to come to the house, wince with compassion, and stick a long stabbing tube right into his belly in the kitchen (away from mother and son) to let the water pour out into a kitchen pail. My father never yelled out in pain, he just winced and groaned and wept softly, O good man of my heart. Then, one morning after we had an argument about how to brew coffee, and the doctor came again to 'drain' him (O Nature go drain yourself you evil bitch!) he just died in his chair right in front of my eyes and I looked at his face in pouting repose and thought 'You have forsaken me, my father. You have left me alone to take care of the "rest" whatever the rest is.' He'd said: 'Take care of your mother whatever you do. Promise me.' I promised I would, and have.

So the undertakers come and dump him in a basket and we have him hearsed up to the cemetery in New Hampshire in the town where he was born and little idiot birds are singing on the branch. At one point the bluejay mother throws the weakling out of the nest and he falls to the foot of the tree and thrashes there dying and starving. A priest tries to console me. I walk with my Uncle Vincent Duluoz after the funeral through the little streets of Nashua and understand, from his silence, why he was always considered the 'mean' and 'uncommunicative' Duluoz. He was the honest one. He said 'Your father was a good boy but he was too ambitious and proud and crazy. I guess you're the same.'

'I don't know.'

'Well, in between. I never disliked Emil. But there you have it, and him, and I'm dying myself, and you'll die someday, and all this, poof, *ça s'en vas* [all this, poof, it goes]. He made a Breton Gallic shrug at the empty blue sky above.

Of Uncle Vincent you could not say that he was a victim of the vanity of Duluoz.

XIV

But I still was a victim, went back to Ozone Park with Ma, she did her spring housecleaning (the old man gone, clean the house, drive the Celtic ghosts out) and I settled down to write, in solitude, in pain, writing hymns and prayers even at dawn, thinking 'When this book is finished, which is going to be the sum and substance and crap of everything I've been thru throughout this whole gaddam life, I shall be redeemed.'

But, wifey, I did it all, I wrote the book, I stalked the streets of life, of Manhattan, of Long Island, stalked thru 1,183 pages of my first novel, sold the book, got an advance, whooped, hallelujah'd, went on, did everything you're supposed to do in life.

But nothing ever came of it.

No 'generation' is 'new.' There's 'nothing new under the sun.' 'All is vanity.'

XV

Forget it, wifey. Go to sleep. Tomorrow's another day.

Hic calix!

Look that up in Latin, it means 'Here's the chalice,' and be sure there's wine in it.

THE LUCK OF GINGER COFFEY

Brian Moore

'Brian Moore is one of the most talented and professional novelists writing today' – *The Catholic Herald*

The Luck Of Ginger Coffey is a brilliant example of Brian Moore's shrewd observation. Ginger Coffey is a thoroughly likeable failure; his new life in a new land (from Ireland to Canada) is hardly off the ground before it starts to crumble around him. At his lowest ebb, Ginger suddenly decides to fight back against his fate, and armed only with the luck of the Irish and a lot of bravado, he starts running uphill in hope, into a hilarious series of misadventures, disasters – and victories. *The Luck of Ginger Coffey* is a superbly entertaining novel.

Fiction 35p

JACKARANDY

Leo Madigan

'Rude, exuberant . . . marks a fascinating debut' – *Daily Telegraph*

Jackarandy is an exhilarating, bawdy, poignant novel about a young Merchant Seaman who, while convalescing after an explosion at sea in which his best friend died, finds himself drawn into the murky, lucrative underworld of the professional homosexual. It brings money and an easy life. Then slowly, and painfully, the realisation dawns that the world he lightheartedly entered cannot be so easily discarded.

'This book, with all its tumultuousness and vitality, seems to me to show that its author is a born writer' – *James Pope Hennessy*

Fiction 35p